**Kerry knelt beside Jess and groaned in anguish. There was nothing he could do to save her...**

His eyes misted as he lifted her into his arms. "It should have been me. That laser was meant for me—"

His voice faltered, and he shook his head to clear his vision. A smear of blood glistened on her lips...a stain on perfection and evidence of his own negligence.

"Please..."

He should have prevented this. Somehow, he should have prevented it! He ran his fingers through the mass of flame-colored hair, golden highlights gleaming in the Phidian sunshine. He buried his face in its softness and held her close to his heart, hoping that somehow his words might filter through to her subconscious mind, as her life slowly ebbed away. "Forgive me, Jess. I love you. I always will...always. I could never tell you how much."

An instinctive sense of danger pierced his grief. He whirled and rolled over his shoulder, just in time to avoid the laser aimed at his back. The blaster he picked up from close to where Jess had fallen made short and bloody work of his would-be assassin, but it seemed even Jess's last moments were to be denied him. He was compelled to leave her and concentrate on destroying the assailants who came at him from all sides.

If they could still rout Ayandos's men and free the Phidians, Jess would not have died for nothing.

**Reviews for *Starquest*:**

"Get ready to travel the galaxy and visit worlds beyond your wildest imagination. Hywela Lyn's *Starquest* is an extremely engaging read, simmering with passion, bold exploration and non-stop action. With an interstellar romance that will keep you guessing until the end, this novel is a true masterpiece!"

~Author *Sky Purington*

"Starquest is a fantastical journey about one strong, brave, and independent woman's search for love that will take the reader to places they've never imagined and reveal insights we all know deep inside. I lost myself for hours in the heroine's action-packed adventures, and knew that when the book ended, she had indeed succeeded in her quest to find the one true home for her heart."

~*Liana Laverentz*, award-winning author of *Thin Ice* and *Jake's Return*

# Starquest

by

Hywela Lyn

This is a work of fiction. Names, characters, places, and incidents are either the product of the author's imagination or are used fictitiously, and any resemblance to actual persons living or dead, business establishments, events, or locales, is entirely coincidental.

Starquest


Contact Information: info@thewildrosepress.com

Cover Art by *Tamra Westberry*

The Wild Rose Press
PO Box 706
Adams Basin, NY 14410-0706
Visit us at www.thewildrosepress.com

Publishing History
First Faery Rose Edition, 2008
Print ISBN 1-60154-355-7

Published in the United States of America

**Dedication**

To my long suffering husband, Dave
for his support and patience,
Graeme Waugh and Caroline Davies
who read and made suggestions to the original draft,
and the many friends
who gave me the encouragement I needed.

# Part One

## Chapter One

The scream of the red alert cut rudely into Jess's dreams, waking her instantly. She sprang from her bunk and ordered the computer to shut off the alarm, then pulled on her bodysuit and raced the short distance from her cabin to the flight deck. She flung herself at the control panels. The flickering lights above the main computer console and the figures on the visual output screen demanded immediate attention.

Her fingers elicited no response when she ran them rapidly over the tactile command pads. She looked up and addressed the main computer panel. "Jaii, these readings are crazy. We're way off course and nothing's working on manual, either. I thought I'd fixed the fault. What's going on?"

The image before her wavered, the familiar features distorted.

*Emergency,* the J.A.II series computer intoned, with what sounded like a hint of panic. *Serious malfunction of auto navigation array, inertia dampers and control systems, including shrouding device failure. Life support systems severely compromised. All systems currently operating on emergency power. Auto-repair systems unable to reverse degradation. Main drive calculated to reach critical mass in fourteen minutes and nine seconds.*

"What? Why didn't you wake me earlier?"

*Such action would have been pointless. You could have done nothing further. I anticipated that the auto-repair systems would keep the situation under control. When the position became unsustainable, I transmitted an emergency beacon before waking you.*

"What are the chances of the signal being received?"

*There is insufficient data to form an accurate prediction.*

"A guess would do."

The image darkened as if about to fail completely, although a moment later it sputtered grudgingly back to life.

"Well, I can't see help reaching us before the ship blows," Jess muttered, her voice grim. She had only one course of action available.

She was heading in the direction of the emergency airlock and her escape pod when the computer's voice made her stop and turn back to the flight deck again.

*It appears...the signal...has been answered. My sensors indicate a large starship on our trajectory. Available data shows that since it would have been outside the range of our sensors when the beacon was transmitted, it must have attained previously unrecorded speeds to reach us so quickly. We are currently being scanned.*

Despite the distortion, combined with the gravity of the situation, Jess had a fleeting sense of something akin to amusement. The computer gave the impression of looking and sounding almost envious as it recited the data relating to the other ship's size and speed. The strange ship was obviously larger and more powerful than anything previously encountered—and phenomenally fast.

"It would help if our scanners were operational," Jess said in frustration. Frantically she activated another control, and the titanium shield covering the observation panel slid back.

"Well, at least something works." She gasped at

the sight of the starship speeding toward her craft. She took in the long, sleek lines of the main hull with its lethal-looking weapons array. The nacelles on each side gave the appearance of the backward sweeping wings of a gigantic bird of prey. Its graceful double tailfins glowed, radiating a pulsing, golden light.

Jess tore her gaze from the panel. Her situation was too critical to muse over the aesthetics of the unknown vessel. She had to leave her ship, and quickly.

*Attention,* the computer commanded. *Imperative you eject in the escape vehicle immediately. Repeat, eject immediately. Life support systems are not sustainable. Drive mass will reach critical in eleven minutes and thirty-seven seconds. All functions deteriorating. I am no longer able...to...stabilise...*

The electronic voice slowed and then faded completely, the image dissipating as if it had never existed. Jess swallowed, hard. For a long time the ship's computer had been her only companion. It was almost like losing an old friend.

She had no time for such sentiments, though. The emergency lighting flickered ominously. The instrument panels were shorting out and gave off a pungent smell of burning. As she sped toward the airlock, she fancied she heard a voice in her mind.

*Listen closely. This is the starship Destiny. You need have no fear of us. Your ship relayed a distress signal, but the communication systems appear to be inoperative. This is the only way we could reach you. Our sensors indicate your drive core is approaching critical mass. You must eject from your ship at once. We will help you on board. You don't have much time.*

After a moment's hesitation, wondering if she was imagining it, Jess felt compelled to obey the 'voice'

*Leave your ship immediately and proceed as follows—*

She stopped abruptly, and half turned. "I need to get something from my cabin."

*There is no time. Whatever you have there will be destroyed anyway, as you will be, if you leave it any longer.*

Reluctantly Jess agreed. She reached the airlock, boarded the escape pod and ejected from the ship. Guided by the mysterious voice, she skilfully manoeuvred the capsule into a position adjacent to the starship's hull. Was she heading into a trap? She had no alternative. Her ship was about to self-destruct and the escape pod was not fast enough for her to outrun the explosion.

The control panel in front of her flashed wildly, a panorama of red telltales. Moments later it died as an unseen force pulled the small vehicle inexorably toward the *Destiny*.

*There is no need for concern. You are in the grip of our tractor beam. Cut the power to your engines and we will bring you in.*

Jess complied, and after a few moments the module came to an abrupt halt. She realised she had passed through the outer hull and was now in what was presumably the starship's main airlock.

She ran a quick sensor scan, which confirmed conditions on the ship were compatible with human requirements. She raised the hatch with some caution, stepped from the escape pod, and glanced around for signs of danger.

The 'voice' appeared to have left her. As she approached the inner lock, it opened slowly and she found herself confronted by a man with long, very blond hair, and a calm air of authority. He smiled reassuringly, but she noted the weapon at his hip. Although his stance was not threatening, she remained on her guard.

"I'm Jon Quinlan, commander of the *Destiny*. You're among friends," he said, using the customary *Common Universal* speech.

"Thank you," she said simply. "I owe you my life."

"Are you all right?"

She nodded. "Yes...I'm fine. But all my ship's control and navigation systems failed at the same time." She hesitated. "There's no reason why that should have happened. There was a slight navigation fault, but I'd rectified it and checked everything else thoroughly a few hours ago. I don't understand, unless—"

She bit her lip and broke off abruptly. It might be better not to mention the thought that only now occurred to her. He and the rest of the crew—and on a ship this size, presumably there was a crew—were strangers to her. Best keep her notions to herself until she was sure she could trust them.

"Was it you who contacted me on my ship, Commander?" she queried instead.

He smiled again. "Call me Jon, we don't stand on ceremony on this vessel. No, I'm not telepathic. That was one of our crew, Delian. You'll meet him shortly."

As he escorted her along a narrow corridor, she wondered again if she'd walked into a trap. For the moment, at least, it seemed she had no alternative but to obey her instincts and accept that they had saved her from certain death.

Eventually they stepped out of the trans-unit, onto what was evidently the main flight deck. She gazed around, trying to take in her new surroundings and the small group of figures ranged around the flight controls, obviously curious to see her.

A vivid white flash lit up the main observation screen. Jess and the others on the flight deck shielded their eyes and looked away for a moment.

*Destruction of the unidentified spacecraft, as predicted, is confirmed. The Destiny is at a sufficient distance from the explosion to have sustained no structural damage. All systems currently register normal.*

The voice was authoritative, female, and, Jess realised, must belong to the *Destiny*'s main computer. Apparently, in keeping with common practice on well-crewed ships, it was deemed unnecessary to provide holographic imaging to go with the vocal interface.

"Thank you, *Metisa*. It appears we only just brought the capsule on board in time." The speaker was an imposing man with dark, slightly curling hair and a sombre expression. Seated before a complex control panel, he did not look up.

At the confirmation of her craft's destruction, Jess felt a sharp pang of loss, for the second time in the space of a few minutes. She remained silent, uncomfortably aware of the curious stares of the rest of the crew.

"Sorry about your ship," Jon said gently. "I wish we could've done something to save her. When we received your distress signal, we ran a computer analysis. The conclusions were obvious. The only option was for you to abandon her before her drive reached critical."

The stern-faced man turned to look at her now. His blue eyes, cool as gunmetal, fixed on her until she felt herself blush under his relentless scrutiny.

He smiled slowly, as if unaccustomed to such an action. He was, in fact, very attractive when he smiled. "Welcome aboard."

The commander nodded in his direction. "Let me introduce Kerry Marchant, second-in-command."

Although Jess still could not help feeling a little suspicious, she managed to smile back at him with a degree of confidence she did not feel.

"I guess you'd better meet some of the others." Jon turned to a girl whose cropped hairstyle heightened her dainty, almost impish looks. "Laitha Callahan's our astro-biologist and ecologist."

A small, neat girl stepped forward, holding out a friendly hand. She appeared to Jess to be barely out of her teens. Despite her rather unprepossessing aspect, she nevertheless radiated a vivaciousness that went beyond physical appearance.

"Hi, nice to have another woman on board. You'll meet Zeldra later on, but she's a lot older than me and I feel kind of outnumbered here." She rolled her eyes disparagingly. "No one ever pays me a moment's attention, that is, unless there's something unpleasant that needs doing, which no one else wants to attend to."

She chortled loudly, and Jon chuckled. Laitha's hearty laugh was infectious. Even the solemn second-in-command had a twitch at the corner of his mouth. Jess could not help adding a smile, and felt she might have an ally in the girl.

Jon indicated two men who stood by the communication panel, obviously brothers. Almost identical, both with short beards, their pale skin created a sharp contrast to their black hair.

"Delian and Ragin," he informed her, "are from Earth Colony Niflheim. They're telepathic and telekinetic, like all Nifls." As the two men smiled in greeting, he continued, "It was Delian who telepathed a message to you so we could get your escape-module on board."

Jess nodded at the brothers, wondering if she would ever be able to tell them apart.

"You'll meet the other two members of the crew, Berne and his wife, Zeldra, when we eat, later on. We all try to take our evening meal together."

Jon paused, clearly waiting for her to introduce

herself in return.

"I'm Jestine Darnell," she announced, after a slight hesitation. "I'm usually called Jess. I'm a citizen of Earth."

"You are rather a long way from home," Kerry Marchant remarked archly, "considering how small your ship was."

"She was a Category 'A' hyperspeedster." Jess tossed back her long hair, a hint of pride in her voice as she defended her lost ship. He was right though. She *was* a long way from Earth. She searched for a plausible explanation. "I'm a...a trader. I was returning from..." she hesitated again, "...from Aquarius Seven."

"Really?"

Was it her imagination, or was there something more than polite interest in Kerry's voice? She sensed he somehow knew she'd lied about her origins. Why did he not challenge her, then?

"We're from Earth too," Jon said. "Originally, I mean."

"Have you heard from Earth lately? How are things there?" she asked. "I...I've been away a long time."

"You've not missed much," the second-in-command commented. "Not a great deal has changed. According to the most recent information, it's still pretty much the same oppressed 'trading post' it always was."

"You don't care too much for Earth, then?"

His glance was frosty as he replied, "Are you surprised? Any scope for initiative or freedom of thought is stifled by the Union and its tyranny. Its petty laws and restrictions do not conform to my idea of what makes an ideal home planet."

"That's partly why the *Destiny* was built," Jon added. "Although she's basically an exploratory vessel, designed to investigate the far reaches of space, I guess we were all beginning to feel our lives had become dull and meaningless. The ship gave us a chance to escape the domination of the Union, to face new challenges."

Jess studied him thoughtfully. He seemed genuine enough. She wanted to trust him, but perhaps she should wait a little longer before telling him about Phidia.

She could not afford to wait too long, however. Who knew what might be happening there now?

****

After the somewhat cramped conditions of her own craft, Jess found the quarters assigned to her on board the *Destiny* frankly luxurious. Everything about the great starship fascinated her, and Jon and Kerry showed her many of its mysteries.

The basic principles of the sophisticated hyperdrive, which enabled the *Destiny* to accelerate from standard cruising speed to many times that of light, together with the highly complicated system of time-dilation stabilisation, the bio-neural cell structures and automated flight controls were similar to those on her own ship. They were refined to such a degree, however, as to make her little hyperspeedster seem almost primitive by comparison.

"The main source of fresh food for the crew is from here," Jon told her as he showed her around the vast hydroponics section. Laid out to represent a garden on Earth, avenues of trees bordered banks of shrubs and flowers. Jess marvelled at the diversity of vegetables and fruit, many of them of extra-terrestrial origin in exotic shapes and colours. A glorious mixture of scents drifted toward her as she took in the almost overwhelming shapes, colours and textures.

"The computer controlled synthe-units, while capable of producing satisfactory foodstuffs, are mainly for the supply of items of clothing, tools and other articles. I guess most of us prefer our food to be natural." He paused. "Did you have a hydroponics unit on your own ship?"

Jess nodded. "Yes, although it wasn't nearly as large and well laid out as this."

She was also impressed by the well-equipped sick bay. Zeldra and Berne Kristiensen, the ship's medics, took pride in showing her around. It contained some of the most advanced equipment she had ever seen, much of it linked to the computer.

"As you can see, we're prepared for any exigency," Zeldra said. Her eyes shone with enthusiasm and her smile dispelled the severe impression she tended to project at first sight.

"*Metisa*'s memory banks contain the knowledge of Earth's greatest surgeons and physicians. Earth's greatest. There's no surgical procedure so complex and dangerous we couldn't deal with it," Berne added, grinning broadly. Built like a small mountain, he, too, had seemed a little intimidating when she'd first met him. Still, Jess found it difficult not to feel at ease with someone with such kind eyes, who radiated such easy-going friendliness.

She could not help feeling a certain apprehension, however, when it came to the telepaths, Delian and Ragin. Could they read her thoughts? The feelings of peace and friendship that filled her mind when Delian "spoke" to her telepathically on board her ship had been so strong, however, she felt sure she could trust them. Nevertheless, she tried to keep her thoughts on purely routine matters when she was near them. Some things she would rather keep to herself.

"Do you ever want to go back to Earth?" Laitha asked, as they relaxed by the viewport after their evening meal.

Jess forced herself to concentrate on what

Laitha was asking. Her mind had been on Phidia, which was always there, impossible to ignore.

"I miss it sometimes," she confessed, "but I love space and travelling. It's something I've always wanted to do."

"Me too," Laitha agreed. "I've no family, no ties, so there's nothing to keep me there, and I was fed up with the conditions there, like we all were. Jon's a very distant cousin and my only living relative. When he asked me to join him on the *Destiny* I was only too glad to get away from Earth." Before Jess could reply, Laitha went on, "What about your family, were they happy about you choosing space as a career?"

"Both my parents are dead now," Jess said, trying to keep the sadness from her voice. "My father was killed when I was a baby, he was lost in a starship accident. Because of that my mother was very much against me training to be a space pilot, but she came around in the end."

Laitha leaned across the table they shared and squeezed her shoulder. "I'm sorry," she said softly, "I didn't mean to stir up old memories."

"It's all right, you didn't know. My mother died suddenly a year ago, on Earth, and I've always regretted not being there with her at the end. We were very close."

"D'you have any other relatives?"

"Not now. My grandfather lived to a great age, but he died just after I graduated from Orion. I was so glad he lived to see it. He persuaded my mother to let me accept a scholarship and attend the Space Pilots academy in the first place."

Laitha shot her a quick, admiring glance before adding, "So you're all alone now, like me."

Jess allowed herself the hint of a smile. "I suppose so—but surely you have friends on board this ship?"

"Yeah, I guess. But no one in particular. What about you, have you any men friends—lovers—stashed away?"

Jess laughed aloud at her directness. "No, nothing like that. I had a few boyfriends at Orion, of course, but that's all they were, friends. There was one...but we were too young, our studies were more important and we drifted apart. There's been no one since."

Laitha drank deeply from her glass. "Good!" she said with her deep, infectious laugh. "Men are more trouble 'n they're worth. We're better off without 'em."

"Does that include your cousin?"

Again, Laitha chortled. "Distant cousin," she corrected. "Nah, he's okay, I owe him a fair bit, and he's a pretty reasonable guy, considering."

Coming from Laitha, this appeared to be high praise and confirmed the conclusion Jess had reached, herself. If there was one person on board the ship in whom she might be able to confide, it was Jon. She knew she would have to tell him the truth soon, though. She'd already been on board the *Destiny* for several days and time was running out. She might be able to persuade him to help her, even though she no longer had anything with which to bargain. The Phidians trusted her. She owed it to them to try to fulfil her promise...their way of life, their very world might depend on it.

She brought her mind back to the present as Laitha drained her glass and, standing, grabbed hold of her arm.

"Come on, let's go over to the recreation deck and see what computer games *Metisa* can rustle up for us."

****

Kerry, by contrast to the rest of the crew, was something of an enigma to Jess. She noticed his attitude toward her becoming increasingly cool. Quietly spoken, often taciturn, he was clearly possessed of a brilliant mind. Although slow to volunteer information, if she asked a specific question relating to either the *Destiny* or *Metisa*, he became completely involved with the subject, explaining simply but precisely.

However, she could not persuade him to talk about himself, which naturally made her all the more curious about him. She frequently felt his scrutiny as if he were waiting for her to give herself away, although she could think of nothing she had said or done to arouse his suspicions.

This was not the only thing about Kerry she found disturbing.

She was coming to know the ship almost as well as she had known her own vessel. A skilled pilot herself, she was happy to tackle many of the routine operating tasks, plus some of those that were not so routine. Despite his aloofness, she found herself learning a great deal from Kerry. She observed the way he handled the ship, the instructions he gave to the computers. It seemed like second nature to him.

On one occasion, at Jon's direction, she was perfecting a complicated navigational manoeuvre with the manual controls, under Kerry's supervision.

"She's a large, powerful ship," he said, "and needs handling with a delicate touch. Too much pressure and you would lose her." Jess glanced at him, frowning. Perhaps the ship wasn't the only thing that needed delicate handling.

He placed his hands lightly over hers to guide them, and to her embarrassment, she felt her heart thud uncomfortably against her ribs and a blush of colour burn her cheeks.

"This is exactly the position these controls need to be in relation to each other, when the readings here, and here, correspond to the coordinates already set."

To her relief, he appeared not to notice her unease. For a moment, his eyes met hers. She saw they were no longer expressionless, but alight with the pride and enthusiasm he felt for the ship. She looked away quickly to concentrate on the data in front of her, forcing herself to ignore the feelings stirring deep within her. She felt privileged that he and Jon allowed her to handle the controls, and determined to make the most of the opportunity to pilot the immense starship, without any distraction.

Besides, she had a mission to accomplish. She had enough to worry about; she didn't need added complications. She thought of the blaster hidden in her cabin. All the crew had free access to the ship's arsenal, and because there was no one else on board the ship, there was no reason for stringent security. She'd found it relatively easy to take the gun when no one was around, but she knew if its loss was discovered she would have to act very quickly.

## Chapter Two

It had been a mistake to bring her on board.

Kerry Marchant studied Jess out of the corner of his eye while ostensibly examining the circuitry in one of the control panels on the flight deck. But of course they'd had no option. She would have died without their assistance.

He was struck by how gracefully she moved, the slender curves of her body accentuated by the dark green bodysuit of clinging, soft synthehide. Her thick, flame-red hair hung in waves over her shoulders and down her back. There was no denying she was pretty. He allowed himself a half smile. No, she was far more than 'pretty.'

He'd had his share of beautiful women in the past, although none of them had made a lasting impression. It was not that Kerry disliked women. There were even one or two, like Zeldra, whom he not only liked but admired and respected. He simply did not trust the majority of them.

"You look deep in thought."

Kerry looked up. Jon was studying him with a quizzical expression.

He said nothing, but shot another covert glance toward Jess. Grudgingly he had to admit that, looks apart, she had a strength—a determination—about her, although paradoxically, at times she appeared strangely vulnerable, naïve, even.

"Care to talk about it?"

"No."

"Fair enough." Jon looked toward the panel Kerry had just replaced. "Is there a problem?"

"I was just checking something."

"Our new crew member seems to be settling in."

"Yes." Kerry could not keep a note of uncertainty from his voice and Jon looked at him sharply. Kerry knew he should tell him about his suspicions. He had no doubt he could forestall any action by Jess that might endanger the ship, but it was not something he should be keeping from Jon. However, he would wait until they had a little more privacy.

Later, as they sat together, relaxing over a drink in Jon's roomy cabin, the *Destiny*'s commander again broached the subject of Jess.

"I get the feeling you know something about Jestine Darnell you're keeping to yourself." He paused. "She seems to learn very quickly."

*Too quickly, perhaps.* Kerry took a long sip of his drink. "Oh. Yes. She's obviously a competent enough pilot, and, to her credit, has been very willing to become an active member of the crew. The *Destiny*'s controls must be infinitely more complex than those of a small hyperspeedster, such as the one she was piloting." He did not alter his expression. "I am concerned about the safety of this ship, Jon. She lied about trading with Aquarius."

Jon nodded. "Yes, I know. That didn't ring true with me, either. Don't you think she might have her reasons for lying to us about her origins? Perhaps she's as wary of trusting us as *you* obviously are of her."

"Have you forgotten Shalina?"

Jon sighed heavily. "No, I can never forget Shalina. But you surely don't think—"

"If you recollect," Kerry said, keeping his face impassive, "No one believed me about her, either, until it was almost too late."

Shalina had been beautiful, too. Tall and statuesque, with hair as black as the void, she had managed to seduce the *Destiny*'s commander, although Kerry had always mistrusted her. Charming the rest of the crew, she'd slowly plotted to bring about the capture of the ship. Kerry had discovered her treachery just in time.

"Supposing Jess is another spy from Grakk, sent to try and steal the ship?" He shook his head. "I'm not going to dismiss any possibilities. We know nothing of her, or where she comes from. I'll not take any chances with the safety of this ship, Jon. I am keeping a very close watch on her."

"If she has any thoughts of stealing the *Destiny*, she might find it difficult to manage it single-handedly now, since it's already been tried once," Jon said slowly. "And I don't really think the Grakks would try the same thing again."

"I'd not be so sure. They would expect us to believe that, so they might just decide to do the unexpected." Kerry still found it astonishing that the normally level-headed Jon could have allowed himself to be taken in by Shalina.

After the discovery of her collusion with the Grakks, she had escaped in one of the *Destiny*'s ferry rockets. They later learnt that, as punishment for her failure, the Grakks had transported her to Salmar, a planet used by them as a penal colony. A fate which, even Kerry acknowledged, was probably worse than execution. He'd always felt there was a possibility the Grakks might try to take the ship again.

Kerry was deep in thought when he left Jon's cabin, his mind still on Jess. He harboured other suspicions about her, which he'd not mentioned to Jon. He did not yet have proof, but when he did, he would have no hesitation in confronting her.

There was a part of him though, which could not help hoping he was mistaken.

****

After their evening meal, most of the crew

relaxed in their quarters or on the recreation deck, but Jess sat enthralled before the main observation panel, watching the rapidly unfolding vista of stars, like shimmering jewels in the black velvet backcloth that was deep space.

There was something about the sheer immensity of the Universe that made her feel very insignificant and, at the same time, very tranquil. No matter how long she travelled in space, she never lost her sense of wonder at its beauty.

The ship cruised under the control of the main computer, and as so often seemed to happen, she found herself alone on the flight deck with Kerry. Was it coincidence, or was he keeping an eye on her? Why else would he be working while everyone else enjoyed their leisure time?

He sat nearby, at one of the consoles, checking the coordinates for the next jump through hyperspace. This would bring them to a previously unexplored sector of space, and the planet Dakkon. Without making it obvious she was looking at him, she watched as he ran his long, slim fingers over *Metisa*'s configuration panels. Although the computer received and relayed most of its information verbally, there were certain functions for which *Common Universal* had its limitations as a computer language.

Kerry's hands fascinated her. She felt such hands should belong to an artist or a musician, not to this stern, logical man who seemed interested only in the ship and its computers.

She turned her attention back to the observation panel and came to a decision. She'd waited long enough to find the right moment to tell Jon about Phidia, and to confess to taking the blaster. She'd tried to return it, but that had proven more difficult than stealing it in the first place. She wondered, not for the first time, if it was even fair to ask him to help her. But time was running out. She sighed softly and decided she could leave it no longer.

Kerry turned and looked at her. "Something on scan that should not be there?" he asked, the brusque tone of his voice breaking into her musings.

"No, it's just...so beautiful out there—and so vast," she replied. How could he fail to be moved by the stars she loved so much? "It makes me think of something my mother told me when I was a child back on Earth."

He raised an eyebrow. "Oh?"

"You wouldn't be interested. It's just a story." She rose from her seat.

"Try me."

"Well..." Noting the cold scepticism in his eyes, Jess wished fervently she had not mentioned it, but it was too late now. Reluctantly she seated herself again.

"I used to spend hours watching the stars, dreaming of one day exploring them," she told him softly. "My mother and I would often watch the night sky together. I loved to see falling stars, and she told me they were the souls of young girls who had died for love. For a long time I believed it."

Kerry regarded her witheringly. "Presumably you do not need me to give you a lecture on meteors and astrophysics?"

"I did say I was just a child. I knew you'd think it ridiculous." She tossed back her hair and looked at him steadily. "But even when I was old enough to know falling stars were merely specks of cosmic dust igniting in the Earth's atmosphere, I still loved watching for them and imagining—"

She broke off with a slight shrug, and gestured toward the scanner. "I'm sure it sounds absurd to you, but I would never be afraid to die if I thought I might become part of all that, even if just for a moment."

"Are you not a little old for such fanciful ideas?"

Jess ignored the scorn in his voice. "Perhaps, but I can't help thinking how fragile life is. I've already cheated death once. My escape module wasn't equipped with interstellar drive. I couldn't have made it to another planetary system before the life support units gave out. If the *Destiny* hadn't picked me up…"

She studied him pensively for a moment. He behaved like part of the ship itself...cold, calculating and unfeeling. Why had he suddenly decided to strike up a conversation with her? What thoughts were going through his head to make him stare at her so fixedly?

"Kerry, don't you believe in anything?"

"Oh, yes," he replied, giving her a very direct look. "Myself and this ship, and the technology that enabled us to design and build her."

"And there's no room in your life for the concept of the Universal Spirit...you think this whole universe was created by accident?"

"I know it goes against all the rulings of the Union, with their insistence on blind obedience to the 'Universal Spirit,' but I trust only in the things I know and can control. I do not waste my time on fantasy or myths."

"It must be very gratifying to be so self-sufficient you need no one and nothing but yourself," Jess said, without trying to suppress the note of scornful resignation in her voice.

"It avoids disappointment."

She shook her head disparagingly and rose to leave the flight deck, taking one last look at the observation panel. To her consternation, Kerry caught hold of her by the shoulder and pushed her firmly back into her seat, standing over her with an attitude of grim resolve.

"Not so fast, you have some explaining to do."

She stared at him, thrown off balance. "Why? What d'you mean?"

"For a start, tell me why you stole *this*." He produced the small blaster from beneath his tunic. "I found it hidden in your quarters."

"How dare you? What right d'you have to go searching my cabin!"

"The safety of this ship and those on board her is more important than your privacy," he stated coldly, placing the blaster out of sight beneath his tunic again. "It would not be the first time a woman tried to take her."

"Is that what you think? I was planning to steal the *Destiny*?"

"When I discovered the blaster was missing, it was obvious who must have taken it. Did you really think a hand scanner would not be able to locate it?" He hesitated, and she thought she detected something other than anger in his voice when he went on, "Jess, why did you lie about trading with Aquarius?"

"How did you find out?" she asked, avoiding his gaze, then, with sudden comprehension, "Of course, Delian and Ragin!"

Kerry shook his head. "The telepaths project their thoughts to each other. They will not use their powers to probe another person's mind without their knowledge." He smiled without humour. "You gave yourself away. Aquarius Seven is an obscure little planet with few resources. I remembered hearing something about it a while ago, so I checked with *Metisa*. As I suspected, it is uninhabited. It was necessary for its handful of settlers to abandon the planet when an accident caused radiation levels to rise to a dangerous level."

He gave her a searching look. "In addition, there were traces of a shrouding device signature, picked up by our sensors just before your ship appeared on our scanners. Now why should a trader need concealment? There have been no reports of hostile ships in this sector. Who were you running from?"

"Does Jon know?" she asked.

"Yes, he did not believe your explanation, either, but he feels you must have had your reasons for lying to us. I've not told him about the weapon...yet."

She sprang to her feet, feeling herself flush with anger and guilt. "I'm sorry I lied. At the time I couldn't be sure I could trust any of you. Aquarius Seven was the first name that came to me. I took the blaster to protect myself—"

"Against us?" Kerry's eyes glinted dangerously. "So that is the thanks we get for saving your life."

His voice had not risen above its normal, well-modulated drawl, but she sensed an underlying resentment, which only served to make her even more angry and defensive. They glared at each other, the tension between them almost electric.

"What's going on here?"

Behind them Jon stood on the flight deck, and Jess could only wonder how long he'd been there and how much he'd overheard.

"When you've finished, perhaps you can both come to my quarters and tell me what this is all about."

****

Jon leaned back in his seat and looked expectantly at her. Jess glanced apprehensively at Kerry seated opposite, before returning her gaze to Jon.

"Kerry told me you know about Aquarius Seven...that...that I lied to you about it."

Jon nodded. "Why don't you tell us where you really came from?"

It was a relief to be able to tell her story at last, although this was not as she'd planned it. It would be easier if she were able to tell Jon in private, without Kerry sitting across from her, his handsome features impassive.

"When you picked me up," she began, "I was on my way from a small Earth-type planet named on the charts as Phidia." She gave Jon a little apologetic smile. "At the time, it seemed wiser not to mention Phidia, so I told you I'd been trading with Aquarius Seven. The Phidians are a gentle and artistic people who want only to live in peace. Phidia was uninhabited when they colonised it a century and a half ago.

"It's the old story. Their own planet was devastated by a global war and only a few thousand of their people managed to escape. They vowed never again to wage war on each other. Once they established a colony, they destroyed the ships that brought them there and devoted all their research to medicine and art. They only developed their technology to a degree sufficient to enable them to live in reasonable comfort."

"This is all very interesting," Kerry interrupted, "but it still does not explain your actions."

She looked across at him. "I'm telling you all this so you'll understand the Phidians have no weapons, and through successive generations of non-violence have completely lost their instinct to kill. This was exactly as they wished it, and Phidia's neutrality has always been respected by Earth and the other civilised planets and colonies in that sector."

Her voice took on an edge as she went on. "Their main settlement, Mirrahn, has been taken over by invaders from the Omega Quadrant, led by a mutant warlord known as Ayandos. He has tremendous power over his own people as well as the Phidians. It's something akin to hypnosis. They seem to obey him mindlessly. He plans to bring in more ships and take over the planet." She clenched her fists until her knuckles whitened. "He's ripping up the land to get at her ores and precious stones and has made slaves of her inhabitants. Worse than this, though, he intends to make Phidia the prime medical centre for that part of the galaxy. They've made tremendous advances in cloning, nano and transplant surgery, bio-regeneration and preventive medicine among other things. He intends to grow rich on their knowledge."

"Surely," Jon put in quietly, "it mightn't be such a bad thing for the Phidians to share their knowledge with other worlds and civilisations?"

"They always have. That's how Ayandos was able to take control so easily. They have never tried to prevent anyone from visiting the planet, and their services are available to anyone who needs them. Now, with Ayandos as dictator, only the wealthiest will be able to afford treatment."

She pushed back her hair and met his gaze. "I've known these people a long time. I've grown to love them and they trust me. They begged me to fetch help before it's too late. They gave me nine perfect and very rare Phidian fire-rubies, each one worth a small fortune, to trade for weapons and people who could use them." Her tone was rueful. "You see, I wasn't being entirely untruthful about being a trader. There's an Earth space station orbiting Ramira 2000. I thought I might get help there. I obtained a permit from the invaders to leave Phidia on the pretext of going on a pilgrimage. I realise now it was too easy. Ayandos must have learnt of my intentions somehow and arranged for my ship to be sabotaged before I left Phidia, after I'd made my final safety checks." She paused. "There's no way all the automatic navigation and control systems could have malfunctioned so suddenly by accident, and it's too much of a coincidence that I lost manual control at the same time."

Kerry gave her a penetrating look. "I wondered about that myself," he acknowledged. "It seems strange he allowed you to leave at all, if he suspected you were plotting against him."

"He's no fool," Jess responded quietly. "The chances of my surviving were very slight. He must have calculated it so the systems would begin to break down when I was too far away from Phidia to be able to return." She glanced across at him again. "I might have been able to repair the damage if it hadn't been so extensive, but once the systems began to degenerate the way they did, I could never have reversed the process single-handed. He probably surmised that when my ship self-destructed, the news of my death would eventually reach the Phidians and they would write it off as an unfortunate accident. Even they might have rebelled if he'd killed me openly."

Jon looked at her curiously. "If you're not a trader, what are you?"

"A missionary with the Universal Sisterhood."

If this information came as a surprise to Jon, he did not show it by even a twitch of an eyebrow. When she looked at Kerry, however, the look on his face was an almost comical mixture of utter amazement and incredulity.

"I suppose you think my conduct hasn't exactly been what you'd expect from a missionary," Jess went on, wishing Kerry would not stare at her so keenly, and wondering just what was going through his mind. "But I felt the Universal Spirit would forgive me if only I could help to save them from Ayandos." She shook her head, lowering her gaze. "Now I can no longer give them the help I promised."

"Even if you did, there is no guarantee the same thing would not happen again in the future, if these people are completely defenceless," Kerry remarked cynically.

She glanced at him, unable to keep a slightly didactic tone from her voice. "Don't mistake a peaceful nature for stupidity. The Phidians wouldn't allow themselves to be taken so easily a second time. Although they forbid weapons of any kind on Phidia, they are quite capable of developing the means of protecting the planet and identifying and preventing any hostile ships from landing there in the future. Until now, because of their neutrality, and the respect with which they are regarded by other planets, they hadn't believed it necessary to take such action."

"Why didn't you ask us to help you before?" Jon queried.

Again, she lowered her eyes for a moment. "At first I didn't know whether I could trust you," she confessed, and looked from one to the other apologetically. "It didn't take me long to realise I had nothing to fear from you. I wanted to tell you, to ask for your help, but...I wasn't sure what your reaction would be when I admitted that I'd lied to you."

She pushed a hand through her hair, looking at Jon uncertainly. "Besides, I can't pay you now. The gemstones were on board my ship. I didn't have time to retrieve them before abandoning her, and I've no right to ask you to risk your lives—"

"If we were not already prepared to take that risk, none of us would be on board the *Destiny*," Kerry reminded her quietly. "And we have little need for precious stones."

Jon nodded in agreement, pressing the tips of his fingers together and looking at her thoughtfully.

"This Ayandos you speak of sounds like an unpleasant character. I guess it might be a privilege to put him out of business. I'll arrange a consultation with the rest of the crew." He glanced at Kerry briefly, then back to Jess. "I won't make any promises at the moment, but I'll explain the situation and ask if they're willing to go to the aid of the Phidians.

"But what about Dakkon?"

"It'll still be there when we get back. If everyone's agreeable, that is."

"Thank you," she said, her eyes misty, knowing the words were inadequate. She reached across and touched his arm in a brief gesture, which she hoped would convey the depth of her gratitude. "I've never wished for the death of a fellow creature before, but Ayandos is evil. If he's not stopped he will destroy the Phidians and their whole way of life."

****

"So that's the situation," Jon concluded, leaning back and surveying the rest of the crew. "What do we do? Take Jess's word and go to the rescue of this little hospital planet of hers? Or do we just offer to put her off at the next planet we come to and let her find help herself?"

"That seems a little harsh," Zeldra said. "Anyway, I for one would be rather interested in visiting this planet...what's it called...Phidia?"

"Me too," Berne agreed. "Me too."

"I take it that's two in favour, then. What about you Liatha?"

"Hmmm. Dunno. I mean, I like Jess, I thought we were friends. But she never told me she was a missionary and she's kept quiet about this until now. Can we believe her? Perhaps Phidia is a trap."

"I must admit I had my own suspicions at first," Kerry put in, "but now, when I think about it logically, I have to ask would she really have sabotaged her own ship and risked her life to attract us? It's unlikely. She had no guarantee we would answer her distress call, and she would not have gone very far in her escape module. I've checked all the available data on Phidia with *Metisa* and although there is not a great deal of information, it would appear to confirm what she says about its medical advances."

"Anything about the invasion?" Jon queried.

"No, but then if she is telling the truth, Ayandos seems to have taken the planet by stealth. He would presumably be blocking any attempted broadcasts or distress calls, which is obviously why they sent her for help."

"What do you think, Ragin...Delian?"

"As far as we are able to tell without entering her mind, she seems completely trustworthy," Ragin said. "Her aura shows no indication of deceit or trickery."

"We believe we should help her," Delian added.

"Laitha...Kerry?" Jon queried.

Laitha tossed her head, grinning. "Oh, let's do it. I was getting bored anyway. I could do with a good fight."

"And I don't like the idea of a defenceless planet being taken over by invaders and subjected to the sort of oppression we left back on Earth," Jon said. He looked questioningly at Kerry.

The *Destiny*'s second-in-command gave one of his uncharacteristic smiles as if there had never been any doubt about his answer.

"Why not? Everyone else seems to be in favour, and I tend to agree with Laitha. I too could use a little excitement."

****

It would take a little over nineteen days to reach Phidia, and life on board the *Destiny* continued its normal routine. Jess had logged the coordinates into the navigation computer and they were on course. The rest of the crew, having agreed to go to Phidia to try to overthrow the tyrant Ayandos, seemed keen to know as much as possible about the planet, Ayandos, and Jess's work. She found it a little wearying to have to answer so many questions, but responded as completely, and with as much good-humour, as she could.

"You're really a missionary, then?" Laitha asked. "I thought they were all old people, wielding Bibles."

Jess smiled good-naturedly. She was always amused at the misconceptions many people seemed to have of her calling.

"Centuries ago, perhaps, but not these days," she assured her. "We never quite know what we're likely to find, or how we're going to be received. It helps to be young and fit enough to defend oneself, if necessary."

"So what do you do then, exactly?" Zeldra enquired.

"Well, we've basic medical training, so we can treat minor ailments and injuries on those worlds where medical facilities are primitive. Our main job, though, is to teach and educate the inhabitants of other worlds, to show them the way of the Universal Spirit."

"Did you always know you wanted to be a missionary?"

Jess thought back to when she first realised what she wanted to do with her life. To travel to distant worlds and spread the message of the Universal Spirit...the true message, untainted by the politics of the Global Union. At the same time, to achieve her ambition of travelling among the stars that fascinated her.

"Not straight away," she confessed at last. After working as a co-pilot for the statutory two years on board a commercial liner to gain her full hyperspacial pilot's licence, she had returned to the Academy of the Sisterhood. She'd been educated there and taught a little, herself before studying at Orion. That was when she had decided to apply to be a missionary. "It's something I thought about after I graduated, and I've always known I made the right decision." She fell silent, deep in her own thoughts. The beauty and immensity of space was all the proof she needed of a Divine Creator. Hers was a gentler Deity than the one the Union expected the masses to worship and obey. One who allowed Earth's children to make mistakes, and Whose commands were simply that they love and respect one another and the creatures that shared their planet. This message had been taught to her by the same man who helped her achieve her dream of becoming a pilot...her grandfather.

She was spared further questioning when Jon appeared on the flight deck. To her relief, Kerry, although his attitude toward her seemed to have softened somewhat, appeared to be keeping his distance. That suited her fine. She was not sure she wanted to face any more questions from him just yet.

****

Alone in her cabin, Jess tossed and turned restlessly, unable to sleep. Her mind kept drifting back to Phidia. Would they get there in time? They had to. They must overthrow Ayandos before he took over the planet completely. If she was honest with herself, she had to admit there was something else troubling her as well. Something that had nothing to do with Phidia and everything to do with the *Destiny*'s second in command.

Eventually she decided there was no point in trying to sleep any more. She dressed and made her way to the flight deck. She had a couple of hours before any of the others were likely to appear. If she took her favourite seat by the observation panel, she might be able to relax and make some sense of the turmoil in her mind.

To her consternation, however, Kerry was already there, standing by one of the control panels, obviously deep in thought, himself.

She turned swiftly, hoping he would not see her, but she was too late.

"What are you doing here?" His tone was one of surprise, an expression on his face that might almost have been concern.

"I couldn't sleep." She hesitated. They had unfinished business between them. There had been little opportunity to talk to him since her confession to Jon. He'd seemed preoccupied and she had not had the courage to seek him out, afraid she might betray what was really on her mind.

"I didn't thank you for...for not saying anything to Jon about the blaster I stole. I realise he has to know, of course, but I'd rather tell him myself."

He was silent for a moment. His eyes scanned her face and once again she felt her cheeks burn under his relentless scrutiny.

"Perhaps that might best be forgotten. However, I fail to understand why you did not put it back when you decided we posed no danger to you."

"Because every time I tried you were watching me," she stated, with simple honesty.

"You might have explained about Phidia when I told you I knew you had taken it."

"Well, you really didn't give me much chance," she retorted, disconcerted by his questions, and wishing she were back in her cabin.

His voice sounded more curious than accusing. "I would like to know the real reason why you took it."

"I told you...to protect myself."

"It surely did not take you long to realise you were safe with us?"

"All right," she confessed reluctantly. "All right. At the time I did have a wild idea of hijacking the *Destiny*. I wouldn't have done anything to harm her, or endanger her crew, you must know I wouldn't. The Phidians were relying on me to bring help and

I'd lost too much time already. I was just waiting for the right opportunity—"

"You are quite a lady, for a missionary." Kerry's eyes were no longer cold. Perhaps there was even a trace of amusement in them. "You only had to ask, you know."

"I do now. I'm sorry. I should have trusted you."

"Yes." He still looked serious. "You should."

****

Kerry turned back to the control panel for a moment, making a few minor adjustments.

"I...I'm sorry," she repeated, and he thought he detected a slight catch in her voice. When he looked around again, she was gone.

He cursed as he left the flight deck. There were things he needed to say to her. There had been something in those large, emerald-green eyes when she looked at him...something she was doing her best to hide...and it was, he acknowledged, beginning to trouble him.

Now that he felt confident she no longer posed a danger to the ship, he admitted to feeling a certain concern for her. She was obviously still anxious about something and he could not surmise what it might be. She was starting to disturb him more than he cared to admit, and it was no longer because he did not trust her. There had been a note of sincerity in her voice when she'd told her story, which was as convincing to him as it obviously was to Jon.

He shrugged. He must have been in space too long. He was growing soft. He had never lost sleep over a woman before and he was not about to do so now. Not even for a beautiful, green-eyed missionary with long, flame-coloured hair.

He narrowed his eyes in sudden resolve. No, especially not for a beautiful, green-eyed missionary with long, flame-coloured hair.

## Chapter Three

Jess reached her cabin and stood with her back to the hatch, her heart thumping uncomfortably. This was crazy. She was not ready for the feelings that clouded her senses, filling her mind. The timing was all wrong. There was too much at stake. She needed her wits about her. She would not allow herself to feel this way...especially about someone who so obviously cared nothing for her, or any other woman, it seemed.

When the soft knock came, she knew immediately who it was. There was no one else it could be at this hour. She activated the remote lock control, turning away as the hatch slid open.

"Jess, we need to talk."

"I...I thought we had."

"There's something you've not told me. I sensed you were holding something back just now." Kerry's voice was soft, almost persuasive.

She turned to face him, although she avoided meeting his eyes. "There's nothing. I'm not hiding any dark secrets from you, if that's what you mean. You needn't worry about the ship any more."

"I'm not. But there *is* something troubling you."

"Even if there were, why should you care?" she asked, a sharp edge to her voice that she hadn't intended. "You've made it fairly clear you don't like me very much. I'll try and keep out of your way, until we reach Phidia." She turned away again, so he would not see the colour she felt once more rushing to her face.

"That won't be necessary. And...it's not that

I...dislike you." He hesitated.

She frowned. Kerry Marchant did not normally appear to have difficulty in finding the right words, but for once he seemed to be struggling.

"Why," he asked at last, "do you suppose I kept quiet about the gun and risked the safety of this ship?"

"I really have no idea," she replied uncomfortably, thrown off-balance by his sudden change of attitude.

"I was hoping you would return it, or hand it over to Jon or myself. I didn't want to believe you were plotting some kind of treachery against us, so I waited. When it became obvious you did not intend to put it back, I decided to have it out with you myself. I was hoping you had a good reason for your actions."

"I know I should've told you the truth in the beginning," she confessed, trying not to let her voice give her away. There was some comfort in the knowledge Kerry's previous cool behaviour toward her had been mainly because he'd known of her deception. "I realise that now."

"It would have saved time if you had not been so suspicious of us."

Interpreting his words as criticism, she hesitated for a moment, unable to cope with the awkwardness between them any longer. She did not understand why he'd come to her cabin like this. He'd said he thought she was concealing something, and yet he no longer seemed to believe she was a threat to the ship.

She turned to face him, while still not quite looking into his face. She ignored the heat burning her cheeks. She tried not to think about the strange sensation in the pit of her stomach, spreading until it tightened across her heart, which insisted on playing a perfidious cacophony against her ribs.

They could not go on like this until they reached Phidia. "Look, I know you and I haven't exactly hit it off. I can understand why you didn't trust me, but now you know my reasons for not being honest with you in the first place, can we at least attempt to get along? Can't we try to...just...be friends?"

"Oh, no, Jess. I doubt if you and I could ever just be friends."

So he would not even give her that. She was about to make a sharp retort, when she saw the expression in his eyes, the way he looked at her, and realised with a feeling of shocked disbelief, what he was implying.

He closed the space between them, placing a hand on her arm, and, taken by surprise, she dropped her guard, trembling at his touch. His blue eyes searched hers, as if determined to see the truth she tried to hide from him...and she knew he would find it, for she could conceal nothing from him now. She closed her eyes, conscious that it was already too late. Very gently, he stroked her face with the back of his fingers, before placing his hands on her shoulders, drawing her even closer to him.

"If I appeared to be...hostile...before," he said, seeming almost uncertain of himself, for the first time since she'd known him, "it was because I had no intention of allowing myself to become involved with someone who might be a threat to the *Destiny*. So I tried to keep a distance between us, to convince myself you meant nothing to me."

She opened her eyes, no longer afraid to meet his gaze.

"You said I needed no one and nothing except myself," he went on slowly, taking both her hands in his. "I thought it was true, but you were wrong, Jess, although I did not realise it until now."

"It seems," she said, her voice unsteady, "we've both been guilty of trying to hide our true feelings—"

"Then...perhaps we'd better make a fresh start." He wrapped his arms around her and she clung to him, finally surrendering to the strange, sweet emotion she had tried to deny. He kissed her, a lingering kiss that sent shock waves through her body, awakening the feelings she had tried to conceal for so long. Her lips responded to his with a fierceness that surprised them both.

Several minutes later, with obvious reluctance, he released her, his eyes still not leaving hers.

"I only came to make sure you were all right. I should leave now. I have heard of the strictness of the Sisterhood. I do not wish to risk compromising any sacred vows or beliefs—"

She smiled, touched by his consideration in giving her the chance to back away, while she still could. "I'm a missionary, Kerry, not a nun! The Sisterhood only condemns casual liaisons, not genuine relationships." She lowered her eyes. "I...I've never been in love before, not...not like this, but I know nothing that feels this way could be wrong."

She slipped into his arms once more. He pressed her body close to his, and kissed her again, with a tenderness she would not have imagined him capable of a short while before, and she wondered how she could ever have thought him cold.

****

Seventeen days had passed since Jess had confessed to her mission. She and Kerry spent many hours talking and working together. Sometimes it was enough just to be together, communing in silence with the occasional glance, or brief touch. It was impossible to keep their growing relationship a secret from the rest of the crew of course, but the others were clearly delighted with the situation.

"It certainly seems," Jon remarked, with some humour, "as if you're having a very beneficial effect on Kerry. He actually smiles occasionally now."

Despite being a little embarrassed by his comments, Jess had to admit it was true. Kerry did, indeed, seem to have mellowed.

As the distance between the ship and Phidia decreased, however, fears and anxieties she was able to repress during her waking hours overshadowed her happiness. They took over her mind when she tried to sleep, invading her dreams and refusing to let her rest.

****

The crew had long since retired to their respective quarters. After sleeping for only a short time Jess awoke. She sat up and ordered the computer to increase the lighting.

"*Metisa,*" she asked, "where's Kerry?" She needed to talk to him...to be near him. Once she had felt uncomfortable in his presence. Now she could not bear to be apart from him.

*He is in the hydroponics unit checking a minor fault,* the computer responded. *Although at present negligible, if ignored it could jeopardise the viability of the unit with serious consequences.*

"Have you any idea how long he's likely to be?"

*There is insufficient data available to make that computation. Shall I inform him you wish to speak to him?*

"No thank you, *Metisa*. I'll wait."

She was reluctant to intrude if he was busy, but she did not want to be alone. Hastily dressing, she paced up and down, clenching and unclenching her fists.

Eventually she could stand it no longer, and made her way to the hydroponics section. She searched the leafy walkways between the trees and flowering plants and shrubs, until she found him. He was completing adjustments to a control panel hidden behind what was ostensibly a stone arch covered with foliage and a profusion of blue and purple blossom.

He turned when she spoke his name. "Jess, I thought you were asleep. I'd not expected to see you here."

"I couldn't sleep. I wanted to be with you." She paused. "Did you sort out the problem here?"

"Yes, it was nothing serious. A slight temperature fluctuation, that was all, although the malfunction that caused it could have become more serious. *Metisa* woke me and alerted me to the situation. I've made sure it will not happen again."

He put his arm around her shoulder and drew her toward a low, comfortably padded seat, beneath a thicket of low bushes covered in a profusion of tiny, multi-coloured blossoms just emerging from bud. Their scent, which filled the air, reminded her of honeysuckle on Earth. A few metres away, a holographic fountain tinkled and splashed, near a discreetly placed observation scanner. On it, she saw Phidia growing almost imperceptibly larger as they hurtled toward the planet at just under light speed.

"You really love this ship, don't you, Kerry?"

"Yes," he agreed. "She is the culmination of years of work and planning, the fulfilment of a dream."

She looked at him quizzically. He seated himself beside her, pressing her head against his shoulder and stroking her hair.

"Oh, yes." He smiled, that rare, flashing smile, which made her senses reel. "I too have had dreams. Jon and I have been friends since we were boys, and long ago we decided we would build a ship as great as any seen on Earth. This ship...a ship to take us away from the stagnation and oppression of the Union."

"It must've cost—"

"The Earth?" he looked amused. "Not quite, although Jon came from one of the wealthiest families in the Union. The *Destiny* was built with his money, plus that of a few other interested parties."

"And your design?"

He nodded. "The initial design, anyway. I know every inch of her, every circuit, every detail down to the smallest component." He held her closer. "I saw her grow from an image in my mind to a ship faster and more advanced than anything in the Allied Planets. I thought it was all I needed...until now."

He looked deep into her eyes. "Jess, the *Destiny* means a great deal to me, but I would give her up without a moment's hesitation, rather than lose you."

"That's a choice you'll never have to make." She was silent for several minutes, lost in her own thoughts.

After a while, he drew her attention to the scanner, the distinctive timbre of his voice breaking into her reverie. "We'll be there in just forty-seven hours."

"I know."

"You don't sound too happy about it. It is what you wanted, is it not? What you were considering hijacking the *Destiny* for?"

"Kerry, don't." She sat up and looked at him in concern, not sure if he was teasing her. "You know I would never have done anything to endanger the ship, even though it's so vital I bring help to Phidia."

"So what's wrong, Jess?"

She shook her head in confusion. "I...I don't know. That is...oh, I'm probably being irrational—"

He studied her solicitously for a moment. "You've not been sleeping well these last few nights, have you?"

She lowered her head quickly. "I've been having strange dreams—"

"Dreams...you mean nightmares?"

"No, not exactly. More like premonitions. I'm

afraid."

His face did not alter expression although his eyes narrowed a little in surprise. "It is understandable. Being a missionary, you can't have had much experience of violence. You don't have to come with us, you can stay on the ship. No one will think any the less of you."

"No, you misunderstand. She shook her head, with a little half-smile. "You have a very old-fashioned idea of my profession, my love. I've seen plenty of violence. I don't hide from it because of my calling, and I've had to learn to fight and defend myself in times of danger. There's no way I'd let you fight Ayandos without me. I'm not unprepared for death, nor do I fear it. I'm not afraid for myself."

"Who, then?"

"You, of course, Kerry. If anything were to happen to you—"

"I am quite capable of handling an adversary like Ayandos, however nefarious."

She shuddered. "You don't know Ayandos. He's treacherous, and although you may not understand the concept, he is evil. And he has others with him."

"Not too many, from what you've told me. We will take him completely by surprise. From what you've said, it seems unlikely he is expecting you to return, with or without reinforcements."

"I know. Common sense tells me there's no reason why we shouldn't overcome Ayandos and his men. That everything will be all right. But in my dreams—I can never quite remember what happens—but I wake up feeling scared and alone. Terribly alone."

He held her in his arms, kissing her face and her hair. "I will never leave you Jess...and nothing's going to happen to me. Nothing. I'll never leave you," he repeated.

Her heart lurched as she looked into the eyes

she had once thought cold, unable to hide the longing, or the anxiety in her own. "Do you mean that? Are you sure this is what you want?" she asked, torn between her desperate need for reassurance of his feelings toward her and a genuine desire to say nothing that would make him feel trapped into giving up the freedom she knew he valued so highly.

He drew her close to him again. "How sure do you think I have to be? I love you, Jess." He kissed the top of her head, her forehead, her lips. "You are the only woman I could ever contemplate spending the rest of my life with." He smiled once more, and she caught the irony in his voice. "The only one I could ever really trust."

He looked at her with a softness of expression she had never seen in him before, as he reached into his tunic and produced a small, antique gold ring, set with Terran diamonds and emeralds.

"I have carried this around with me for a long time. It belonged to my mother. I don't remember her, she died when I was very young. I want you to have it, now."

She gazed at the ring he held toward her, suppressing a gasp of admiration. It was exquisite.

"But...I can't let you give me this," she whispered, placing her hand over his. "You say it belonged to your mother—"

"It's yours now."

She looked up into his face. He had a faraway look in his eyes, as if remembering something painful. There was still so much about him she did not know—so much he kept hidden. She hesitated a moment. "What about your father?"

"I never knew him, never found out what happened to him. An aunt brought me up until I was old enough to go to a formal State learning centre." He placed the ring on her finger. It slipped on easily, as if it were meant for her. "I always swore, if I ever found a woman I could love...really love, I would give this ring to her." He kept hold of her hand. "It could have been made for you, Jess, it suits you. The emeralds match your eyes."

"It's the most beautiful thing I've ever seen," she breathed.

"Then wear it for me."

****

Jess slipped her arms around Kerry's neck and kissed him wordlessly. "We have something in common," she murmured, her gaze returning for a moment to the scanner and Phidia, drawing ever closer. "I never knew my father, either. I was just a baby when he was killed in an accident. My mother told me what happened as soon as I was old enough to understand. The ship he was piloting disappeared with all on board. The last, uncompleted message he managed to transmit to Earth indicated that the time-dilation stabiliser on the ship was malfunctioning uncontrollably. The obvious conclusion was that instead of stopping at the programmed time zone, it took them back to the beginning of time itself...to the formation of the Universe."

She stopped, her voice trembling slightly. "A terrible but rather wonderful way to die, don't you think?"

He said nothing, merely holding her closer to him.

"The Titan series of ships was discontinued after that, although there had never been such an accident before. No one ever discovered what caused it. The TDS system had never been known to fail before then."

"I'm surprised I have not heard about it before," Kerry remarked slowly, his voice sympathetic.

"The Union hushed it up," Jess said. "It was

unthinkable that a ship of the Global Union and Allied Planets should ever meet with such an accident."

"Yet that did not stop you from wanting to be a pilot?"

"No, I told you, I've loved the stars ever since I was a child. All I ever wanted was to travel to distant planets, visit new worlds."

She smiled a little sadly. "Like you, I thought my work and my love of travelling was enough. But space can be very lonely sometimes, however beautiful it is. I hadn't realised how lonely."

"How long have you been a pilot, Jess?"

"Seven years, allowing for the vagaries of Time-Dilation and FTL travel. I graduated at eighteen from the Orion Space Training Centre and then, after my two years practical space flight experience, joined the Sisterhood as a missionary. Apart from a year's intensive training with them, I've been travelling in space since I qualified."

"You went to Orion?"

She nodded, enjoying the quick look of approval he gave her. Orion was notorious for the difficulty of its entry requirements and the rigorous training undertaken by its student pilots.

"Seven years is a long time," he said softly. "I promise you Jess, while we both live, you will never be alone again."

## Chapter Four

Kerry scowled in frustration. So this was Phidia. He cast an appraising eye over the alien but starkly beautiful landscape, suffused with a delicate glow from the first rays of the early morning sun. The rolling blue-green grassland, devoid of any buildings or artificial structures, was marred only by deep holes and fissures in the ground, unsightly confirmation of what Jess had told them about Ayandos's illicit mining operations.

They'd thought they had everything planned so well.

"Ayandos is allergic to strong daylight," Jess had said when they were working out their strategy. "He's likely to be in the underground quarters he's taken over, once the sun is up. If we land just after dawn we'll be able to spring an attack before he realises we're there, and before it gets so light any of his men on the surface spot us. I've a security implant, which will get us past the main entrance."

It should have been easy. Kerry, Jess, Berne, and Ragin would enter the underground complex near the main Medical Centre and take Ayandos and his henchmen captive. Since the Centre had only one entrance, there was no way the mutant and his men would be able to escape. Meanwhile Jon, Liatha, Delian and Zeldra would keep guard at the entrance until the rest of the crew emerged with their prisoners, when they would round up any of Ayandos' men who were on the surface supervising the slaves in the mining areas.

At least that had been the idea.

Unfortunately, it seemed the mutant had set up a sophisticated sensory and tracking system while Jess was away, and Ayandos was waiting for them as they set foot on the red Phidian soil.

"Your weapons. I order you to remove them and place them on the ground—now." he said, while one of his men pointed his gun at the crew.

"How did he manage to override our scanners?" Kerry hissed in Jess's ear, throwing down his blaster in disgust, as the others also surrendered their weapons to Ayandos's men. Jess gave Kerry a look of despair and whispered, "I've no idea. He seems to have powers I wasn't aware of."

Kerry glanced at Ragin, who was standing motionless, and surmised from his stance he was conversing telepathically with Delian.

*I have told Delian to remain on board, in the armoury. We're maintaining contact. We detect that Ayandos is not telepathic, so he will be unaware there is someone left on board,* Ragin telepathed in answer to Kerry's covert look.

Ayandos was tall, well over two-and-a-half metres, dwarfing his own men. An albino, with white, flowing hair, his face was a ghostly mask, his lips colourless. His crimson eyes seemed to glow with malevolence. Kerry avoided the temptation to look at those eyes for more than a moment. Jess had warned them about this, reminding them the mutant was rumoured to have hypnotic powers. He wore a swirling cape of a rich, many-hued material, which seemed to shift and alter in the luminous light of the Phidian dawn. Ayandos appeared to be unarmed himself, although several of his men stood to the side, and slightly to his rear, and carried lasers or blasters, as well as the electronic nerve-whips they used to goad the Phidian slaves.

In the distance, Kerry saw a miserable group of Phidians working under the supervision of two of

Ayandos's men. They used their whips frequently, eliciting sharp cries of pain, which drifted on the still air.

Ragin telepathed another message. *Be careful, my friends. He is not to be trusted. There is something...something hidden...I cannot tell what it is.*

"The girl, I want her." Ayandos's voice over Kerry's translator sounded harsh and unnatural. "My laws she has violated, and she must be punished. Hand her over to me. The rest of you I will spare and you may depart."

Kerry willed Delian to hurry, casting another discreet glance to where Ragin stood out of the range of the mutant, his eyes shut in concentration.

Jon stepped forward to speak. "You are referring to a missionary with the Terran Sisterhood of the Global Union and Allied Planets. If any harm comes to her the Union won't rest until they find and destroy you—"

"Enough," the albino interrupted, raising his hand in a gesture of impatience. "Little is known to me of this 'Union' you speak of. You are interlopers on this planet. Your lives I have offered you, on my terms. Accept them, or with the girl you will die."

"No. She stays with us!"

Without warning, Ayandos leapt forward in a fluid movement that was almost too fast to comprehend, and caught hold of Jess's arm, dragging her back to where he'd previously stood.

"Let me go!" Jess lashed out with her free hand, struggling to free herself, but she was no match for the strength of the mutant. Kerry lunged toward the albino, as Jess cried out, the dread in her voice tearing through him like blaster fire. "Kerry, no—*he has a gun!*"

Too late, Kerry saw what she had seen and Ragin sensed, a tiny laser concealed in the alien's palm and aimed at his chest.

Jess twisted in Ayandos's grasp, trying to wrest the small weapon from him, and kicked out. Ayandos staggered a little from the blow, and she pulled herself free and sprang toward Kerry. A beam of almost invisible laser light struck her between the shoulders and she fell at his feet. Ayandos again raised his laser, and in the same instant Delian's and Ragin's combined telekinesis resulted in each of the *Destiny*'s crew finding themselves once more in possession of a weapon. Kerry unleashed the whole force of his blaster at Ayandos, firing repeatedly at point blank range.

The mutant screamed, a hideous, unearthly sound, as his body flared briefly with a blinding white light before falling, blackened and lifeless. The *Destiny*'s crew, now joined by Delian, turned their weapons on the rest of Ayandos's men, who scattered in fear and confusion. The air shimmered and burned with green blaster fire.

Kerry knelt beside Jess and groaned in anguish. There was nothing he could do to save her. His eyes misted as he lifted her into his arms. "It should have been me. *That laser was meant for me—*"

His voice faltered, and he shook his head to clear his vision. A smear of blood glistened on her lips...a stain on perfection and evidence of his own negligence.

"Please..."

He should have prevented this. Somehow, he *should* have prevented it! He ran his fingers through the mass of flame-colored hair, golden highlights gleaming in the Phidian sunshine. He buried his face in its softness and held her close to his heart, hoping that somehow his words might filter through to her subconscious mind, as her life slowly ebbed away. "Forgive me, Jess. I love you. I always will...always. I could never tell you how much."

An instinctive sense of danger pierced his grief. He whirled and rolled over his shoulder, just in time to avoid the laser aimed at his back. The blaster he picked up from close to where Jess had fallen made short and bloody work of his would-be assassin, but it seemed even Jess's last moments were to be denied him. He was compelled to leave her and concentrate on destroying the assailants who came at him from all sides. If they could still rout Ayandos's men and free the Phidians, Jess would not have died for nothing.

Kerry was only vaguely aware of his companions fighting beside him, and that several Phidians had joined in the fray, retrieving their former masters' weapons when they fell, to use against them.

It was clear Ayandos had felt secure with only a small contingent of men to control the weaponless Phidians, but now that their leader was dead, they were undisciplined and disorganised. They ran without direction, firing their blasters wildly in confusion, as if unable to believe these people they had made their slaves could possibly rise up against them.

Kerry barely noticed the crack and whine of blaster fire, the screams, oaths and commands that filled the air. He fought like an automaton, dispensing death to his opponents. It might have gone on for minutes or hours, for all he knew. He discharged his weapon mechanically, and when it failed at last, used it as a club to shatter the skull of his last remaining adversary.

The blaster dangling from his hand like a broken limb, he surveyed the aftermath of the battle, as if watching a scene on a holocast. His mind still numbed by grief, he peered through the curtain of blaster smoke that hung heavy in the air.

The stench of burning flesh was all-pervading, thick and choking. Bodies lay congealed in their own blood, those still on fire scorched the sward beneath. It appeared none of Ayandos's men remained alive.

The Phidians who had participated in the fighting, turning on their oppressors, were congratulating each other and pointing toward the *Destiny*'s ferry, in obvious jubilation. Others tended their wounded comrades or helped them to the underground medical facilities.

Blinking in an effort to focus, Kerry stared through the haze. In the distance he could see Jon helping Laitha to her feet. Delian and Ragin stood close by, Ragin inspecting an injury to Delian's arm.

Kerry looked all around, refusing to believe Jess was lost to him. He scoured the ground. The Phidians had swiftly removed the dead and injured from the battlefield. To his consternation, he realised during the confusion her body had also been taken, and a cold despair took hold of him.

He stumbled toward his crewmates as Berne and Zeldra ministered to their wounds. "What have they done with Jess?"

Berne turned from examining Jon's shoulder, and placed a sympathetic hand on Kerry's arm. "There you are, Kerry. There you are. For a moment, we were afraid...I'm sorry, but I doubt if there was anything even the Phidians could have done for her. You know as well as I do the damage a laser—"

"Berne, what have they done with her?" Kerry's voice was harsh with emotion.

"I'll find out for you, but you must let me have a look at that blaster burn on your face—"

Kerry pushed him aside, ignoring the wound that burned down the side of his face, starting just below his left eye. "I will not leave her on an alien planet."

A solemn-looking Phidian of uncertain age and dignified appearance approached. "You wish to know what we have done with the young woman, Jestine

Darnell," he said, in good *Common Universal*. "She has been taken to the Medical Centre. Her body will be properly prepared with due reverence and—"

Kerry's voice was soft, almost menacing. "She died for me. I will not leave without her."

The Phidian studied him for a long moment, then nodded. "Forgive me, I was not aware...you and she cared for each other?"

"More than you could begin to understand."

"True. We do not feel the need for such emotions on Phidia." Even so, his voice was sympathetic. "We will return her body to you when the hours of darkness have given way once more to the light."

"Why not now?" Kerry controlled his anger with an effort.

"She cannot be moved until the dawning of the new sun," the Phidian said with polite resolve, his voice respectful but firm. "Until then you are all welcome to our hospitality. We would deem it an honour to be allowed to treat your injury and those of your companions."

Kerry would have protested, but Jon silenced him with a hand on his arm.

"It must be some sort of religious custom," he said quietly. "I guess we'll have to respect the conventions of these people. They loved Jess too, remember."

Despite his seething emotions, Kerry had no choice but to accept Jon's reasoning. He endured the treatment for his wound in a state of suspended consciousness, speaking and reacting automatically, with no real awareness of what he was actually saying. He slipped away from the meal that was provided afterward as soon as courtesy would permit, seeking the solitude of the underground apartment which had been put at his disposal.

He slept little that night, although the quarters allocated to the *Destiny*'s crew were comfortable enough. His mind would give him no rest and it was only when Jess's body was delivered to him at daybreak that he realised, with a dark sinking of spirit, he had been hoping for the impossible...

A miracle from a Divine Presence in whom he did not believe.

****

The *Destiny* sped through the heavens, leaving Phidia far behind. Although the Phidians had been sincere in their gratitude, they had also made it no secret that they were anxious for the *Destiny*'s crew to leave. While relieving the planet of its dictator, they had also brought violence, something which had never before been known on Phidia.

Their gift of several containers of a colourless salve healed the crewmembers' injuries overnight. Kerry's grief was such, however, that not even the almost miraculous properties of the salve, or even the small bio-regenerators they were also given, could arouse his interest.

He languished in his cabin, battling his wretchedness until he could take it no longer and went to the flight deck to speak with Jon. There was one last thing he could do for Jess.

****

A few hours later, Kerry again made his way to the flight deck. It seemed Berne and Zeldra had arrived moments before him, and both looked perplexed.

"We have subjected the salve to a detailed analysis," Berne was telling Jon. "It is mainly composed of substances already found in the human body. However, there are traces of something else. Something the computer is unable to identify and which is far in advance of our current medical knowledge. Far in advance. We only know its purpose seems to be to greatly accelerate the body's natural healing processes."

"Pity," Laitha said. "We could've made a fortune out of it if we'd been able to find out what it was."

"Then perhaps it's just as well we'll probably never know," Jon reproached her. "I guess that's not quite what the Phidians had in mind when they gave it to us."

"Well we did save their planet, didn't we?"

"Yes, and as far as they're aware, we've already been paid well for it," Zeldra put in. "Don't forget they weren't told the jewels they gave Jess were lost with her ship. To them we're just a bunch of mercenaries—"

She stopped as if only then aware of Kerry's presence.

"I have completed the preparations. Everything is set up."

Jon left the controls. "The ship's flying on automatic." He nodded toward the others. "If you all head for the ferry launch area Kerry and I will be with you shortly."

Taking the hint, the others left the flight deck.

Jon looked across at Kerry. "You sure you're up to this?"

Kerry brushed his fingers through his hair. "It is what she would have wanted. We had each other for such a short time. Perhaps this seems a little dramatic, but I could not have left her on Phidia, even though I know how fond she was of the Phidians."

Jon hesitated, seeming to choose his words. "I understand, Kerry. I realise nothing anyone can say could help at the moment, but I do know something of the pain you're feeling."

Kerry glanced at him sharply. "You're thinking about Shalina? At least you know she's still alive!" he added bitterly.

Jon sighed. "Yes, she's still alive, as far as we know. But what will the Grakks have done to her? I guess it would probably have been better for her if she had died."

"I'm sorry." Kerry meant it. No one deserved the kind of treatment Shalina probably suffered at the hands of the Grakks. "You still care for her, don't you? After all this time, and what she tried to do."

"It still hurts," Jon admitted. "Jess gave her life for you, because she loved you. Nothing can alter that. The only thing Shalina left me is the memory of how she tried to betray this ship and its crew, and use my feelings for her to doublecross us. I can't help wondering where she is now, what happened to her. The Grakks don't deal lightly with those who fail them."

As they left the flight deck, he placed a hand lightly on Kerry's shoulder. "I understand what you must be going through, but thankfully, at least you know nothing can ever hurt Jess again."

Kerry had to admit he was right, but at that moment, it gave him little comfort.

****

The ceremony conducted by Jon, as commander of the *Destiny*, was short and simple. Each of them said goodbye to Jess in their own way.

"She was only with us for a short time," Jon concluded his eulogy, as they stood grouped around Jess's escape module standing in the launch area, "but I think we were all moved by her compassion and courage, and were the richer for having known her. Today we not only mourn her death but celebrate her life, and the fact we've all been touched by her love and her zest for living."

The crew was silent for a few moments, perhaps lost in their own thoughts and memories. Then Kerry reached into the little vessel and gently fastened the straps securing Jess into the seat in front of its control panel.

The Phidians had dressed her in a long, hooded

robe of a white velvety material shot through with an incandescent thread. A few fiery curls of hair escaped from beneath the hood to frame the exquisite beauty of her face. Her closed eyes, with their long, dark auburn lashes gave her a tranquil appearance. She looked as if she were merely asleep.

With infinite tenderness, Kerry removed the small gold cross from around her neck. Taking hold of her left hand, he pressed his lips to the ring he'd given her, fashioned from the same precious metal, with jewels the colour of her eyes.

He slipped the cross into his tunic and kissed her lips, before sealing the vessel's hatch and returning with the others to the flight deck. There he instructed the computer to make the necessary preparations for launching the projectile from the *Destiny*.

The capsule headed into the void and as the *Destiny* moved rapidly away, Kerry turned to the scanner. Stars filled the screen, countless suns of unseen worlds, which Jess had loved. The beauty which, until he had known her, he had taken for granted.

Perhaps she was right. Perhaps such beauty was, after all, more than a mere cosmic "accident."

He allowed himself a slow, sad smile of satisfaction when the atomic charge he had placed on board the module detonated, exactly as programmed, the dazzling flash of the explosion resembling a miniature supernova.

A vision filled his mind of a young girl, flame-coloured hair touched by the moonlight, searching the night sky for a falling star. "Farewell, Jess," he whispered. "Join the stars you love so much, and know I will *never* forget you."

# Part II

## Chapter One

### Extracts From A Journal

157-35.01 (Post-Alliance Calendar)

I have decided to keep a record of everything I remember and everything that happens to me from now on. I've invested some of my savings in a personal holocorder for the purpose. There is something reassuring in being able to record my thoughts and feelings without having everything I say constantly analysed. I mean to make this journal as full and honest an account of my thoughts, and what happens to me, as I can. Although I have lost some of my past, I intend to lose none of my future.

It's now several months since I regained consciousness in this medical centre below the surface of Phidia, with no memory of who I was or how I came to be here.

"Your memory will return," Yan Kloor assured me. "It would be harmful for you to remember too much too soon."

I should have accepted his words. He is a wise and skilled physician. I realise he was only trying to protect me.

But no...I had to find out. I wanted so badly to know who I was and what had happened to me. I felt as if I'd been robbed of my identity, and at last, after much pleading, I persuaded Yett Sitta, my nurse, to tell me about my "treatment." She did not realise the processes regarded as normal and humane on this planet are almost unknown on Earth, since the Commission set up after the Revolution banned them as being immoral and against nature and the commands of the Universal Spirit.

At first, I could not believe what she was telling me. Then, after a while, I began to remember the waves of red-hot pain, sensed rather than felt. The hideous, terrifying nightmares—dreams in which I'd wanted to scream and been unable to, where I'd been incapable of movement, living in a world of darkness and yet, in some strange, uncanny way, still aware of everything around me. Perhaps they were, after all, more than mere products of my imagination. Can it really be true? Even now, I shudder at this thing they have done to me, even though it was apparently the only way to save my life.

From what Sitta told me, it seems I was a member of the crew of a starship called the *Destiny*. How then did I come to be here on Phidia, alone? What happened to me that I needed such radical treatment? She could not tell me, she didn't know. Apparently, that information is 'classified.' As she spoke, vague, shadowy memories began to whirl around in my head. I strove to remember. The images were blurred. It was like having a piece of familiar music playing in my mind and not being able to recall the words. Faces half hidden in shadow began to dance before my eyes and at last...I remembered.

I remembered the *Destiny*'s crew, their names, their faces. I also remembered how my feelings for one of them had grown into something much deeper than friendship.

I had known love...a love so intense that now it felt as if I had lost a part of myself.

My heart pounded against my ribs and my senses swam. I buried my face in my hands in complete and utter despair. My skin felt icy cold as I drifted into unconsciousness. And I had such dreams—not the terrible visions of my nightmares, but beautiful, sad dreams. Dreams of the *Destiny* and her crew, so vivid that when I awoke, my face wet with tears, I could not believe I was not in my own cabin on board her.

Yan Kloor looked down at me, his long, silvery-blue tinged face sympathetic.

"So...you now know what has happened to you."

"Yes, I know. I wanted to remember. Now I wish I could forget."

"You could have destroyed everything we have tried to do for you. We partially suppressed your memory to protect you."

"You mean," I asked, unable to keep a note of horror from my voice, "my memory was wiped out...on purpose?"

Yan Kloor looked offended. "Not wiped out, merely temporarily suspended. It was for your own good." He frowned. "Yett Sitta was very wrong to tell you. I intended to explain everything to you gradually. However, you should have been prepared first, with proper counselling and—"

"I don't need counselling. All I wanted was the truth!"

It was no good trying to explain my frustration. I'd thought I knew these people. Now I wondered if I would ever fully comprehend the way their minds work.

****

Yett Sitta has been transferred to another part of the sanatorium, something I deeply regret and blame myself for. She nursed me when I first recovered consciousness, and apart from Yan Kloor she was my only real friend. I could confide in her in a way I couldn't do with Yan Kloor. I had grown very fond of her and I miss her so much.

Gradually, some of my memory has returned. I

still can't remember how I came to be here, though, or how I became separated from the *Destiny* and her crew. Yan Kloor refuses to tell me. He believes my own mind is 'blocking' these particular memories, and they will return when it is 'right' for me. Until then, he says, I should accept it and be patient.

I still have the occasional bout of nightmares and headaches, which he tells me will pass. He assures me I will hasten my recovery by trying not to worry about my past.

But I can think of nothing else. Now I know what I have lost—the man I loved—it is like a physical ache deep within me. I see his face everywhere I look. I hear his voice in the soft winds that blow from the Northern Cansarvian Mountains. Sometimes I imagine I see him standing in the shadows. I dream of him at night and wake feeling desolate and alone. This is not the infatuation of some silly girl. He came to mean more to me than life itself. I think I will lose my sanity if I don't at least try to find him again. I have to find a way to leave this planet to search for the *Destiny*.

****

157-02.02

Soon after Sitta's revelation, when I felt strong enough to face up to what I imagined to be the worst, I asked for a personal monitor and gazed at myself, for a long time. I'm not sure what I expected, and I hope I am not a vain person, but I have to admit that I was not displeased with what I saw.

I imagined my face would show the strain of what I had been through. Mentally I felt as if I had aged several years. Physically...physically I looked, if anything, less than my natural age.

Sitta did not go into too much detail about my actual treatment, and I have only a vague idea of what it must have entailed, but I was grateful for the fact I appeared to look perfectly 'normal.' I could not have contemplated facing the crew of the *Destiny* again if I were disfigured. No, my love, I do not think you would reject me. What we had went beyond mere physical attraction, but your eyes would remember, and I would know. I couldn't live with your pity.

Although many of my memories are still hazy, the *Destiny* and her crew are as vivid to me now as if I had never forgotten them. Surely they would not—could not—have coldly left me to my fate if they had known the truth? I still don't know how I came to be separated from them, or why they left without me. Did they know what the Phidians were going to do? I have to find them again...take my place on the *Destiny* once more, if they will accept me. I mustn't allow myself even to think of the alternative.

When I told Yan Kloor about my decision to search for the *Destiny*, he wasn't enthusiastic about the idea, but I think he could see I'd made up my mind.

"I suppose, if you are so determined, you will find a way, with or without my help," he said with the faintest of smiles. "I'll see what I can do to help you find work. You will need money if you're really serious about doing this."

So I've been working at the Medical Centre, and saving every credit I earn to buy my way off this planet. I have a little medical knowledge and, after some further training, have been working on the accident wards. In the main, my duties involve dealing with minor wounds and occasional broken bones. I enjoy the work although it's exhausting. The hours are long, but the satisfaction in being able to return some of the care given to me has been immeasurable. The Phidians have almost eliminated disease from their planet, but accidents still occur with depressing regularity.

I've been paid well, far better, in fact, than I

would have expected. I feel sure my generous remuneration has something to do with Yan Kloor, who obviously has a lot of influence at the centre, although I'm not quite certain why he should be so charitable. He seems to be taking a special interest in me and I will always be grateful to him.

I will work as long as necessary until I have enough money to buy my passage on board a starship. Yan Kloor has agreed to help me find a suitable craft for my search, although he warns it may take some time. Apparently, no spacecraft of any kind are built on Phidia. Although the Phidians would be quite capable of the technology required, they have channelled all their scientific knowledge into medical research and into building magnificent medical centres like this one. However, since treatment is available to anyone who needs it, from anywhere in the galaxy, provided they come peaceably and unarmed, they do have a large space terminal not far from this institution.

My main concern is that I may not be able to find the *Destiny* after so long. I have, I'm informed, been on Phidia for nearly a year. She could have travelled vast distances in that time. But I must try. Somehow, I must find her again.

****

157-30.08

At last I have enough saved to buy my passage off this planet. However, it's proving more difficult than I had expected to find a suitable ship. I visit the space terminal as often as I can, and sometimes Yan Kloor comes with me, but so far I've had no success.

The first time I visited the terminal I was filled with hope that I would soon find a ship to take me on my search for the *Destiny*. There were many crafts arriving and departing. Ships from Draton and Karangh, Nitte-Eng, Salmar and Trantona, and planets with strange, exotic-sounding names I've never even heard before. None of those suitable seem interested in taking on an extra passenger, though. This morning, after unsuccessfully approaching several visiting ships, I eventually stopped at a vessel whose identification symbols proclaimed it to be Salmaran. I asked the pilot if I could buy a passage off Phidia. In response, the Salmaran caught hold of me and began to pull me toward his ship. I shook his long, claw-like fingers off my arm angrily.

"No, let go of me!" Backing away swiftly, I glared at the off-worlder, tall and muscular, with shiny bronze skin, dark hair and the black, elongated eyes of his species beneath hooded lids. Salmarans are humanoid in many respects, and I'm sure he would have been attractive to many women. But those cold eyes, and the cruel set of his features gave him a sinister aspect and his manner was now distinctly menacing. "You said you needed passage on a ship. Mine will suit your purpose perfectly. Come with me an' I'll show you." He lowered his voice suggestively, setting his lips into a smile. "I'm sorry if I startled you, my dear. Come, I'm sure we can do business together."

I gritted my teeth. It was obvious I'd made a mistake in approaching him and offering to work as well as pay for my passage. I'm desperate to find a ship for my search, but not so desperate I'd resort to what I was beginning to realise was his idea of payment. I was trying to think of a way of extricating myself from this embarrassing and potentially dangerous situation when I saw a tall, familiar figure making his way toward us, and I breathed a sigh of relief. Not that I'm unable to defend myself, of course, but the last thing I wanted to do was provoke an incident on this planet that abhors violence of any kind.

"Senior Medical Administrator, Yan Kloor," he

stated with authority, as he reached us. "Is there a problem?"

"No," I said, moving swiftly to his side, and flashing a look of contempt at the Salmaran. "No problem. Just a misunderstanding, that's all."

"In that case," Yan Kloor told me with a stern look, "we had better return to the Medical Centre." He nodded curtly in the direction of the Salmaran ship's pilot.

As we walked away, I glanced over my shoulder. The Salmaran's face wore a furious expression, and I was aware that if it had not been for the intervention of Yan Kloor, I could have been in real trouble.

"Of what were you thinking?" Yan Kloor demanded, his oval, dark purple eyes growing dark with concern. "Don't you realise how dangerous the Salmarans are? Who knows what would have happened to you if you'd gone on board his ship with him."

I lowered my eyes and tried to look suitably repentant. It doesn't do to argue with Yan Kloor. Besides, I knew he was right.

"Salmar," he went on, "is a penal planet, belonging to a distant planet called Grakk. The Salmarans subject the prisoners to brutal tortures and mind-probes if they refuse to divulge information, or obey their rules."

I couldn't hide my shock and he paused for a moment.

"If they go too far with an important prisoner, he—or she—is brought here, to Phidia, for treatment. These prisoners are then 'reconditioned' by the Salmarans before being returned to Grakk." He paused again, looking at me meaningfully. "The Salmarans on the whole are a cruel race and best avoided."

I was appalled his people could condone such

things by continuing to associate with the Salmarans.

"We don't condone them," he assured me in answer to my protests. "But neither can we interfere in the affairs of other worlds. The Grakks feel this is the only way they can control crime, and those who might rebel against their leaders. We can't refuse to treat those who've broken down under—what is the term you would use—under the Grakks' 'brainwashing.' It would not be ethical to refuse them our help. They explain the treatment of the prisoners as 're-education.' When they have accepted and understood what is expected of them, they're taken back to Grakk where they will work peaceably for the rest of their lives."

"I think I would rather die than live like that," I said bluntly. He did not reply, but his expression implied he agreed with me.

I realise that I've been naïve in thinking that all ship owners are to be trusted. This morning's incident has shown me I need to be much more careful in my approaches.

It's growing late, and now I have brought my journal up to date I must try to sleep, if I can. I am beginning to despair of ever finding the means to begin my search.

****

157-05.09

It does no good to sit around brooding, so this morning I decided to take a walk to clear my thoughts.

The Phidians build their cities below the ground, so the surface remains green and unspoiled and in many areas almost gives the impression of being uninhabited. It is a beautiful world, with rich, rolling grasslands, as I imagine the prairies and steppes on Earth must once have been. In the distance, jagged mountains, rugged yet majestic at the same time, reach toward the sky.

Phidia derives much of its energy from the sun and wind. The solar panels set into the hillsides and the graceful, almost transparent wind turbines are constructed in such a way as to cause the minimum encroachment on the landscape. Even the sails turn almost silently.

The animals of this world are completely unafraid, since the Phidians are not meat eaters and have devised methods of amusing themselves other than hunting the wild creatures that share their planet. I spent a long time watching a herd of long-necked, deer-like animals. They lacked horns or antlers, but had enormous, almond-shaped golden eyes and long, pointed ears.

They grazed the lush grass by a tuneful waterfall, which tumbled recklessly down a steep cliffside. They were so tame they ate from my hands, even the young ones. Overhead, a large golden bird, with black wingtips soared and swooped, and the hum of myriad brightly coloured insects filled the air.

I felt my spirits lift as I took in the peace and tranquillity of my surroundings. I noted with some surprise, however, that in certain places large areas of land look scarred and the vegetation is more sparse and of a lighter colour. It gave the appearance of having recently been torn up and then re-seeded in an attempt to repair the damage.

I found this curious since the Phidians are particularly conscientious about their environment and take pains not to disfigure their surroundings. The workings of the few mines, for instance, are so well camouflaged as to be almost undetectable. They have learnt that greed is self-destructive and take from their planet only those minerals essential to their way of life, and necessary for trade.

I wonder what could have happened here to

cause this kind of damage, which seems quite extensive.

I walked for several miles, completely losing track of time. Then I began to feel the need for something a little more substantial than the succulent fruits and berries which grow everywhere in abundance, and remembered my promise to Yan Kloor. I reluctantly turned back, but it was already early evening when I returned to the Medical Centre.

Close to the entrance that leads down to the main medical areas, I saw Yan Kloor waiting for me. Beside him stood a tall, slim stranger, dressed in crisp, white spacers' overalls. Fair hair, cut to just above his collar, and with a tendency to wave, fell in a slightly unruly fringe above friendly grey eyes, and served to heighten the youthfulness of his appearance.

Yan Kloor took a step forward. "I'm glad you have returned at last. I was beginning to worry." He inclined his head in the direction of the stranger. "This is Dahll Tarron, from Anraat. He has a small ship which he is willing to charter."

## Chapter Two

I stared at Dahll and found him gazing just as fixedly at me. He looked hardly older than about eighteen or nineteen Earth years, yet there was an expression of absolute confidence in his eyes, which I noticed had flecks of gold in them. Furthermore, he held himself in a way that defied anyone to challenge him.

As Yan Kloor introduced us, I smiled, and held out my hand. Dahll raised it to his lips, in what is apparently as common a custom on Anraat as it once was on Old Earth in ancient times.

"When," I asked, slightly disconcerted by this charming and unexpected gesture, "can I see your ship?"

He grinned boyishly. "Whenever you wish, the sooner the better, in fact. I don't want to hang around this planet any longer than I have to," he added, with an apologetic glance in Yan Kloor's direction.

I looked at him excitedly. "What about right now? Can we go this evening?"

"It's late," Yan Kloor stated firmly. "We will go at first light of the new day. I don't expect you have eaten since you left this morning?" He was right but I found it very hard to say goodbye to Dahll and follow the Physician-Administrator back down to the Medical Centre.

Recording this before settling down to try to sleep, I can hardly curb my impatience until tomorrow. I've waited for so long to find a ship to take me in search of the *Destiny*. I'm almost afraid to hope that here, at last, may be the answer to my prayers.

****

157-06.09

*It is beautiful!*

My first sight of Dahll's hyperspeedster, as it stood silhouetted against the early morning sky of pink and gold, is something I will never forget. I caught my breath as I took in the smooth, slender lines and glistening hull. Graceful atomic shields and neatly folded-back solar sails back up the propulsion systems, in addition to the elegant fins she is equipped with for flight within a planetary atmosphere.

"Would you like to see inside?"

I nodded slowly, feeling a little anxious. It was surely too much to expect that the interior could be as perfect as the exterior suggested. To my delight, however, it was. The living quarters are more than just comfortable. The hydroponics unit, although small, is efficient and adequate and the sophisticated sensors and tracking equipment, linked to an advanced computer system, are impressive.

"Well, what d'you think? Will it suit your purpose?" Dahll queried, although I'm sure he already knew what my answer would be.

"She's perfect," I told him enthusiastically. "Exactly what I've been looking for."

Dahll glanced across at Yan Kloor. "Good, then that's settled."

I smiled wryly. "All except for the matter of your payment."

"I'm sure we can come to some arrangement."

I let my eyes wander over the little ship once more. Recording this in my room, I can picture her, sleek and streamlined, and if what Dahll says is true, faster than anything of comparable size.

Surely, with such a craft, I will be able to find the *Destiny*.

****

157-08.09

Things have happened so quickly over the past couple of days. Dahll appears to be impatient to leave. He has already stocked his ship with provisions, in addition to the food supplies and hydroponically produced fruit and vegetables already on board. These will be a welcome alternative to the replicated meals served up by the ship's catering unit.

I have amassed a stock of my personal requirements, clothing and so on, bearing in mind I don't know how long our journey will take or what conditions we are likely to encounter. I've tried to restrict myself to essentials, although I did allow myself one luxury by purchasing a small vial of my favourite fragrance. The synthe-unit will be able to produce as much of it as I want, while we are in space.

Now that the time is nearing for me to leave, I feel a strange regret, almost as if I were deserting Phidia. Can it be that Yan Kloor is right after all, and I really do belong here? I shall miss him and I'm sad I won't be able to see Yett-Sitta again, to say goodbye. I still feel guilty about her and wish there were something I could do to re-instate her. I've caught glimpses of her now and then but have had no chance to speak to her.

Yan Kloor again asked me to stay. Despite the help he's given me, he thinks I'm setting myself an impossible task. He finds it difficult to comprehend why I should wish to search the galaxy for a ship I may never find and a man who may no longer love me.

"Why," he asked me this morning, "should you go to so much trouble to seek out one man, when there are so many others to choose from?"

I found it impossible to explain. The Phidians seem unable to comprehend or appreciate love as we think of it, or the concept of a lifelong union between a man and a woman. They obviously feel friendship, and a sort of universal concern for the welfare of all Phidians as individuals. However, marriage as such is nonexistent on this planet. That's not to say they have no concept of morality, though, and the few children I've seen have been well cared for by the community as a whole. They simply feel no need to form permanent relationships.

Perhaps such a passionless society is a good thing. It certainly avoids many problems, and there is no lack of concern or affection on Phidia. I can't help feeling, however that they are missing something we humans still manage to retain, despite the frailties and weaknesses inherent in our emotions.

****

I have taken to walking on the surface each evening, at sunset, before the three moons have risen. The planet is very beautiful. Earth must have been like this in the old days, before her atmosphere became poisoned, and the global climate so unstable her cities had to be built beneath huge transparent domes. I've grown to love Phidia, although I still don't fully understand it.

Although I'm longing to set off on my search, I shall miss the peace and tranquillity of this world. As I walked this evening, along the shore of the lake, I looked back toward the hills with their strange, jagged contours. The sun had set now, but the sky seemed almost as bright as it was during the day. The three moons rose, casting a brilliant bluish-white light over everything, throwing intriguing shadows. I imagined Dahll's ship, somewhere beyond those hills, standing silhouetted in the moonlight waiting to begin her journey.

We've been so busy making preparations for our departure, Dahll hasn't had time to demonstrate her control systems yet. I know I'll be able to handle her, though. I'm determined to do my share of piloting her on our voyage. I intend to show Dahll I can be more than merely a passenger.

****

157-09.08

We finalised our agreement this afternoon. The sum Dahll asked is substantial but reasonable, considering I have no idea how long my search is likely to take. He has set a time limit of two Terran years, which seems fair. If I haven't found any trace of the *Destiny* by then, I probably never will.

Yan Kloor told me the Anraatians as a race are highly honourable. I have confidence in his judgement, of course. He went on to tell me Anraat is globally an almost matriarchal society with a thriving economy.

"The Anraatian laws relating to important matters such as marriage are very strict," he said. "And once an agreement of any kind, business or personal, has been entered into, whether verbal, or recorded in writing or on disc, it is irreversible. All Anraatians have strict moral and ethical codes instilled in them from early childhood. Their word is completely binding. I think you'll be able to trust Tarron implicitly."

I already feel as if I know Dahll, and I like what I see. I think we'll get along well together. There is, however, one point on which I intend there to be no misunderstanding. I tackled him on it, as he keyed his confirmation code into the Agreement with something of a flourish.

"Dahll, I've paid you the amount you stipulated," I started, rather self-consciously, "and I think we'd better make one thing quite clear from the very beginning."

He waited, politely attentive.

"The contract I've signed with you is purely a business arrangement. I'm more than willing to do anything you ask of me with regard to the piloting and maintenance of the ship, but that's as far as the relationship goes, while I'm on board her." I hesitated awkwardly. "It wouldn't be fair to let you think otherwise. Also...my reasons for setting out on this search are personal...and private—"

Somewhat to my consternation but also, I must admit, to my relief, Dahll gave a soft chuckle.

"Don't worry. I reckon I get the message. I shall respect your...privacy."

"Good, then we understand each other." I held out my hand. "It is customary on my world to shake hands on such an agreement."

He looked slightly quizzical, but took my hand solemnly.

"Our customs are a bit different on Anraat. We've a lot to learn from each other, I think." His clear grey eyes with their gold flecks met mine, and I found myself wondering just how much he knows about me, and the *Destiny*. What has Yan Kloor told him? I was glad he didn't take offence at my words. Perhaps I was presuming too much anyway, but after my narrow escape from the Salmaran, I wanted to be quite sure there are no misconceptions about my role on board the ship.

****

SHIP DATE: 157-10.02

Much has happened since my last entry, but I must start at the beginning.

Yan Kloor woke me a few hours before dawn. He told me to dress and meet him in his office. I had to be ready for liftoff immediately. Hurriedly I did as instructed. I knocked softly on his door and he pulled me inside, shutting it silently behind me. In answer to my rather bewildered questions, he explained that some members of the Supreme Council of the Medical Institute had decided I should not be allowed to leave yet. They claimed my treatment could not be considered complete until my memory returns fully.

"Tarron refuses to delay his departure by longer than another few days, and there is no telling when your memory will return. The best course of action is for you to leave immediately. The Council will not be expecting such a move, and by the time they find out it will be too late."

I had noted upon my return from my customary walk the previous evening that Yan Kloor was not around. Apparently the Council, when informed of my imminent departure, had summoned him to an urgent meeting to discuss the matter.

I can't help wondering why they are so concerned for me. I feel fine now and am beginning to accept what's happened to me without the feelings of revulsion which used to overwhelm me.

"Won't you get into trouble when they discover I've gone?" I asked anxiously. "They're bound to connect you with my disappearance."

Yan Kloor smiled reassuringly. "No one is a prisoner on Phidia. They cannot force you to stay, although they could make things difficult for you. I'm afraid they might even consider re-admitting you for further treatment."

"But there's nothing wrong with me now. You said yourself my memory will return naturally."

"Yes, I'm sure that is the case. You must not blame them for being so protective of you, though. They have their reasons." His purple eyes had a glint of humour in them as he continued, "Don't worry about me. I am not without influence on the Supreme Council. I can hold my own if there's an investigation."

"Why are you doing this for me?"

Yan Kloor did not reply immediately.

"I suppose I admire your determination," he said at last. "For many months you have worked here under Administrator Yett-Anghaar. I know she has not given you an easy time, yet not once have I heard you complain. I have never seen you spend anything on your own pleasure or comfort, instead you've saved every exchange disc you've earned to hire your passage on a ship. If you are forced to remain here until your memory returns fully, it may be another year, or even longer, before you find another suitable ship." His expression became very serious. "Also, there are some on the Council who would prefer you to stay on Phidia indefinitely."

I hesitated for a moment. "Can you give me some idea of how long it's likely to be before I regain my memory completely?" I asked.

"That is another reason why I feel you should be allowed to leave. I do not believe this block in your memory, this gap that you still have, is anything to do with us. I think your own mind has blotted out the events that brought you to this Centre. It seems likely you will only be able to recall them when you are back with your own people once more."

I had to be content with that. I now recall nearly everything of my past life, except the events immediately preceding my arrival at the Medical Centre. They remain, stubbornly, a mystery to me. And whatever Yan Kloor knows he is obviously not going to tell me.

He looked at me gravely. "There is just one thing I want you to do for me. I realise I may be asking a great deal of you, but it might be better if you did not return to Earth."

"I have no great desire to go back to Earth," I replied, "but suppose I find the *Destiny*'s crew has returned there?"

Yan Kloor squinted, which I knew meant he was thinking deeply.

"If you must go, then let your identity be known to as few people as possible and only those you know you can trust. There could be trouble for Phidia if the Authorities on Earth ever learn what's happened to you."

I realised he was worried about the nature of my treatment since such processes are illegal on Earth, so I agreed to his request. After ascertaining that I had everything with me I would need, he hurried me out of the room and back along the narrow corridor. The passages leading to the various levels and up to the surface were deserted, as was to be expected at that hour. No one challenged us. As Yan Kloor had told me, I was not a prisoner on Phidia. Nevertheless, rather than risk disturbing anyone by using one of the hydrogen-propelled transport vehicles, he decided we should walk to the place where he'd arranged to meet Dahll.

We approached the low fence that marked the end of the confines of the underground hospital complex and a bright red warning light flashed. Yan Kloor stepped up to a small panel set into a metal column. There was a pause of a few seconds, while the computer system analysed the data from Yan Kloor's microchip implant. Eventually the lights changed to yellow to indicate the force field guarding the entrance had been de-activated.

Once outside, I stopped and turned back for one last look at the grassy landscape and the mountains, beneath which was the only home I'd known for so long. In a strange way I think I'll miss it, although the memories I hold of it aren't all happy ones.

"Come," Yan Kloor urged. "We must not keep Tarron waiting."

We walked briskly in silence, both of us engrossed in thought. The nights on that part of

Phidia are warm, and the moons cast a gentle, almost protective light through the fine, feathery branches of the trees, throwing intricate lacy patterns on the ground before us.

We stepped into a clearing and there was Dahll, and standing next to him a slim, fair-haired young woman.

"Sitta," I exclaimed as we hugged each other. "I was afraid I'd have to leave without saying goodbye to you."

"Yan Kloor arranged it as a surprise. I wanted to see you, to ask you to forgive me for being so stupid. If I'd known how it would affect you, I'd never have told you—"

"It's all right," I assured her. "It was a shock, that's all. It was my own fault for making you explain what had happened to me before I was ready to accept it."

"I hate to break this up," Dahll put in dryly, "but when you two have finished apologising to each other, you might remember we're supposed to be leaving this planet before daybreak."

I turned. In my excitement at seeing Sitta again, I'd almost forgotten Dahll's presence. The smile on his face belied the sharpness of his words.

"I don't want to rush you too much, but it'll take us some time to get to the terminal, even by hydro-car."

"Of course." Now the time had finally come to leave, I realised it wasn't going to be quite as easy as I had imagined. I gave Yett-Sitta another hug. She'd nursed me through all the pain and trauma when I first regained consciousness after my treatment. Without her skilful and dedicated care, I'm sure my recovery would have taken much longer. It was hard to express my gratitude.

"I have something for you," she said a little shyly. The hydro-car was parked a short distance away. She went over to it and, after removing something from the back, returned with a soft, white bundle, which she held out to me.

As I took it from her, it unfolded to reveal itself as a cloak of fur-like material, white and soft as the finest down. It had a hood, lined with the same soft material.

"It's a special thermal material," she explained, "developed for its supreme insulating properties."

I gazed at it admiringly, and there was a lump in my throat. I've always loved beautiful things. "Thank you Sitta," I said quietly, "but I couldn't possibly accept anything like this."

Her eyes widened in disappointment. "You do not like it, then?"

"I love it," I told her quickly. "It's just that it must be worth a great deal of money, it wouldn't be right for me to accept it."

"I will be very unhappy if you don't take it."

She was so obviously set on making me a gift of the beautiful robe I couldn't refuse any longer.

"Then, thank you," I said, my voice faltering. "It's a long time since I wore anything so lovely."

Sitta smiled broadly again. "Yan Kloor has a gift for you, too."

Wordlessly Yan Kloor handed me a small silvery box. Inside was a transparent triangular crystal, within which minute fragments of coloured vapour moved swiftly to form a picture. Distant Phidian mountains, their tips covered in snow, and in the pastures below, a small herd of the deer-like creatures I'd become so fond of, moving slowly and cropping the lush vegetation.

I've seen these moving cloud pictures before, but not on such a small scale. It's an art form peculiar to Phidia, and I've never been able to determine whether or not it's an illusion. Whatever the truth, the pictures appear quite real to the beholder, and are very beautiful.

"Thank you, thank you so much, it'll always remind me of Phidia." Tears sprang to my eyes. "I'll never forget you and Sitta!"

Impulsively I kissed him on the cheek, a thing I would never have contemplated doing previously, but he seemed quite pleased, and grasped my hand warmly. He'd become almost like a father to me during the time I'd been on Phidia, if such relationships had been recognised there. I wondered how old he was and whether he might have a daughter of his own somewhere on the planet.

There was the wisdom of many years in his eyes and I felt he had an 'old soul,' although he did not look old. It's not easy to gauge the age of any Phidian, and I suspect many of them must be far older than their appearance would suggest.

"I hope you find your starship and your companions, but remember there will always be a place for you here, if you need one."

"I'll remember," I told him softly, knowing in my heart how unlikely it was I'd ever see him or Phidia again.

****

It's not easy to remember accurately the events leading up to the present time. As soon as we reached the space terminal and Dahll completed the many checks and formalities, we boarded the ship. Dahll seemed anxious to leave, and I was just as keen to start our journey.

The take-off from Phidia was uneventful. I watched the planet dwindle from a large, pale green sphere, circled by her three small moons, until she was no more than a distant star. Then she became lost among the hundreds of thousands of other stars visible through the viewport. Only when I was no longer able to see the speck of light that was Phidia did I look away. I was about to release my seat harness when Dahll asked if I was prepared for hyper-acceleration.

"Of course," I replied. I hadn't expected him to go hyper this early, but if he felt it was right to do so, it was fine by me. On the flight deck, the pilot and passenger seats on the ship are positioned one behind the other, unlike the arrangements on most Earth ships. I couldn't see Dahll because of the high back to his seat. I checked my safety harness and braced myself for the acceleration to light speed.

The whine of the powerful ion-drive rose to a screech. The pressure pushed me back into my seat. I closed my eyes and gritted my teeth. It's been a long time since I travelled in hyper-space, but I couldn't recall experiencing anything like that before...and I could now remember what it was like to pilot a ship, myself.

The weight on my chest increased and pain flooded over me. The screech became a scream that rang in my ears, but I was unable to tell whether the sound was the hyperdrive or my own voice.

My vision blurred. Vaguely, at first, I began to perceive a hideous, demonic form, the spectre that haunts me, hunts me down in the hidden corridors of my mind. Its flaming eyes seemed to bore into my soul. A bolt of raw fear ran through me, a fear that is no stranger to me.

But each time I experience it in my dreams, it's as if I'm feeling it for the first time. The fear tightened itself around me like a metal band.

I felt as if I were choking. I tried to cry out...no sound came. Pain again...a flash of light...white, then crimson, then myriad swirling, blinding colours. More pain, intense, burning...

Drawing me into the familiar land of my nightmares.

## Chapter Three

Slowly...painfully...I fought my way out of the blackness. As if from a great distance, I heard someone repeat my name insistently. With an effort, I opened my eyes. Dahll was bending over me, holding a vessel of something warm and syrupy to my lips.

"Here, drink this."

I obeyed, swallowing reluctantly at first, choking a little, then more eagerly as I began to feel life flow back into me. The remnants of my nightmare visions slowly faded. My aching body seemed to become weightless, the pain miraculously ebbing away, leaving me with a peculiar but not unpleasant floating sensation. I looked around, half-dazed.

"I must've blacked out. How long have I been unconscious?"

"Not long. I came to you as soon as I could." He was studying me with a curious expression—a strange mixture of fear and concern...and something that might have been anger, but whether this was at me or himself, I couldn't tell. If it was directed at me, I was at a loss to know what I had done to incur it.

"I thought you said you were used to hyper-travel?"

"I am," I said weakly, "Although it's been a while."

"Then why didn't you activate your shield?"

I looked at him blankly. "My what?"

"Your shield?" he repeated patiently, as if telling me something I already knew. "To counteract the effects of hyper-acceleration."

By way of demonstration, he touched a control in my seat's armrest. Immediately I found myself under what appeared to be an oval, transparent bubble. I felt a warm, soothing breeze on my face. My eyes felt heavy, so I closed them. In another moment, I would have been asleep, but then the shield slid back and I was alert again.

I shook my head in amazement. "I've never seen anything like that," I admitted frankly. "The ships of Earth are constructed so the effects of acceleration are hardly felt by the crew."

Dahll looked impressed, then concerned once more.

"I'm sorry. I should have explained. It never occurred to me our ships might be constructed differently from yours."

"I'm as much to blame as you are," I said. "I just thought one hyperspeedster must be designed very much like another. Perhaps if we hadn't left in such a hurry...why did we go hyper so soon? The Phidians haven't any ships to follow us, even if they'd wanted to."

Dahll hesitated for a moment. "There was a Salmaran slaver trailing us. He left Phidia shortly after we did. Even the Salmarans can't track a ship through hyper-space."

I shuddered as I realised how close I'd come to putting myself at the mercy of the Salmaran back on Phidia. It had to be the same one, since Yan Kloor told me it was the only Salmaran vessel to have landed on Phidia in several weeks.

"But why?" I asked, slightly bewildered. It hardly seemed likely he would have gone to the trouble of trailing a small Anraatian speedster on my account. "What reason could he have for following us from Phidia?"

"There's a score I have to settle with Narhjohol and he wants to get to me first," Dahll stated, without expression. Before he finished speaking, something that had been at the back of my mind, vaguely puzzling me, formed itself into a question.

"Dahll, you didn't activate your shield, either, did you? I'd have seen the shield forming before we accelerated to light speed, if you had. Yet you weren't affected by hyper-acceleration."

Dahll grinned. I could see the relief in his gold-flecked eyes.

"You *are* feeling better, aren't you? I'll explain later, but you should go to your quarters now and rest, I think."

"I'm fine," I assured him a little impatiently. "Please tell me what it's all about."

Dahll seemed to be doing his best to look stern, but somehow the expression didn't quite come off.

"I'll explain everything after you've rested."

I couldn't force him to tell me, so I decided to take his advice. Despite my words, when I reached my cabin my head was beginning to throb and I also had a pain behind my eyes, which I knew would become excruciating if I didn't do something about it quickly. I haven't had any pain for so long I was beginning to hope the attacks might have ceased altogether.

The ship's small infirmary is well stocked. Yan Kloor personally added many items before we left Phidia. I quickly found what I needed and went back to my cabin.

Once removed from the refrigerated unit and exposed to the ship's atmosphere, the protective wrapping of the analgesic capsule evaporated. I inserted it into the auto-spray. As soon as I activated the spray against my arm, the medication penetrated painlessly beneath my skin and began to take effect. I lay on my bunk for what I intended to be a few minutes, meaning to rejoin Dahll on the flight deck as soon as my migraine subsided. I must have dozed off because when I opened my eyes again, several ship's hours had elapsed and all trace of pain had gone.

I freshened up and ran a comb through my hair. I changed into one of the long, comfortable, sleeveless shifts I had brought with me from Phidia, choosing a dark green, which shimmered in the light, its soft material flaring out to just above my ankles. Clipping a narrow, metallic belt around my waist, I checked my personal monitor and decided I was presentable. Space overalls and bodysuits are all very well for practical purposes, but I don't intend to spend my leisure hours in them.

When I reached the control deck, Dahll was engaged in a game of concentration and skill with the computer. It looked rather complicated. The Tri-D board projected was hexagonal in shape and the strange-looking pieces appeared to move upon it at random. He glanced up as I came on deck and stared at me so intently I felt the colour rising to my face.

"How're you feeling now?" he asked at length, as he froze the programme.

"Hungry!" I told him with feeling. He grinned, that boyish grin that is somehow very endearing, and put me at ease once more.

"In that case, there can't be much wrong with you. We'll eat now and talk later."

Our first meal on board the ship was a pleasant and relaxed affair. The computerised catering facility produced a delightful concoction of hydroponically grown vegetables for a very satisfying main course. There followed the lightest, most delicious compote, washed down by a fruity Anraatian wine, which complemented the meal perfectly. Afterward, when we'd checked we were on course and everything was functioning normally, we sat in the recreation area. I gave Dahll a long, hard look.

"Right, then, you promised to tell me about the Salmaran...Narhjohol, and why *you* weren't affected by hyper-acceleration."

"Oh, that can wait."

"You promised."

He frowned, and I could see he was reluctant to tell me, but in the end he gave in. Anraat, he said, is in the same star system as Grakk and Salmar. Although not actually at war with each other, there is a certain amount of rivalry and animosity between his home world and Grakk. The Grakks had developed their own ships in a similar manner to the Anraatians.

"Because their ships are modelled on ours," Dahll went on, "the Grakks and Salmarans are faced with the same problems regarding hyper-acceleration. While the hyper-shield protects the passengers and crew of a starship, it also means that for a short time they're unconscious. Even with the ship under computer control, this can be inconvenient at times...and could be crucial in an emergency."

I nodded in agreement. The problem was obvious. This was something I'd never had to face on Earth-built ships, which have an in-built dampening system.

"A few years ago," Dahll went on, "my father developed a formula, which protected the user by temporarily altering their metabolism, thus enabling them to remain conscious throughout hyper-acceleration."

He paused meaningfully for a moment. "When he heard of the Phidians' great advances in medicine, he contacted them and they agreed to collaborate with him to perfect the drug.

"While I was on Anraat, completing my study of advanced astrophysics and the finer points of flying one of these—" He made a gesture that encompassed the whole ship— "he, my mother and my sister visited friends in a hamlet on Dolsimerh, a small neighbouring planet. Two weeks after they arrived, Narhjohol raided the village and captured my sister. When she resisted him, he subjected her to brutal mind-manipulating procedures, in order to make her more amenable. In so doing, he inadvertently learnt of my father's formula. Then he used a probe on her to try to find out where the formula was hidden. However, that was known only to my father."

Dahll stopped speaking for a moment, his expression troubled. "Not many people survive a Salmaran mind probe. When she died, Narhjohol went after my father and tried to make him sell the formula to him, knowing he could demand his own price for it from the Grakks. When he wouldn't cooperate, Narhjohol killed him. My mother killed herself rather than be taken by him."

The look on his face was now one of bitterness...and hatred. I touched his arm lightly in sympathy.

Dahll's clear eyes darkened for a moment, and he hesitated slightly before continuing. "I only learned what happened afterward, when it was too late. My father arranged for me to receive a coded message should anything happen to him. It took a while, but I was eventually able to work out where to find the formula. Also who to contact on Phidia to produce samples for testing."

"And Narhjohol's been coming after you for the formula ever since?"

Dahll grinned humourlessly. "More like me being after him. He knows the first chance I get I'm going to kill him."

I shivered slightly, he looked so grim, not at all the carefree, gentle boy he'd seemed up until now.

"But he was on Phidia when you were. If you're so determined to avenge your family, why not then?"

"Have you forgotten the Phidians' laws against violence and the carrying of weapons? I'd have been arrested immediately if I'd tried to bring a weapon down to the planet, or even just confronted Narhjohol without one. That's why I was so anxious to leave Phidia. I knew if I left first he'd follow me, but if he got away before me, he'd extrapolate my course and lie in ambush. I'd rather keep one step in front of him."

"But this ship's armed. You could have opened fire on him."

Dahll looked me straight in the eyes. "Risking my own neck's one thing. I don't intend to take the slightest risk with yours. Narhjohol's ship is large and fully manned. He's not going to stand quietly by and be blasted out of the ether without taking retaliatory action, although he won't fire first. I'm no good to him dead."

"Well there's no need to be concerned about me," I said quietly. "But I'm sorry, I didn't realise—"

"Of course not," Dahll assured me hastily. "I reckon I'd best be straight with you, though. When Yan Kloor asked me if I'd consider chartering my ship to you, I nearly refused. I didn't want to risk getting you involved with Narhjohol. There's no telling how long it'll be before we catch up with the *Destiny,* and I didn't want to chance losing him, either."

"Then why did you agree?"

"I needed the money," Dahll stated candidly. "Unfortunately, my father ran up a lot of debts while he was perfecting the formula, and I had to pay them off. I couldn't consider selling it until I knew it was completely reliable, so I couldn't count on the proceeds. I decided Narhjohol would have to wait. He wants me alive for the formula, so I don't think you're in any danger, and I don't think it'll be hard to shake him off our tail for a while. His ship's large but not nearly as fast and manoeuvrable as this one."

While Dahll was speaking, the reason why he'd not activated his own shield had been dawning upon me.

"Is that why you've been testing it on yourself?"

He glanced at me sharply, then nodded slowly. "The Phidians subjected it to numerous clinical tests under computer simulated hyperspacial conditions to ensure its safety, but since they no longer have any ships of their own it's never actually been tested in space."

I shook my head in mock despair. "And of course you have to be the one to give it its maiden test."

"Why not? It's my formula now. It's only right I should be the first to try it out in practice."

I gave him my most direct look. "I want to use it, too."

"Sorry, not until I'm absolutely certain it hasn't any side effects, although there's no real reason why there should be. The Phidians were very thorough."

"You didn't suffer any side effects, did you?"

Dahll's lips formed a half smile. "You don't get round me like that. I've used it under the supervision of the Phidians before they would allow me to use it under hyperspacial conditions. I may be lucky, or it might affect you differently—we're from different worlds, remember. I want the scientists on Anraat to test it, as well, before it's released for general use."

I glared at him in exasperation. "Dahll, you said the Phidians tested it. I know how they work. They wouldn't have agreed to let you try it on yourself if they weren't convinced of its safety."

"The answer's still no."

But I could see by his expression he was beginning to weaken.

"I promise I'll tell you at once if I feel any

unpleasant side effects, but I'm sure it'll be all right. Please let me try it...just once. It'll be a much better trial if we both use it, and compare notes."

The smile hovering on Dahll's lips allowed itself to become a grin, but his eyes were still serious.

"Persistent, aren't you! All right, you win. I'll let you use it once, after we've done some tests to ensure your compatibility, but if you feel the slightest discomfort—"

"I'll let you know immediately, of course," I promised. I've been secretly dreading using the shield, ever since Dahll showed me how it works. I'm afraid any artificially induced sleep, however short the duration, might precipitate one of the horrifying nightmares that torment me. I'd rather take my chances without the shield.

"I'll take your word. Just remember I might have to answer to Yan Kloor for your welfare, some day."

"Does he know about Narhjohol and your parents and sister?"

"I told him everything when he first asked me if I would take you along. I didn't want him to be under any misapprehensions, and I was a little worried about your safety if we ran into Narhjohol. He seemed to think you'd be safe with me. Although we can't track each other through hyperspace, once we've found the ship you're searching for, I'll find *him*. A Salmaran slave ship isn't the easiest thing to hide."

He smiled again, beginning to look more like his old self, so I refrained from repeating that I was quite capable of looking after myself.

"I'm sorry. I would have told you about Narhjohol before we left, given you the chance to change your mind. But Yan Kloor seemed to think it important that you left at once and there was no time to find another ship—"

"It wouldn't have made any difference," I told him. "I'm not afraid of Narhjohol. I just want to find the *Destiny*."

"Now I've told you my story, perhaps you'll trust me enough to tell me yours...when you're ready," he said quietly.

I didn't answer. He knows it's important to me to find the *Destiny*. I haven't told him why, nor have I said anything about the nature of my treatment at the Medical Centre. Perhaps it would be fairer to tell him, but at present I still find it too difficult to talk about.

****

157-13.08

It's now three days—Anraatian ship's time—since we left Phidia. The ship handles beautifully and I love piloting her, when Dahll will let me, that is. Her controls are not so different from an Earth ship, although they seemed a little strange at first, and there were some features Dahll had to explain to me.

I asked him if I could name her the *Quest*, since the symbols emblazoned on her hull, which he reels off automatically, are totally incomprehensible to me. I think he found my request amusing, but he agreed readily enough. The Anraatians don't name inanimate objects, which they regard as purely functional, but already I have come to love this little craft and feel at home in her.

I'm beginning to realise how much I owe to Yan Kloor for recommending Dahll and his ship to me. I know how difficult things would be if Dahll tried to put our relationship on anything more than a friendly business footing.

From what I have learnt of Anraatian culture, women on Anraat are treated with the greatest courtesy by the males of that planet. Even, it seems, with a degree of reverence. They are highly respected as individuals, and most occupy positions of power and privilege.

Dahll behaves toward me with a courtesy that, at times, I feel almost borders on patronising, but I can't help liking him. He is very self-assured, and I have absolute confidence in his ability as a pilot. Despite his apparent youth, he is a master spacer and has taught me much about the ship in the short time we've been on board.

The computer predicts it will take just over twenty-one ship's days to reach Niflheim at our present speed. Niflheim. Planet of telepaths and home of Delian and Ragin, two of the *Destiny*'s crew.

It's a start.

****

157-05.09

Life on board the *Quest* has been purely routine. We've made regular entries in the ship's log, of course, but there has been nothing of importance to record in my journal. Niflheim fills the main scanner screen now and I can hardly take my eyes off it.

Surface conditions are difficult to predict because of the vapour clouds surrounding the planet. However, the computer indicates the following: It has a breathable atmosphere, although the oxygen content is rather low, especially on higher ground. It has no natural satellites and animal life is minimal, except in the more temperate areas. There is little variety in the vegetation, which nevertheless is plentiful where conditions are favourable, and most of the populated areas are on the far side of the planet.

Deceleration and entry into normal space will be in precisely twenty-three minutes. Dahll reluctantly administered the serum, as promised, after first insisting on an analysis of DNA, blood and tissue samples from us both. The results are highly favourable. Biologically, Dahll and I are as human as each other, and I foresee no complications arising from my use of the formula. Certainly, at present, I don't feel any ill effects.

The real test will come, of course, when we are actually decelerating. I can't feel apprehensive. I am too excited at the thought that every second brings us closer to Niflheim, where my search will begin in earnest.

## Chapter Four

Computer Reference Ec34-76801

*NIFLHEIM: Colonised in the year 2173(old calendar) it was named after the mythical Scandinavian land of mist and cold because for much of the year low vapour clouds cover many parts of the planet. The early settlers made an intense study of ESP and eventually developed telepathy and telekinesis to a high degree. By the second half of the twenty-third century, telepathy had become their natural means of communication*

Date As Before

We made planet fall ten hours ago, according to the timepiece Dahll gave me as part of my travel pack. (Based on Anraatian time, ship's time is divided into twenty sections, each section roughly seven minutes longer than an Earth day.) I'm happy to record that the formula did its work with no apparent ill effects. I ached slightly for a while after we'd re-entered normal space, but Dahll says it's usual to experience some slight discomfort at first. It was certainly nothing to complain about compared to what I'd experienced without it.

The *Quest*, unlike the *Destiny*, is small enough to land and lift off from a planet without it being necessary to use ferries. We touched down on a vast plain, devoid it seemed of any life and with only a sparse covering of short, purplish vegetation scarcely visible beneath a fine powdering of snow.

The computer indicated that in the areas of densest population the temperature is cold, although not extreme. There is, it informed us, a settlement, large by Nifl standards, situated on the other side of the mountains. Because of the dense cloud cover, the sensors were unable to confirm whether there is a suitable area there to land the ship. The *Quest* is equipped with a hover-hopper though, so it shouldn't be too difficult to reach.

We adjusted the thermostats of our suits to a level that was pleasantly comfortable, and in addition, I wrapped myself in the cloak Sitta gave me on Phidia and pulled on long, insulated boots.

Dahll handed me a chronograph-like object. "Sims-translator."

"Is it necessary?" I queried. "Being an Earth Colony, surely the Nifls will speak *Common Universal*?"

"Well, they don't take up much room," Dahll pointed out, strapping his own onto his wrist. "I've never been to Niflheim before, and since it has no links with Anraat there's not much data on it. Some of the Nifls might've stopped using *Common Universal* by now. Besides," he added, touching it briefly to demonstrate, "it's also a communicator, so if we should get separated we can keep in touch with each other."

We made one more check with the computer and equipped ourselves with sidearm, wrist flares and survival packs. Then we hauled out the hopper, and prepared to set foot on Niflheim.

To the north, beyond the ship, a range of high, denticulate mountains stretched into the distance, cutting across the plain like giant dragon's teeth. Their summits were half-hidden in swirling mist. To the east and west, the featureless plain stretched out endlessly. Straight ahead stood a forest of tall, needle-leafed trees, covering the slopes of the mountains beyond which, the computer indicated, lay the Nifl settlement.

"It looks pretty dark in there," Dahll said,

folding his long legs into the hover-hopper and drawing his blaster. "I think it's best not to take any chances."

I put my hand lightly on my own weapon, hoping I wouldn't have to use it. Activating my wrist flare, to augment the lights of the hopper, I settled myself beside Dahll. It was easy going, at first. There was little undergrowth, and the trees did not crowd too closely together at the edge of the forest. After a while, however, the land began to slope sharply upward, and the trees grew closer together. The thin air made it difficult to breathe and I was glad we did not have to walk. Even with the vehicle, it seemed to take a long time before we reached the edge of the forest.

When the trees thinned out at last, we found ourselves on a high plateau. Looking back, we could see the mountains beyond the *Quest*. The rocky floor before us spread out for several metres and on one side rose again to form a low cliff studded with dark holes that appeared to be caverns.

I turned to Dahll. "According to the computer, the settlement is on the other side of these mountains. I wonder if these caves go through to the other side?"

"It's quite possible. You keep watch here and I'll check them. If nothing else, we might need to take shelter in them for the night."

I nodded. While we had been working our way through the forest, hovering a few feet above the forest floor, the steady decline in the amount of daylight filtering through had scarcely been noticeable in the murky gloom between the trees. Now, however, I became aware that both the yellow G-type sun and the much more distant red giant were rapidly sinking on the horizon.

"If you see or hear anything, contact me on the communicator," Dahll said, jumping down from the vehicle. "I'll try not to be too long. I just want to make sure those caves are uninhabited."

I watched him stride off into the nearest cave. I guided the hover-hopper to the mouth of the cave into which Dahll had disappeared and left it next to the rock face, just inside. If we had to go through the caves, the small vehicle would be safer here than out in the open. I turned back to scan the mountains, straining my eyes to try to find the *Quest*. The red sun cast an eerie pink glow over everything. At last, I picked out the ship, standing in the clearing beyond the forest, her hull catching the last dying rays of both suns.

The mist almost completely enveloped the mountains now and was rapidly sweeping down toward the forest. I noticed it was no longer white but pink and attributed the change in colour to the setting suns. Suddenly I felt a wave of unexpected homesickness sweep over me as I remembered there are still a few places left on Earth where one can watch the clouds turn rosy at sunset, without being poisoned by her polluted atmosphere.

I don't know how long I stood there, staring at the mountains, but when I looked away, Dahll was standing beside me once more.

"Your thoughts were far away from this planet, I think," he said softly.

I nodded. "I was thinking of my own world," I told him. "In some ways Niflheim reminds me of Earth." I shivered and drew my cloak closer around me. While I'd been standing there, the air had grown noticeably colder. I turned for another look at the *Quest*. I could no longer see her. In fact, the clouds of pink mist now completely obliterated the forest and the mountains. The sky had lost its colour and become a dull, metallic grey.

"That mist is getting closer," I told Dahll. "Perhaps we'd better find shelter before—" I stopped as the true nature of those rolling pink clouds struck me.

"That's not mist," Dahll said, "it's snow!" He took hold of my hand and pulled me in the direction of the caves, just as I felt the first flakes fall on my face. The thin air made it difficult to run. The snow was getting thicker every second.

We were within yards of the caves when I stumbled and nearly fell. Dahll grabbed hold of me around the waist and half carried me the rest of the way. We dived inside the first cave and sank down onto the ground near the entrance, gasping for breath.

After my head stopped spinning, and once my lungs had ceased straining and my heartbeat was close to normal again, I glanced at Dahll. As our eyes met, we burst out laughing. Perhaps it was weakness from lack of food and our exertions in the rarefied atmosphere of the planet, but it took several minutes for us to regain control of ourselves.

"What was so funny?" Dahll asked when he could speak. I shook my head, wiping the tears from my eyes. "I don't know," I confessed. "I just realised what a pair of idiots we were, running away from a little snowstorm, like that."

"Little snowstorm?" Dahll retorted. "Just take a look outside."

I went to the cave mouth. The snow fell in a thick, pink sheet, already piled high in front of the cave. Its colour had nothing to do with Niflheim's red sun.

"You're right," I said soberly. "It wouldn't have been very funny if we'd been out in that for long. But...pink snow? Have you ever seen such a thing before?"

"No, I haven't, but then it's rare to see snow at all, where I come from."

"Coloured snow isn't unheard of on Earth," I

mused. "It's very uncommon, though, and I've never seen it myself." I realised I was very hungry. We hadn't stopped for a meal since we'd left the ship.

"Perhaps we should have something to eat while we're waiting for the storm to pass?" I suggested.

Dahll frowned. "I'm not too keen on survival rations, but you're right, we need to keep our strength up."

While we sipped the self-heating protein and vitamin mixture and nibbled on the somewhat tasteless nutrient bars, we debated our next course of action. The snow outside showed no signs of abating and it was already quite dark.

"I think we should follow the caves back as far as we can," Dahll said. "I've had a quick look around and there seems to be a network of passages and caverns. They're faintly illuminated somehow, so I think we can assume they're in regular use. From what I've seen so far I reckon there's a good chance the caverns go right through to another part of Niflheim.

"Perhaps," I agreed cautiously. "But we don't know what might be lurking in some of these caves, either."

"Well, there's not much animal life in this region, according to the computer," Dahll reminded me. "And we can be pretty sure the Nifls themselves, if we come across any, will be friendly, from what you've told me. Besides, we have our blasters, and anything's better than sitting here indefinitely, waiting for the snow to stop."

I had to agree. So, having finished our meal, we checked our blasters and switched on our wrist flares again.

As Dahll pointed out, the cavern we were in had some form of dim lighting, although from what source we couldn't tell. The extra light from our flares sent the shadows leaping and dancing wildly around us.

The cave was much larger than I had supposed, with huge stone pillars and rocky outcrops.

"Keep close behind me," Dahll cautioned unnecessarily, "and be prepared to use your blaster if you have to." The cave narrowed at the back into a tunnel slanting gradually downward and growing steeper as we progressed along it. The passage was wide enough for us to walk in single file quite comfortably, although there would not have been enough room for two to walk side by side. As we walked, I became more and more convinced Dahll's suppositions were right and the passage was in regular use. The floor was smooth beneath our feet and there was none of the usual debris which one would expect to find in a deserted network of caves.

After walking for about thirty minutes, the light became much stronger, and we stepped into a natural amphitheatre. At least we assumed at first sight it was natural, but it's possible the inhabitants of Niflheim could have hewn it out of the solid rock.

For several seconds we stared in awe, not speaking. The soft, golden light appeared to come from the walls themselves. It struck flashes of diamond bright light from the most beautiful stalactites and stalagmites I've ever seen, their crystal formations glinting and sparkling with rainbow colours.

Ranged around the sides of the arena, as if to form seats, were smooth, greenish-white slabs, like pale onyx. At one end, a fountain set in a deep pool shimmered as if composed of liquid gold and threw up spray that gleamed like precious molten metal.

I looked at Dahll in awe. "What is it?" I asked softly, for some reason feeling I shouldn't raise my voice above a whisper.

Dahll shook his head. "I'm not sure. It almost seems like some kind of temple." At the far end was a high dais, on either side of which ran a passage. We looked at each other.

"It appears we're going to have to separate," I said. Dahll shook his head.

"No, we stay together."

Why?" I demanded. "If there's any danger, we have the blasters, so why waste time?"

"We're on a strange planet and we don't know what we might encounter. Until we're sure what we're up against, we should stay together."

"Dahll, I know you think you need to protect me, but it's really not necessary. I can take care of myself. We can keep in communicator contact. If either of us does run into trouble, surely it's better for the other one to be free to help, if possible, and if not, to return to the ship?"

I could tell by Dahll's expression he could see the sense in this, even though he obviously didn't like it.

He favoured me with that look he gives me occasionally, and which I must admit I find a little disconcerting. "Tell me," he said, smiling to take away the edge to his words, "are you always so stubborn?"

"I just feel it would be sensible to split up and explore the passages separately," I insisted, ignoring the affront on my character, "so long as we can still keep in touch."

"Perhaps you're right," Dahll admitted grudgingly. He peered along the nearest passage, to the left of the dais.

"I'll take this one. If you see or hear anything, contact me at once."

We took one last look at the wonders of the cavern and prepared to separate.

"Don't take any chances," was Dahll's parting shot. "If we should lose contact, return to the ship."

He disappeared into the passage before I could

argue. I listened to his footsteps getting fainter and fainter and forced myself to shake off the sudden feeling of isolation that descended on me. After all, it *had* been my idea.

The right-hand passage was wider than the one we had just travelled along and seemed to be more brightly lit. Probably why Dahll had chosen to take the other one himself.

The going was easy. The passage sloped sharply downward, as had the previous one, and it also appeared to be in regular use.

I wondered why we hadn't seen any Nifls and where their settlement might be. I would have thought that with their telepathic powers they would have known of our landing some time ago. I would have expected them to have made contact by now. Then again, if my memories of Delian and Ragin were anything to go by, the Nifls were a rather quiet and introverted people. Perhaps they were waiting for us to make the first move. It might be that, gauging our presence on Niflheim as posing no threat to them, they were not even interested in making contact with us.

As I rounded a bend in the passage, deep in my own thoughts, but with my blaster poised ready for trouble, a distant blood-curdling screech shattered the silence. I shrank back against the wall, holding my blaster in both hands, expecting at any moment some gigantic creature to materialise and launch itself at me.

After a few minutes, when nothing had appeared, I continued cautiously along the passage, blaster still at the ready. I had only gone a few hundred yards when the tunnel divided without warning, forking obliquely to the right. I hesitated a moment, before continuing straight ahead. As I progressed along it, the passage began to narrow, and to my concern, the light faded out. Also, I noticed the ground had become very uneven and boulder strewn. I decided to go back and try the other branch of the passage. Then it came again, that shrill, wailing cry.

I braced myself for another of those unearthly cries, as I activated my communicator.

"Dahll," I said, anxiously. "Are you all right?"

Dahll's voice held a note of surprise.

"Yes, of course. I haven't come across anything interesting so far. What about you?"

"You didn't hear it then?"

"Hear what?"

"There was a strange sort of animal cry just now. It seemed to come from somewhere ahead of me."

Dahll's small holographic image hovering above my communicator seemed to stiffen and his voice registered concern. "I haven't heard anything this side. You may be in danger, I think. You'd better come back. I'll meet you in the cavern."

"No, Dahll. If there is a creature of some sort in the passage, I might lead it to you if I came back now, and then we'd both be in danger."

The image was too small for me to see Dahll's expression clearly in the dim light of my wrist flare. I could imagine it, though, in the brief pause that followed.

"It would be better to have two weapons against it, if it's dangerous."

I thought for a moment and decided perhaps he was right after all. "All right," I said reluctantly. "I'll come back now. This particular passage doesn't look as if it leads anywhere anyhow."

"Good," Dahll said, sounding relieved. "I'll wait for you in the cavern."

I was about to retrace my steps when the creature shrieked again, this time sounding much closer. I wasn't sure of the direction because the rocky escarpments sent echoes reverberating in all directions. I flashed my wrist flare in front of me, straining my eyes in the semi-darkness, trying to see beyond the shadows.

I moved forward a few metres. The surface was very uneven. I stumbled, and the ground gave way beneath my feet. I felt myself slipping and stifled a yell, dropping the blaster as dust and pebbles rained down on me. I slid down a steep slope and when I scrambled to my feet at the bottom was relieved to note that at least my wrist flare was still intact.

My descent had been brief, and I was shaken more than hurt. However, the walls of the declivity down which I had fallen were several metres above my head and looked none too safe to attempt to climb. I was about to contact Dahll to explain my predicament when I became aware of something moving behind me.

I turned sharply, and came face to face with a huge, bear-like creature, with luminous green eyes that seemed more feline than ursine. As I looked around in desperation for my blaster, the beast raised a giant paw. I shrank back against the cold stone wall, realising I was completely at its mercy.

# Chapter Five

I tried to quell the feeling of panic, which threatened to deprive me of my ability to think. My heart thumped in my chest and I was aware of beads of perspiration on my brow. I slowly brushed my sleeve across my forehead, taking several deep breaths as I did so. The beast would smell my fear, and I knew I had to try to remain calm.

It was not the first time I'd stared death in the face. I'm not entirely unprepared for it, but neither am I in any particular hurry to meet it.

I reflected upon the irony of having survived the trauma of all that happened to me on Phidia, only to have my search for the *Destiny* end here, on the very planet where I'd hoped to pick up her trail.

The light from my wrist flare showed the creature crouched, pale and ghost-like, the tip of its short tail twitching spasmodically. Its brilliant eyes had an almost mesmerising effect. I forced myself to look away, trying desperately to think of a way out of the situation. If I attempted to contact Dahll now, the sound might alarm the beast and cause it to spring.

Very, very slowly, I ran my hand down my leg toward my boot knife. On more than one occasion, it has been invaluable in an emergency. I was not prepared to stand and allow the creature to tear me to pieces without making at least some attempt to protect myself. At the same time, I hated the thought of killing such a magnificent animal. However, sentiment can be a dangerous companion in times of crisis.

All at once, it inclined its great head to one side, for all the world like a domestic dog on Earth listening for its master's call. It growled deep down in its throat, the sound ending in a long, drawn-out shriek. My fingers closing around the knife, I stood motionless, expecting at any moment to have the creature spring at me, its claws tearing at my throat.

Instead, I began to experience a feeling of great calm. The tension left my body and my breathing, which was still laboured from lack of oxygen, became easier. Another mind was reaching out, touching my own. I must relax, it told me. The animal meant me no harm. There was nothing to fear.

My mind became a blank, my body weightless. I closed my eyes and had a momentary, strange sensation of floating upward. When I opened my eyes again, I found myself standing on the edge of the pit beside a dark-haired man with a neat pointed beard. Next to him stood a striking-looking girl, her black hair worn in a braid that nearly reached her feet. They smiled at my obvious bewilderment.

"Levitation," the man said, speaking slowly and carefully, as if not used to the spoken word, "is not so far removed from telekinesis, and such things are commonplace to a telepath."

"But I'm not telepathic."

He smiled again. "No, but you are very receptive. Once we calmed your fears, it was easy for us to manipulate you in order to help you."

In another moment, my blaster sailed through the air, to settle snugly in my hand.

"Perhaps you feel more at ease, now you have your weapon?"

I lowered it to my side. The Nifls were both unarmed and would hardly have returned the gun to me if they intended any harm.

"Thank you," I replied, speaking in *Common*

*Universal*, as he had. "My companion...is he all right?"

"Your friend is quite safe," he assured me. "We have contacted him, and my sister is guiding him here." I glanced at the young woman, who stood absolutely still, with her eyes closed and a look of rapt concentration on her face.

"We'll take you to our city, Gladsheim, and after you have rested and refreshed yourselves you can tell us how we can help you."

Gladsheim—the great *Hall of Joy* of Asgaard in the mythical Niflheim. Strange, my memory has retained such information, presumably learnt from my childhood, yet I still have no recollection of the events that separated me from the *Destiny*'s crew. Will I ever know, or will it always remain a mystery, like the meaning of the hideous dreams that used to haunt me?

Footsteps sounded in the passage, and a moment later Dahll appeared. He looked at me, staring straight past the Nifls, hidden in the shadows.

"Thank goodness you're all right," he said quietly. "I had some sort of telepathic message, but I wasn't sure if it was a trap."

He holstered his blaster. "I said we should stay together. I knew you'd find trouble."

"I also found the locals," I retorted, smiling, too pleased at seeing him again, unharmed, to resent his words. "Or rather, they found me."

The telepaths stepped out from the darkness. The man extended his hand to touch Dahll's fingertips in the Nifl manner.

"Welcome. I am Gullin of the House of Yarvi, and this is my sister, Tamarith."

Dahll returned the greeting politely, before adjusting his flare and glancing warily into the pit where the great bear-like creature still crouched, making a sound that was surprisingly like a cat purring.

"You left your communicator on audio transmit," he said. "When I heard the animal, I was afraid it'd attacked you."

"Malmooth would not hurt anyone," Tamarith said. "See, I will show you." She went to the edge of the crater and stood in silence for a moment.

She must have spoken to it telepathically, for the next instant it leapt out of the pit to land softly at her feet, sitting with its head inclined and one huge paw slightly raised. Dahll eyed it suspiciously and I stepped back a little.

"You see?" Tamarith scratched the beast behind its ears and again it made that deep rumbling in its throat like a contented cat. Apart from its eyes, it resembled a bear more than anything else. Its shaggy coat was a creamy yellow colour and it had four long, hooked claws on each paw, which did not appear to be retractable, like a true feline's. It seems the Nifls call them 'ice-cats' and keep them as domestic pets. Apparently, soon after colonisation, while they were still experimenting with telepathy, they discovered that these creatures were easily tamed and very responsive to telepathic commands.

"So much for the computer's prediction of minimal animal life," I murmured to Dahll.

"Even a computer can't be right all the time," he said defensively. He looked at Gullin enquiringly.

"Many parts of Niflheim have very little in the way of animal species," the Nifl told us. "But in areas where the climate is less severe and some variety of plants can be found, there is quite a diversity of animals. The ice cat is the largest animal native to Niflheim. Despite its size, it *is* herbivorous, which is fortunate," he added with a wry smile.

He looked at his sister. "Come, Tamarith, we're being poor hosts. Our guests must be tired, and hungry also."

The young woman ceased petting the ice-cat and turned to Gullin. "Of course. I've already sent word to Gladsheim to tell them we found the strangers and are bringing them to the city."

I was happy enough to allow them to lead us back to the fork in the passage, which obviously I should have taken instead of continuing straight ahead. I couldn't answer for Dahll, but I was certainly both tired and hungry. Our meal in the cave seemed to have taken place a very long time ago.

Also, the low oxygen atmosphere, which appeared to have no effect on Tamarith and her brother, was starting to make me feel distinctly light-headed. I was feeling the chill slightly, too, despite the warmth of Sitta's cloak, for I had only set the controls on my suit to minimum. It was, of course, even colder in the labyrinths than it had been on the planet's surface. I adjusted the suit temperature from the small control panel on my sleeve and followed Gullin.

The tunnel along which we now progressed was illuminated much more brightly than the one in which Gullin and Tamarith had found me. At length we came to a place where it opened out into another large cave, through which ran a swift river. Moored on the shingle were two small boats.

Tamarith stepped into one, holding out her hand to Dahll to help him in beside her. Gullin and I took the other. I was a little surprised to find the Nifls use boats, since they have the power of levitation. My curiosity getting the better of me, I said so to Gullin.

"We do not normally use levitation as a means of transport," he explained. "Rather, it's a form of meditation and relaxation. If necessary, some of us use it to travel short distances, but we prefer to use more conventional modes of transportation."

The river carried us along at a rapid pace. Each boat was equipped with a single paddle, enabling the Nifls to keep the boats from getting too close to the shore.

Malmooth had plunged into the icy waters, apparently quite unconcerned. He swam strongly behind the boats in a most un-catlike manner, seemingly quite unhampered by his thick, woolly pelt.

The water shimmered in the golden, phosphorescent glow from the walls, like the pool in the cavern where Dahll and I had separated. Beautiful, delicate stalactites hung from the roof of the tunnel, looking like the branches and flowers of some exotic forest. Here and there along the banks of the underground river were peculiar gigantic stone figures. I asked Gullin if they were natural.

He said the figures had been in the underground caverns when the original settlers of Niflheim had first explored them. They were roughly human in shape, and although crudely formed, had a strange beauty. If they were not natural, Gullin went on, the civilisation that had fashioned them must have died out long before the first Terran set foot on Niflheim. No other trace of it had, as yet, been found.

At length we came to a huge wall of water cascading down from the roof of the cave in an awesome, iridescent waterfall. The Nifls steered the boats to the side and we disembarked, hauling the boats up onto the shore. Ahead of us was another tunnel, well lit and wider than any we had yet passed through. After we'd been walking for a while, Gullin looked at me reassuringly.

"There is not much farther to go now. A short ride and we'll soon reach Gladsheim." I glanced back at Dahll, wondering if he was as tired as I was. We seemed to have travelled for much longer than the five hours indicated by my chronometer since we left the ship.

Another turn in the passage and we were out in the open once more. While we were in the caves, night had fallen and the mountains were in darkness. Near to the entrance of the cave from which we'd just emerged stood a young boy. He held the reins of several large, sturdy-looking, sandy-coloured ponies. Tamarith told us they were descended from genetically engineered Fjord and Icelandic stock brought with the first settlers in cryogenic suspension.

As soon as we were mounted, Gullin led the way and we set off on the final stage of our journey. The ponies picked their way delicately down the narrow trail, which zigzagged down the mountainside. Niflheim's moon and the countless stars shed a silvery light over the snow-covered landscape. I was grateful for the sure-footedness of the ponies, which never once missed a step or stumbled on the slippery track. As we reached the foot of the mountain, they sprang into a gallop that ate up the metres. I have not had the opportunity to ride a horse since I left Earth, but it felt good to be in the saddle again.

The saddles themselves were deep and comfortable, the seats covered with soft fleeces, woven, I'm told, from the fur shorn from the ice cats. The gelding I rode was very responsive, moving low to the ground, with steady, rhythmic strides. I found the ride across the snow-covered plain exhilarating, dispelling my earlier weariness.

I wasn't sure if Dahll was used to horseback riding, but he seemed to handle his own mount well enough. I was almost sorry when Gullin reined in his pony at last and announced we'd reached the city of Gladsheim.

A minor shift of my weight and a slight tightening of my fingers on the reins was enough to make my pony slow down and stand obediently for me to dismount. I patted him gently by way of thanks, and stared around, marvelling at the beauty of the scene before me.

Gladsheim is set around the sides of a deep valley. The area in the centre comprises a long, narrow ornamental lake, flanked by mosaic paving with fountains and flowering shrubs. The jagged mountains, which form the walls of the valley, are so high I could scarcely see their snow-covered peaks, which made a sharp contrast to the soft lines and curves of the buildings below.

I was surprised to see flowers everywhere, pushing themselves out of the snowy ground as prolifically as anything growing in a more temperate climate. My first impression of the various dwellings themselves was that they were so graceful they appeared as if the slightest breeze would blow them away. The tall spires and turrets of many of the structures made it look like a scene from a fairy tale, such as the ones pictured in the holobooks I watched as a child. They must have been constructed or overlaid with the same substance as the walls of the caves, since they glowed with a similar soft luminescence, without the need for additional lighting.

The young Nifl lad, who had ridden with us, came forward to lead the ponies away and Gullin gestured to Dahll and me to follow himself and Tamarith. A high, delicate bridge spans the lake, and as we crossed it, it produced a low, musical sound, like little tinkling bells. The shining metal from which it is constructed flashed and sparkled with many colours in the reflected light from the buildings, reminding me of the Rainbow Bridge of Scandinavian mythology. Ranged outside the houses were small groups of Nifls, obviously curious about us. They stood politely aside to let us pass, and some murmured soft words of greeting.

One, an elderly, distinguished-looking man with grey hair, stepped forward.

"This is Liftrar, one of our Elders," Gullin said, and we again exchanged the Nifl form of greeting. He joined us as we walked toward a large, elegant dwelling on the other side of the lake. When we reached it, he and Gullin stopped and appeared to be 'conversing' wordlessly. Tamarith put her hand lightly on my arm.

"Come," she invited, "you will stay with us."

We entered the building and I found myself separated from Dahll as Tamarith escorted me to a spacious, comfortable room, sparsely but adequately furnished. An enormous dining table was set for a meal, with several chairs as well as a long, low couch at one end. We walked through, into a narrow corridor and through a low archway.

Tamarith opened a door at the end of the corridor to reveal a fountain playing into a pool of clear water. "You can bathe and refresh yourself before we dine, but first I'll show you the room that will be yours during your stay."

She led me up a steep ornamental staircase to what were obviously the sleeping quarters, and showed me into a room whose window looked out across the lake.

A light, refreshing fragrance filled the air. It came, I assumed, from the creamy gold and pale pink blossoms arranged in bowls and vases all around the room. The floor covering was soft to the tread, the bed large and inviting.

"I hope you'll be comfortable here," she said with a smile. "When you are ready to bathe, you will find everything you need by the pool."

I thanked her, and she left after instructing me to be sure to call her if there was anything else I should require.

I laid my pack down at the side of the bed, and removed my travel-worn clothing. A long robe hung on the back of the door, and I slipped it on and went back down the stairs to the pool. A pale, green light illuminated the bathing chamber. The pool itself was formed from smooth, olive-veined stone, which looked like marble. It was shallow at one end, with a very gradual downward slope. Drying cloths and several bottles of coloured liquids were arranged on the low shelf that ran around it.

I removed the robe and uncorked one of the bottles, sniffing curiously. It smelt of pine forests and sea winds, and something else I couldn't quite place. It foamed on my skin, tingling slightly. Still clutching the bottle, I stepped in at the shallow end and waded in deeper, following the slope. Warm and refreshing, the water flowed gently in, at one end of the pool, and out the other, continually being replenished but remaining at a constant level.

I sang softly to myself as I washed...oh, the indulgence of limitless fresh water! The sonic shower on board the *Quest* is hygienic, but hardly luxurious. I had to remind myself sharply that our hosts were expecting Dahll and me to dine with them, soon. It wouldn't be courteous to keep them waiting.

I left the water reluctantly, and dried myself by the poolside, smoothing some of the scented oil from another bottle into my skin. My hair, which when I first regained consciousness on Phidia was quite short, has now grown long and thick. I knew it would take time to dry properly, but I rubbed it until it was merely damp and I was able to run a brush through it.

I put on the robe again and went back up to the sleeping chamber. My clothes, which I had folded carefully and placed on a seat near the window, now lay spread neatly on the bed. They had obviously already been cleaned and pressed. They were clearly not quite suitable for a family meal, and beside them, I found a long, elegant gown, made from a pretty, cream-coloured fabric. A pair of soft, comfortable house shoes completed the outfit. Tamarith has certainly taken great pains to ensure my physical comfort and I feel almost as at home here as if I were with my own friends back on Earth.

****

I enjoyed my first meal with the Nifls. Dahll appeared, looking as relaxed and refreshed as I felt. Tamarith gestured to him to sit beside her and I was placed next to Gullin.

We were introduced to their younger brother and sister, the twins Rhenn and Melind. They look a few years younger than Tamarith who is, I think, about seventeen or eighteen years old, while Gullin seems about nine or ten years Tamarith's senior.

Although barely more than children, Rhenn and Melind are as friendly and interesting to talk to as their siblings. There is a strong family resemblance between all four. Gullin told us their parents were lost several years ago in an accident in the mountains, and he and Tamarith have taken care of the two younger children ever since.

After our meal, we talked for a long while about Niflheim and Old Earth. I told them of my search for the *Destiny* and they have promised to help me.

Tamarith paid a great deal of attention to everything Dahll said and seemed to be very taken with him. He appears to enjoy her company as much as she does his. She is certainly very beautiful. She is petite—the Nifls as a race tend not to be tall—and has a good figure. Her pale skin is flawless. She has high cheekbones with large black eyes and thick lashes, and masses of long black hair. I can't blame Dahll for being attracted to her.

Supposing he decides to stay? It would be very difficult to find another ship. I wonder...on further reflection, however, I'm sure that as an Anraatian he would never break our contract. And I don't really think he'll settle anywhere until he's accomplished the task he's set himself. He hates Narhjohol too much!

I am recording this before settling down to sleep. Tamarith came to my room a short while ago to ask if there was anything I needed.

"Are the sleeping arrangements satisfactory for you?" She asked politely.

I gave her a grateful smile. "Yes, perfectly, thank you. It's a long time since I had such comfort."

"Please don't think I pry," she began, "but since you and Dahll travel together I thought perhaps—"

I smiled reassuringly. "I hired Dahll and his ship to help me find the *Destiny*, that's all. It's purely a business arrangement, nothing more."

"Then you don't find Dahll attractive?" she asked with simple candour, and I found it impossible to be offended by her directness.

"Yes I do...very," I said, with equal honesty. "But there is only one man in my life."

"And he is on board the *Destiny*?"

I nodded. Tamarith smiled a little self-consciously.

"Perhaps you think it strange I should have need to ask you such things, but the telepaths of Niflheim don't normally pry into the minds of non-telepaths. Such minds are usually closed to us anyway. However," she hesitated slightly, "we also possess ESP, which enables us to discern the aura which everyone projects to some degree. I feel a closeness between you and Dahll, which perhaps you are not yet aware of. Also—"

"Go on," I prompted gently, sensing there was something else, something she seemed reluctant to tell me.

"I would not wish to frighten you, but I sense

something. I feel danger threatening you both, but especially Dahll."

I recalled that Narhjohol was still out there somewhere in space, awaiting his chance.

"Is there anything more you can tell me?"

She shrugged. "I wish there were, but I'm a telepath, not a prescient. I only know what I have told you."

"Have you told Dahll?"

"Yes, but he doesn't take me seriously. He is used to danger, he says. Please," she went on urgently, "be careful. And try to stop him from taking any unnecessary risks."

"Of course," I assured her. "But he's not likely to act recklessly, you know, or to risk his life without knowing exactly what he's doing."

"This I know too," Tamarith said quickly. "But the evil that threatens you may not be where you expect it." Her smile, though still friendly, seemed a little strained.

I had the feeling she knew—or sensed—something about Dahll, which she was determined to keep to herself.

"Perhaps I am wrong. Perhaps a threat is seen by me where none exists."

"It exists all right," I said, and explained about Narhjohol.

"Maybe that is it," she agreed quietly. "You, too, must be careful. The aura of danger surrounds you, as well as Dahll."

As she rose from her seat near the window, she touched my shoulder lightly. At once my mind became calm and I was filled with the feeling that whatever threatened Dahll and myself, we would be able to overcome it.

"I didn't mean to worry you or to cause you any distress, but it is better you are warned."

"I understand...and thank you."

Tomorrow," she said, "we will try to contact other Nifls who might be able to help you to locate your starship. Gullin is seeing to the arrangements tonight."

I thanked her again, and when she left, undressed and slipped between the warm sheets, to update this journal. The delicate scent of flowers still fills the air. I feel deliciously warm and at ease, despite what Tamarith told me. I thought it would take a long time to sleep, but I find I can hardly keep my eyes open.

****

157-06.09

This morning, I woke early. I dressed and flung wide the drapes at the window. The red sun had just risen, and not long after, the golden G-type appeared over the mountains. Mist filled the valley, drifting like a soft, pink and white cloud, completely obscuring the lake.

Only the roofs and spires of some of the tallest buildings were visible. I have rarely seen such a beautiful sight. The red giant is spectacular. I find it sobering to reflect that if it were as close to Niflheim as Sol is to Earth, it would consume the planet. Thankfully, however, it is a safe distance from Niflheim.

I went down the staircase, treading softly so as not to awaken the rest of the household, and as I reached the door leading to the lakeside it swung quietly open. I heard a soft laugh and, turning sharply, saw Tamarith standing just behind me.

"Good morning, you rise early."

"It's such a beautiful day," I said, "I couldn't stay in bed any longer." We walked outside into the soft light of dawn. The ice-cat came lolloping from somewhere, and Tamarith stooped slightly to pet it for a moment.

"You have chosen the best time to visit. We are

entering into our summer. For most of the year," she went on, "the days are very short and cold, and it's difficult to get around, even though temperatures are much less extreme here than in some other parts of Niflheim."

"It's certainly very pleasant now," I agreed. "I wasn't so sure yesterday!" I told her about the pink snowstorm.

"That was what we would term a summer shower," Tamarith said, smiling. "You should be here in the winter, when it really snows."

"But the colour?"

"It's caused by minute plant forms. That is how the species propagates itself. It disperses the young shoots that detach themselves from the parent in the wind that brings the snow. They'll lie dormant until the snow melts and then take root and grow."

Just then Gullin and Dahll appeared. By now, the yellow sun had risen fully, and I could see movement along the lake as the inhabitants of Gladsheim went about their daily routine.

"Good day. It is well you are early risers," Gullin said. "I have just received word from Thorren, a settlement on the other side of the Gunaran Mountains. The others will be arriving soon now, so I suggest we have our morning meal." He met my eyes and his own were very serious. "We want to help you find the *Destiny*, but to do so we require your assistance...will you allow us to enter your mind?"

## Chapter Six

I knew what Gullin was asking. It's no small matter to open one's mind to another, with all that implies. I also knew how telepaths dislike probing a non-telepathic mind. But they were willing, it seemed, to go to a great deal of trouble for me, a stranger. How could I refuse? Besides, I was determined to endure anything, if it would help me find the *Destiny*.

I nodded agreement. "Of course, I'll go along with whatever you suggest."

"Good. Then we'll leave as soon as we have eaten."

By the time we reached the amphitheatre, which was more brightly lit than I remembered, the morning was already well advanced. A number of Nifls now occupied the stone seats ranged around the sides. I recognised Liftrar from the previous evening.

Dahll glanced at me dubiously. "I know it's none of my business, but are you sure you know what you're letting yourself in for?"

"Dahll," I chided, "why are you so sceptical?"

"Am I? I just don't reckon I'd enjoy opening my mind to a telepath."

I have to admit that at that moment I was not as confident as I tried to sound. I was, after all, putting my trust in people I hardly knew. Logic told me, however, they had no reason to deceive me or mess with my mind. I posed no threat to them or their way of life.

"They're trying to help, and Gullin tells me they

just want to tap into my memories of Delian and Ragin."

Dahll looked unconvinced, but at that moment Gullin, who had apparently been communicating with a group of Nifls from the settlement of Thorren, approached me. It's a little disconcerting to see the Nifls obviously 'conversing' animatedly, yet to hear no sound.

"We are ready," he said. "The Thorrens have heard of the two brothers who went with the *Destiny,* and it is their opinion that, with your assistance, we should be able to trace them, or at least contact someone who knows them and may have been in touch with them recently."

I looked around at the assembled Nifls, finding it hard to believe they were all here just to help me achieve what many might consider to be an impossible task.

"Thank you. But...why are you going to so much trouble for me?"

Gullin gave me a very direct look. "Why not? Frequently we assemble here to make contact with those of our kinsfolk who have migrated to other worlds. We are all glad to have the chance to help someone who is a friend of our brothers, Delian and Ragin."

He explained it was not usually necessary for them to come together in one place in order to communicate with each other, that each inhabitant of Niflheim could make contact with any other on the planet, regardless of how far distant they were. However, physical contact through a group greatly increased the telepathic intensity, and, by working together, they would be able to transmit thought waves for immense distances through space.

"Is there any chance you might be able to unlock the memories in my mind? The things I can't remember about myself. The way in which I became separated from the *Destiny*?" I asked, a little hesitantly.

"To do so, we would have to probe too deeply. It is likely the memories you refer to are hidden far back in your mind and your subconscious has blocked the events too painful to recall."

"That's what Yan Kloor said." I shrugged in resignation. "I hope you're both right and I *will* remember in time."

"Patience," Gullin said gently. "The human mind is a wonderful thing. Whatever has happened to blot out your memory of those events must be for your own protection. You will remember when you are mentally able to accept it." He led me over to the dais, where Tamarith, Rhenn and Melind already sat, with several other Nifls, most of whom seemed quite elderly. After nodding briefly to the others, Gullin mounted the dais and gestured to me to stand beside him.

"First we have to make contact with as many of our people as we can, in order to unite our minds and search space for your ship. You may come with us if you wish."

I looked at him enquiringly. He spoke almost as if they were going on a journey. He took my hands in his.

"Close your eyes and allow your mind to become blank...like a sheet of unused parchment. Just relax and listen to my voice."

I obeyed. It was easy, listening to his soft, strange accent, to let my thoughts drift away until there was nothing left but his voice in my head. I don't remember the actual words he spoke, but it doesn't matter. It might have been a few minutes or much longer, but suddenly I felt I was no longer in the underground chamber, but flying high above the sweeping, snow-capped mountains of Gladsheim. I sensed, but did not see, Gullin beside me, guiding my mind with his own.

The mountains below were beautiful, but there was little time to stop and admire them. We moved on, over icy seas and mist-filled valleys, through immense stretches of dark forestland and across vast, snowy plains, past settlements and a few isolated homesteads. Whenever we passed over an inhabited area of the planet, I seemed to hear voices.

No, that's not entirely accurate. I was conscious of many beings, communicating with Gullin and each other, but there was no actual sound and often they did not even use words or language, as non-telepaths would understand the term. On the other side of the planet, where night had fallen, we did not disturb those who lay sleeping. I became aware, through Gullin, that he'd already contacted their representatives the previous evening. They were now prepared for the time when they would be called upon to unite their minds with Gullin and his fellow Nifls.

Many parts of Niflheim are unpopulated areas of intense cold, miles of barren land; grey and windswept valleys so full of mist and icy darkness that not even the simplest lichen is able to take a hold in a crevice in the frozen rock. Other areas of the planet, however, are much more temperate and indescribable in their mystery and beauty. I longed to linger awhile, but Gullin was anxious to return.

It might have been hours or just seconds later when I found myself back in the underground cavern again...if, in reality, I had ever been away from it.

"It is for the next stage we need your cooperation."

I opened my eyes. Gullin looked tired and a little strained, as if he had, indeed, just returned from a long journey. Rhenn, Melind and several of the other Nifls also seemed a little travel-weary. Only Tamarith seemed completely fresh and at ease.

Gullin hinted to me that she possesses considerable powers in excess, even, of his own.

"How long have we been away?"

Gullin smiled at me, seemingly amused at my question.

"You have not been anywhere. We only projected our minds to the far corners of Niflheim."

"I felt as if I were really there...and it was one of the most beautiful experiences I've ever had," I said truthfully.

He smiled again. "That is good. As I told you before, you are very receptive, but we are now ready to begin the search for your friends." He told me to sit, and then Tamarith knelt in front of me and placed the fingertips of both hands on my forehead, bowing her head in rapt concentration.

"Close your eyes," she said. "Clear your mind of everything except the *Destiny*." I obeyed, and my mind conjured a picture of the immense ship. A great surge of nostalgia, swept over me, just thinking of her. The *Quest* is a magnificent little craft, but the *Destiny* is far superior in both design and speed. And she holds so many memories, memories I can now recall. After all this time, I can still visualise her in so much detail, and it's easy to imagine myself back on board her.

"Now concentrate your thoughts on Delian and Ragin."

Tamarith's voice was inside my head now, softly persuasive. "Visualise them going about their routine tasks. Talk to them as if you were still on the ship...ask them where they are."

*That's all very well,* I thought, *but I'm not a telepath.*

Tamarith chuckled softly, and I remembered my mind was now open to her.

*No, but you are not alone. Each of us is here, with you. We can amplify your thoughts and together project them through space. But you must concentrate... concentrate.*

I tried. I really tried. But however hard I attempted to direct my thoughts toward Delian and Ragin, another face filled my mind, blotting out everything else. I told myself fiercely I'd never find him again unless I followed the Nifls' instructions.

Again and again I strove to make my mind a blank, to forget everything except the *Destiny* and try to concentrate my thoughts on the two brothers. The result was always the same. However hard I tried, I could not vanquish him from my mind, could not let go the image of him in my memory. At last, Tamarith called the proceedings to a halt, promising we'd make another attempt to trace the *Destiny* tomorrow.

When everyone had left the underground chamber, Tamarith took me to one side.

"Don't look so discouraged. I'm sure we will have more luck the next time."

"I feel I've let you down. You were all trying so hard to help me."

Tamarith shook her head. "No, if anything, we let you down. We should have taken into account the fact you are not used to concentrating your thoughts on one thing for such a long time—not to the intensity needed for our purposes, anyway. We will try it another way tomorrow."

"But how long are your people prepared to help me? They must have other, more important things to do."

As I was speaking, Gullin joined us. "They will stay for as long as it is necessary," he said. "As for there being more important things to attend to..." he paused significantly. "You may have noticed an absence of workaday routine here. Each family group is self-sufficient, or very nearly so. We grow our own crops and harvest them, spin ice-cat wool into yarn, which we dye and weave ourselves, and trade between ourselves the varied skills that each individual can offer. Our needs are simple. Because we spent many generations developing the power of our minds, we can perform many tasks without effort, and since we do not regard wealth as being of any importance, we will not count the hours spent with you as wasted."

He smiled encouragingly. "In addition, the inhabitants of Gladsheim and Thorren can make use of the opportunity afforded to trade with each other, so you see there's no need for you to be concerned."

I could only thank him, and hope that some day I might have the opportunity to repay their kindness. Both of them tactfully refrained from referring to the object of my thoughts when I should have been concentrating on Delian and Ragin!

I realise I've misjudged the Nifls as a race. I understand now that what I took for reticence and a certain aloofness in Delian and Ragin on board the *Destiny*, was, in reality, a deep respect for the privacy of others—a desire not to intrude, however innocently, into the mind of another person.

When we returned to Gladsheim I was amazed to realise it was already late afternoon. Although we hadn't eaten since early morning, it was only then I began to feel the first pangs of hunger. Melind and Tamarith informed me the evening meal would be served shortly. I said I would like to walk beside the lake while I was waiting, for I'd spotted Dahll standing, looking out over the mountains. I badly wanted to speak to him.

I haven't had much opportunity to talk to him alone since we entered the 'city,' as the Nifls call their chief settlement. In reality, it is nothing more than a collection of dwelling houses and other buildings, arranged around the lake, but a more beautiful settlement than anything I can recall seeing on Earth. He turned as I approached, and together we walked along the edge of the lake. We were silent, for a minute or two, watching the setting suns turn the placid waters to deepest pink and purple.

"It seems we're likely to be here for a while," I said.

He nodded, seeming a little distracted.

"I suppose I thought we'd be able to make contact immediately, but it doesn't seem to work that way," I went on.

"The Nifls seem to take things at a fairly leisurely pace anyway," he observed dryly.

"What about you? How do you feel about having to wait around while we try to establish contact and pick up the *Destiny*'s trail?"

"It doesn't matter what I think. We have an Agreement. No matter how long it takes, we have to stay here until we can pick up a lead on her. We certainly can't head into space blindly." He regarded me with those compelling eyes of his. "The one thing I'm worried about is the *Quest*. I don't like leaving her unguarded and out of sight for so long. It's possible Narhjohol might manage to trace us to Niflheim. He frowned, his eyes darkening in annoyance. "The computer topography analysis wasn't very helpful. If we'd known there was such a vast expanse of plain on this side of the mountains we could've landed here."

"Do not worry," Tamarith had come up, unnoticed, behind us. "Forgive me, please. I came to tell you it's nearly time for us to eat, and I could not help overhearing your conversation. After you told me about Narhjohol, I arranged for a shield to be put around your ship. She will be quite safe."

Dahll looked rather dubious. "Thanks, but what kind of shield? To generate a force field around the *Quest*, you'd need some pretty sophisticated equipment, and I've not seen anything of that nature around here."

Tamarith laughed gently. "You still don't know our ways very well—the shield we use to protect the *Quest* is of the mind. Anyone approaching her without authorisation will see nothing but a large outcrop of rock. Should he still approach, he will be overwhelmed with the desire not to advance any further. He will be quite certain the outcrop is, after all, just rock and not worth investigating." She hesitated. "If that fails, then I'm afraid we will have to resort to more drastic measures. We're capable of inflicting pain, if necessary. The effects are temporary but very effective. You need have no fear for your ship."

I was a little startled by the revelation this seemingly gentle people could, after all, resort to violence. I have now had time to think about it, however, and realise they can't be condemned for evolving the means to protect themselves and their property. If I'm honest, I have to admit their "weapons of the mind" are no worse than many of Earth's weapons. An ordinary blaster is capable of killing or horribly injuring a person, yet according to Tamarith, the pain they would inflict would last only as long as the recipient posed a threat.

****

157-09.09

We landed on Niflheim four days ago, and as I record this, we have still not made a contact or picked up a lead on the *Destiny*'s likely location.

The day-to-day routine of the community continues, much as I imagine it does on any world boasting a civilisation of any kind. It takes a little while though, to get used to doors opening and shutting, apparently by themselves, and objects floating through the air, seemingly of their own volition.

Their society is very democratic and so well ordered there appears to be no need for official titles or positions of authority. But I notice Gullin and Tamarith seem to command great respect from the other Nifls, even the oldest among them, including Liftrar. It seems their powers of telepathy, especially Tamarith's, are even more developed than those of the rest of the community.

On the second day of our attempted contact, at Tamarith's suggestion, I allowed myself to be placed in a semi-hypnotic trance and this is the method we also employed today. Afterward I remember nothing of what has happened, so there is very little to record. Tamarith says while I am in this state of trance, they are able to extract information about Delian and Ragin and the *Destiny* from my mind and collectively project it into space. The hope is that some distant Nifl will recognise the two brothers and be able to give news of their present whereabouts.

I can't help wondering what else they have seen in my mind. They say they concentrate only on the two crewmembers of the *Destiny,* though, and do not try to see any further. I have to accept this, although I long to know what happened before I arrived on Phidia, and how I came to be there alone. But they are adamant I should not try to force myself to recollect these events, whatever they were, but wait until the rest of my memory returns naturally.

I try not to let Gullin and his family see how despondent I feel. They have been so kind to me and are determined to keep on trying. I can't push to the back of my mind, however, the thought that space is vast and full of danger. There is always the possibility, however difficult to face, that the *Destiny* may no longer exist.

****

157-13.09

Our ninth day on Niflheim: just when I had

given up hope, when I felt it was pointless to keep on trying, we have a clue as to where the *Destiny* might be headed. A telepath on the planet Antargonn received the message transmitted by the linked Nifls and informed them the crew of the *Destiny* landed recently on his planet. Their next destination, it seems, was Osind, in the constellation the Nifls call Hvergelmir, named after the Norse 'cauldron of seething cold.'

I can't express the elation I felt when Tamarith told me the news. For eight days we had been trying, and I was beginning to think our task was hopeless, but she never doubted for a moment that we would find success in the end. It was, she kept assuring me, just a matter of time.

I think Dahll is as pleased as I am to have a definite lead at last. I know he is anxious to return to the ship, despite the Nifls' efforts to ensure her safety. Gullin showed us the position of Osind on their star charts, and we tried to correlate them from memory to those on the *Quest*. Dahll made many notes and calculations.

It will take some time, and many more calculations, to correctly set our course, but that shouldn't pose any great problem for the *Quest*'s navigation computer. At least I now have a tangible point of reference, something to base future extrapolations on, even if they have left the Hvergelmir constellation by the time we reach it.

Tonight the Nifls held a farewell banquet for the Thorrens and us. Of course, all my clothes, except the ones I have been wearing, are on board the *Quest*. Tamarith lent me a gown of finely spun ice-cat wool, in the most beautiful shade of sapphire blue. Apparently, the wool is taken from the ice-cats in the Nifl summer, rather as sheep used to be shorn on Old Earth. It's spun and dyed using natural vegetable dyes. Indescribably soft, it feels like the purest silk.

I am taller than Tamarith, so we needed to let down the deep hem to its fullest extent. After taking it in a little at the waist and shoulders, it fit almost as well as if it were my own. The prettily shaped neckline was off the shoulders and tastefully low-cut without being *too* revealing.

My hair I left loose, but I braided a few strands from each side, fastened at the back with one of the dainty cream flowers with which Tamarith fills the house.

I don't normally use any makeup, but I borrowed some lip colour from Tamarith and used just a little, with a touch of dark colour on my eyelashes. Tamarith wore a dress of the same material but in a slightly different style to the one she lent me, in deepest crimson. It perfectly set off her black hair, which tonight she wore coiled high on her head in a very elaborate and striking style. We admired and complimented each other when we were ready, like a couple of young girls going to their first grownup dance!

Dahll wore formal attire for the occasion, although he is so tall by comparison with the Nifls I can only assume his clothes had been made especially for him; they certainly suited him well, and he made a dashing figure. He and Gullin were waiting to escort us as we entered the Banqueting Hall. After some polite, complimentary remarks, Gullin introduced me to several Nifls whom I hadn't previously met, before escorting me to my place at the vast banqueting table. Tamarith had, of course, ensured that Dahll would be her escort for the evening, and he seemed happy enough with the arrangement. He laughed at her jokes and obviously enjoyed the occasion and the company as much as I did.

It was good to be able to relax after the strain of

the past few days. Gullin, who until now has seemed rather reserved and serious, proved himself a delightful and witty companion. We were entertained by the most gifted and accomplished musicians, playing on unfamiliar and melodious stringed instruments, and the meal we were served was superb, even by Nifl standards. The time passed with incredible swiftness, until, in the early hours of the morning, we made our way to our respective sleeping quarters.

I am recording this before going to bed. I feel tired, but it's a pleasant sensation, and with the prospect of soon being on our way to take up the trail of the *Destiny*, I have a feeling I won't sleep very much before dawn.

****

157-14.09

Despite the words I recorded earlier, I soon fell into a deep, dreamless sleep, as on every other night I've spent on Niflheim. I woke early and refreshed. Dressing quickly, I made my way to the lake to look for the last time on a red Nifl sunrise.

The whole lake was shrouded in a cloud of white mist, which flushed pink as the early sunlight touched its edges. Gradually, the suns rose higher in the sky and some of the mist dissipated. A small, oddly rigged boat sailed out on the calm water, which shimmered cerise and gold, reflecting the strangely-shaped sails in hues of white and silver.

I drank in its beauty, reflecting how different Niflheim was from what I had expected. I'd thought the world would be cold and cheerless. Instead it is filled with beauty and its people seem both happy and at peace.

Of course Gladsheim is situated in the most temperate area of the planet, and I know from my "journey" with Gullin that parts of Niflheim are very inhospitable. In the early days of colonisation, he told me, many pioneers perished and life was far from easy. Balancing this, though, as time passed it became apparent Niflheim imparted the gift of longevity on her settlers and their descendents. In addition, they are almost entirely free of the diseases and ailments that beset the people of Earth. Airborne bacteria are unable to breed in the cold Nifl atmosphere.

I took one last look at the lake and made my way to the barn at the back of the house. I wanted to spend a few minutes with Dancer, the pony I've ridden every day when we crossed the plain to the amphitheatre in the mountains. Today would be my last ride on him, when we returned to the *Quest*. He whickered softly when I entered his stall, turning his head and nuzzling me gently. I patted his neck and gave him some slices of a tasty root vegetable he's very fond of, before making my way back to the house. I have a feeling I'll miss him almost as much as the human companions I have met during my stay here.

We left almost immediately after our morning meal, saying goodbye to Rhenn and Melind and the many friends we've made on Niflheim. The whole settlement appeared to have turned out to bid us farewell. Gullin and Tamarith accompanied us on our journey back to the place where the *Quest* waited patiently for our return. It took us several hours and the trip was pleasant although, for me, anyway, tinged with sadness at having to say goodbye to Gullin and Tamarith.

Once we reached the ship, we invited them on board, and Dahll seemed to enjoy himself immensely, showing them around. Then we applied ourselves to the serious business of programming all the relevant data into the navigation computer.

Tamarith was strangely quiet, and I didn't have to be telepathic to realise her sombre mood was the result of Dahll's imminent departure. I will not dwell on our parting with her and Gullin. I've fallen in love with these people and their beautiful "mist home," and I shall probably never see them again.

We have waited until we are well into deep space before administering the formula to ourselves and preparing to enter hyperspace. Seeing Dahll was immersed in his own thoughts, and since there was nothing useful I could do, I decided he might prefer to be alone. I've spent much of the time since we left Niflheim in my cabin, making this entry, and thinking about my experiences there. Now I must rejoin Dahll on the control deck.

I wonder what's made him so preoccupied. I thought perhaps he was thinking of Tamarith, but maybe he's considering the information she gave us before we departed from Gladsheim. Last night someone was seen prowling near the shielded *Quest* but disappeared before he could be apprehended—someone answering the description of the Salmaran, Narhjohol!

## Chapter Seven

158-03.06

It's been a long time since I was able to bring my journal up to date, for reasons that will become apparent later, but I must start at the beginning. As recorded in the ship's log, nothing of any significance occurred to affect the routine on board the *Quest* during our journey to Osind.

We were half-expecting Narhjohol's ship to be on our tail, but our computers indicated nothing, and when we made our reconnaissance orbit around the planet, the *Quest*'s sensors detected no craft of any kind. If the *Destiny* had been in this sector of space, she had obviously left before we arrived, but I wanted to investigate the planet in the area where the Nifls had told us she had originally landed. It's possible someone here might remember something or know where the ship was headed. After all, I had not really expected to find her on the first planet we traced her to.

The computer informed us Osind was the second of its sun's three planets. Of the other two, neither were uninhabited by intelligent life forms although one had, apparently, a few species of flora and fauna, while Osind had an abundance of both. It had two moons, and the atmosphere, pressure and temperature were compatible with human requirements.

The climate in the area where, according to the Nifls on Antargonn, the crew of the *Destiny* had intended to land, was semi-tropical, with medium rainfall, and there were two distinct indigenous intelligent life forms. There was, it informed us, insufficient data to enable it to give more information regarding either of these species.

We landed on a flat area near the coast, and armed with our blasters, sim-translators and life-support packs, descended from the ship. Dahll had spent much of the time since leaving Niflheim in perfecting a small explosive device that would detonate immediately if anyone attempted to enter the *Quest* in our absence. He made a great show of setting up his invention.

"There," he said when he was finished. "Anyone trying to snoop around is likely to blast himself to pieces!"

"As long as they don't do the same to the *Quest*, in the process," I muttered, out of his hearing.

I looked around at our surroundings. Osind glittered in the bright sunlight, like a rare jewel. The sky was a richer blue, the grass more lush and of a more intense green than on any planet I could recall. Large insects, giant, brightly painted butterflies, and tiny, jewel-bright birds hovered over sweet-smelling, brilliantly-hued flowers, flashing and shimmering in breathtaking splashes of colour.

In the distance a small group of animals, looking something like Terran goats but much bigger and with strangely elongated noses, grazed peacefully. I took a deep breath of the fresh, tangy air. It was almost too perfect.

As usual, Dahll was restless, anxious to find a settlement and establish whether the inhabitants were disposed to be hospitable. Having quickly scanned the area and ascertained that there were no dwellings and no evidence of intelligent life in the immediate vicinity, we decided to make for the beach. The computer had indicated the seas of Osind were rich in fish. Therefore, there seemed a good chance many of her inhabitants would be fisher folk and might have built their houses near the shore.

We approached the beach cautiously, but if the natives of the area were aware of our presence, they were obviously not over-anxious to show themselves. The tide was coming in rapidly, although there was a broad expanse of pinkish-coloured sand still exposed. It coarsened out into a low bank of shale and pebbles beneath a sheer black cliff face that swept round in a broad curve, forming a small bay. We advanced warily. Glancing up at the cliff, we noted several zigzag paths leading up the steep, shiny escarpment, and small stone constructions built onto natural ledges jutting out from the cliff face. If the computer records were right, the inhabitants of this planet were not technologically advanced. It must have taken considerable time and much physical effort to build this compact, cliffside community.

We walked for some time. Dahll seemed distinctly uneasy and I noticed he kept glancing up at the cliff dwellings.

"Doesn't it strike you as strange," he observed when I asked him what was worrying him, "that we haven't seen any of the inhabitants of this planet yet?"

"What did you expect—a welcoming committee?" I teased lightly. "Besides," I went on, more seriously, "we'd been on Niflheim several hours before the Nifls showed themselves."

"That was different. We were pretty sure the Nifls were friendly. Also, Gladsheim was some distance away from where we landed." He nodded toward the cliff.

"We can see the dwellings of the Osindians, so why don't they show themselves?"

"Perhaps these dwellings have been abandoned?" However, I had no sooner spoken the words than I dismissed the idea, since the small houses showed no sign of decay and gave every impression of being in regular use.

"There's something else," Dahll said, sounding apprehensive. "I'm sure I spotted movement on the ledges, once or twice."

I nodded. I too had caught a flash of quick movement out of the corner of my eye, but when I looked again, there was nothing.

We approached a rocky promontory, jutting from the cliff, far out into the sea. As we scrambled over it at a conveniently low point, we saw what had been hidden by its rocky contours. Shielded by the headland and situated on top of the cliff that rose on the other side was a small village. It was comprised, not of simple, single-storied dwellings, like those we'd already seen, but of far more impressive structures, three and sometimes four stories high. Dominating the village, while standing a little apart from it, was a brooding and imposing castle, black against the brilliant blue sky. A road ran from the entrance, winding down the steep cliff until it reached the beach.

The tide was rising fast now, so we had to walk along the shingle bank. Just then, two things happened almost simultaneously. The first was the appearance at the entrance to the castle of a rider who, having passed through a gateway, paused for a moment before galloping down the steep pathway toward the beach. The second occurrence was a great heaving and churning of the water a short way out to sea as a huge, monstrous creature waded ashore.

I reached for my blaster, then remembered the ice-cat on Niflheim and reminded myself of the advisability of not judging by appearances. Dahll also had his hand on his weapon, and I heard his sharp intake of breath as the creature advanced toward us through the shallow waters of the advancing tide. Dahll was a little ahead of me, and I took a step or two forward, but he stopped me with a peremptory wave of his hand.

"Stay back," he hissed through his teeth, glancing up at the cliff. "If that thing makes any threatening gestures, we'd best find a cave to hide in—it's too big to fight!"

He was not exaggerating. It was certainly enormous. Standing erect as it was, it must have been at least four metres high. It was now only a short distance away, and it seemed as interested in us as we were in it.

"I'm not sure it means us any harm," I said softly. "Perhaps it's just curious."

The creature's eyes were large and dark in colour. Its body was completely covered in shimmering black armour-like plates, similar to the scales on a fish, and triangular scarlet wattles ran from the top of its head down to its shoulders. The head itself was, disconcertingly, almost human if one discounted the feathery gill tufts sprouting from either side of the short, stumpy neck. At least, they looked like gill tufts, but there wasn't much time to ponder upon their exact nature or purpose. Its hind legs ended in flipper-like feet, which made its movements awkward, but it still moved surprisingly quickly, for something so large.

It was now so close we could have reached out and touched it. Dahll took several steps backward and I followed suit. A sudden clatter of hooves on rock made us both look sharply toward the castle. The rider was now on the shingle bank, rapidly bearing down on us. The alien creature, too, must have heard the sound of hooves. Opening its mouth it made a mournful cry that reminded me vividly of sound recordings of the dolphins and whales of Old Earth. Its plaintive resonance mesmerised me for a moment, making my blood run cold with the eeriness of it.

Dahll turned his head swiftly to glance at me and then, to my horror, the creature stretched its hand toward him. It had five webbed fingers, the shortest being almost a thumb, and "hand" is the only word that describes it accurately. Leaning forward, it picked him up as though he were a child, pinning his arms to his sides so he was helpless to defend himself.

I drew my blaster and set the intensity control to full, aiming the whole force of the charge at the monster. To my incredulous despair, it bounced off the armour plating of its scaly skin, dissipating in a glare of energy. I tried again with the same result. Dahll seemed to be shouting something at me, but I couldn't catch the words. As the creature stooped closer and was about to reach for me with its other hand, I heard another voice to one side, speaking in a language I couldn't comprehend.

I leapt back rapidly, out of the sea creature's grasp, and as I did so I turned, and gazed into the hypnotic blue eyes of a mottled grey-and-black horse. A horse with a single, short glossy horn in the middle of its brow, bearing an uncanny resemblance to the mythical unicorns of Old Earth's legends, except for its size and colour.

Looking closer, I saw it had a stiff, spiky mane and its ears were tufted. It differed from a Terran horse in other ways, too, but at that moment I had other things on my mind. The animal was kneeling, and its rider, pale and silver-haired, although his face and form were those of a young man, gestured frantically for me to mount in front of him.

I aimed my blaster once more at the creature that had Dahll in its grip, and the strange rider shouted impatiently. The next moment I found myself being grasped firmly around the waist and lifted into the saddle.

I struggled. I kicked and shouted, and gestured

wildly toward Dahll. The rider took no notice, but turned his mount's head toward the castle, and the beast stood erect. It was taller than any horse I have ever seen. It must have been about nineteen or twenty hands high, but its master seemed to have no difficulty in controlling it. He was still talking to me, but the words were unintelligible.

The animal leapt immediately into a smooth gallop, its hooves, hard and black, like ebony, speeding effortlessly and unhesitatingly over the rough, pebble-strewn ledge. I remembered the sim-translator, activated it, and waited impatiently through the jumble of strange tongues until the words the man was speaking began to make sense to me. I locked the translator onto the setting and tried to control my voice, which seemed to my own ears to be shrill and hysterical.

"Please, turn back! Please, you have to understand. My companion—"

"I'm sorry. I regret I can do nothing for him, my lady."

"But you can't just leave him to the mercy of that—that monster!"

He reined in the 'unicorn' so sharply it reared, front legs pawing the air wildly as he swung it round to face the beach. The creature, still clutching Dahll, had climbed onto the ridge and was shuffling awkwardly behind us, periodically uttering that weird cry.

"You wish us both to be killed, as well? You saw how powerless was your own weapon against the Gru. We can only fight them with fire-cannon or a skilled rider with a laser."

He wheeled his mount around again. "Come, my lady. The Gru cannot move fast across the rocks. My shanya will soon outdistance it." He slackened his grip on me in order to soothe his steed, which once more plunged and reared. Eventually we left the ridge and sped across a wide expanse of flatland beneath the citadel on the cliff. The hard ground seemed to pose no problem to the sure-footed animal.

I waited until the stony ground levelled out and I saw an expanse of what looked like green vegetation. Wrenching myself from the rider's grasp, I leapt to the ground. It was a long way down but the soft ground broke my fall, as I'd intended. However, the green was deceptive. The ground beneath the leafy foliage was almost liquid. The more I struggled to find solid ground beneath my feet, the more I found myself being sucked deeper into the ooze.

I looked up helplessly as the shanya's rider wheeled it round.

"That was a foolish thing to do, my lady. You might have been hurt."

There was little choice but to grasp the hand he held out to me as the animal he called a shanya knelt at the edge of the morass. He once more swung me into the saddle behind him.

"You don't understand," I said desperately, "Dahll...I have to try to help him!"

"I regret it is probably already too late. The Gru delight in killing. Sacrificing ourselves as well could have done nothing to help your friend."

"Then...then there is no hope for him?" I stammered, as I realised the full significance of his words.

"I am sorry, my lady, but at least I arrived in time to save you from a similar fate."

We were now climbing the steep and twisting road that led up the side of the cliff to the castle. At the top, we passed through the heavy iron gate, which took two men to open. We clattered across a stone bridge spanning two jagged pinnacles of rock, into a large courtyard.

A youth ran to take the reins of the shanya as it knelt for us to dismount. My rescuer, whose name it appeared was Jarrok, helped me from the saddle. He shouted a few orders and a young, olive-skinned girl, with hair as yellow as the pale gold flowers that grew everywhere, came running across the yard.

"This is Leihdannah. She will show you where to bathe, and you will have a change of clothing. After refreshing yourself and resting, we will eat together." He turned to the girl.

"Take care of my lady and see she has every comfort. She is my guest. If she has need of anything, alert me at once."

I allowed the girl to lead me through a door in the castle and along a narrow, winding corridor. The sudden and tragic events of the past hour or so had left me in something of a daze, so I was only vaguely aware of my surroundings. Eventually my guide showed me down a flight of worn steps hewn from the rock. We passed through a door at the bottom and into an anteroom, through which I could see another chamber, lit by lamps set high up in the ceiling. The whole room appeared to be carved straight out of the black rock. The bathing area consisted of several small and irregularly-shaped pools, around which smooth rounded stone slabs were laid to neaten the outlines.

Leihdannah crossed over to where a number of recesses were set into the wall of the anteroom, and withdrew drying cloths and cleansing oils. She handed me the former wordlessly and poured the latter into the water of the nearest pool, where it immediately became a rich and aromatic foam. To my discomfort, it soon became apparent she not only intended to help me undress, but expected to have to assist me in the actual bathing process, as well. As I wriggled out of my mud and slime encrusted outerwear, I tried to make her understand I was used to bathing in private.

She looked puzzled. "You mean you don't have

any servant to wait upon you?"

I explained that this was indeed the case, and an expression of contempt passed across her otherwise rather pretty face.

"Then you're no more'n a common serving girl like me. I thought you were a lady, from the way my Lord Jarrok spoke."

I told her I was neither servant nor mistress, that where I come from no one keeps servants or slaves. Leihdannah looked unconvinced.

"If I don't follow my Lord Jarrok's instructions, I'll be punished."

I couldn't really imagine my rescuer being cruel or unjust, and picturing once more his pale, handsome face and bland expression, I decided she was probably trying to play on my sympathy for some reason of her own. At last I managed to persuade her I was quite capable of washing myself. Placing the drying cloths on the edge, where I would be able to reach them easily without assistance, I stepped into the soothing waters of the pool. She stubbornly insisted upon hovering about at the edge, and I tried to ignore her.

I scrubbed the grime from my body and then applied myself to doing the same to my hair. Afterward, while I dried myself, Leihdannah disappeared into the anteroom. She came back with sandals and a bundle of clothes, which she told me Jarrok wished me to wear. My own, she said, had been removed while I was bathing, so they could be cleaned.

I was grateful for Jarrok's thoughtfulness, but a little dismayed when I discovered how revealing the clothes were. A sleeveless top, cut very low, left most of my middle region bare. Next, a long, flimsy, wrap-around skirt so designed that however much I tried to adjust it, it always revealed one leg. A pair of the briefest of panties was the only underwear. Both the skirt and top were woven from a silky, bluish-purple material, encrusted with gemstones and gold and silver embroidery. The skirt was girdled with a jewelled belt. A gossamer fine cloak completed the outfit, fastened at one shoulder by an ornately carved clasp, which gleamed and glittered as if from some fiery force within the metal.

On Earth, in ancient times, before the revolution, I understand such attire would have been quite commonplace. These days no respectable woman would have worn such clothes, and I felt like a wanton. However, the garments Leihdannah wore were very similar, albeit the material lacked the embroidery and gemstones, and she had no cloak. As a guest of these people, I naturally had to conform to their customs.

I was concerned to discover my journal, which had been in my tunic pocket, had disappeared, along with my clothes. I'd laid the sim-translator on the edge of the pool when I was bathing, but I'd had no reason to remove the recorder from my tunic. I explained to Leihdannah and she promised to make sure it was returned to me. She told me Jarrok was expecting me to dine with him. I slipped on the sandals and followed her back up the steps and along the corridor.

At last she showed me into a large room with heavy, rich-coloured drapes at the windows and soft animal skins on the floor.

Jarrok sat at a long, marble-topped table piled high with food. He nodded curtly at Leihdannah and she left, closing the door. The last thing I felt like doing was eating, but I couldn't refuse his invitation for fear of offending him. It was impossible for me to do justice to the lavishness of the meal, however. For one thing, the food before me consisted of several different kinds of meat. I have no taste for animal flesh, having become accustomed to the mainly vegan diet of all who travel in space for any length of time. Far more than this, though, was the fact that I was still numb from the events of that day.

I found it hard to accept Dahll's death. It seemed so unfair. I have been lucky. Despite everything, and my partial loss of memory, I know I have had moments of great happiness—and I have experienced love. Even death could not have robbed me of that, the death I have already cheated more than once, so it seems. I was the one who should have been taken, not Dahll.

His friendship had come to mean a great deal to me, and I couldn't believe I would never see him again. I tried not to think about how he might have died. I had not the courage to contemplate it. I could only hope the end came quickly.

Jarrok noticed my lack of appetite and asked if I would like the food on the table to be sent away and 'something more to my taste' brought in. I assured him the fault was entirely mine and there was nothing wrong with the meal.

"Then perhaps it is the wine that is at fault. I think I have something to sharpen your appetite."

He gestured to a serving lad who stood nearby and spoke to him quietly. The boy nodded and returned a few moments later with a small flagon, which he handed to Jarrok. He poured me a generous cupful, and then one for himself. He smiled as I hesitated. "Please my lady, it will be good for you."

He took a long sip and, out of politeness, I followed his example.

It tasted sweet, but with an aftertaste of sharpness that was wonderfully invigorating. It was like all the sweetest, most exotic fruits I have ever tasted, and I finished the cup almost before I realised. Already I could feel my spirits beginning to lift a little. Jarrok refilled the cup, and after that things began to get a little hazy, although I tried to concentrate on what Jarrok was saying to me.

He asked why Dahll and I had come to his planet, and I told him about the *Destiny*. How we had reason to believe her crew might have recently visited Osind. Jarrok said there was someone he knew, a trader, who might be able to give me news of them. Tomorrow, he promised, he would try to contact him.

"It is most unfortunate about this friend of yours," he added. "Was he a very...close friend?"

By now, I was feeling extremely lightheaded and nothing seemed to matter any more.

"No," I said airily, "he was just a boy I hired to help me find the *Destiny*. I paid him well. He knew the risks."

Jarrok nodded wisely. "Then matters could have been worse, my lady. But you are tired. I will bid Leihdannah show you to your quarters."

I allowed Leihdannah to lead me down a dark corridor, to a room whose main feature was a low, comfortable bed. I collapsed onto its softness and, wrapping myself in the fur covers, fell at once into a heavy sleep.

I woke when the sun had been up for many hours. The buoyant, almost carefree sensation I felt when I wrapped myself in the sleeping furs the night before had gone. In its place was a hollow emptiness. I bowed my head in shame as I remembered my conversation with Jarrok the previous evening.

If the effect of the strange wine he calls 'vyrminth' was to make me so insensitive I could dismiss Dahll's death in one short, uncaring sentence, then I would never touch it again. I could manage without the accompanying uplifting of spirits it bestowed.

I stood at the window, parting the heavy, woven drapes to look out on the tranquil blue-green sea. I prayed to Dahll's spirit to forgive me, and made a silent vow that, if it were at all possible, I would take his formula to Anraat for the benefit of his people. At least his death would not be entirely in vain.

I left the chamber and made my way to the bathing area, which I was relieved to find deserted. After a long soak, I felt a little better, and it was good to be able to bathe in privacy without Leihdannah hovering close by.

Later that morning Jarrok and I talked again. He informed me he had made contact with the trader he'd mentioned, and he would be arriving in about two days' time. Meanwhile, Jarrok said, I was welcome to stay on as his guest, and I was to be sure to tell him if I needed anything.

I asked him about my journal, and he assured me it was quite safe and would be returned to me along with my clothes.

The next two days dragged by. I was impatient for Jarrok's trader friend to arrive so, if he really was able to give me some information on the *Destiny*, I could return to the *Quest* and leave this colourful, treacherous planet.

There was very little to do except talk with Jarrok or sit in my room and mourn for Dahll. Always, my mind returned to the *Destiny*. With a heart that felt as if it were breaking, I wondered if I would ever find her, and my love, again. Jarrok insisted I stay within the castle confines, since he seemed afraid I might be in danger from the Gru if I ventured outside the castle walls. If I walked in the courtyard, his men stared at me and made insolent remarks, so I remained inside the castle.

Jarrok spent a lot of time with me and explained some of the history of Osind and her people. The cliff dwellers, he told me, were a timorous race, perpetually going in fear of the Gru. Jarrok and the other leaders of his people had built their fortresses high on the cliffs, to protect themselves and the cliff dwellers. The latter showed their gratitude by giving the only thing they could—their labour—enabling the castle lords to live in almost feudal splendour. From what I'd seen, it seemed the cliff dwellers were willing to submit to virtual slavery in order to ensure their own protection. The system appeared to work well enough, however. It was not my place to make judgements.

On the evening of my fourth day on Osind, I took my meal with Jarrok as usual. When we'd eaten, he offered me a cup of vyrminth. I refused, politely, and instead he poured me some of the creamy milk from the herd animals that graze in the pastures behind the castle at the top of the cliff.

We were interrupted by a young man, with the olive skin and fair hair of the cliff people. He spoke a few words softly to Jarrok, who dismissed him with a nod, then leaned across the table to me.

"The trader I told you about arrived a short while ago. If you have finished, my lady, he would like to speak with you."

"Of course," I smiled, rising from the table.

Jarrok crossed over to the door and threw it open.

I found myself looking into the cruel face and black expressionless eyes of Narhjohol.

## Chapter Eight

I looked desperately in Jarrok's direction. Surely, he couldn't be aware of how ruthless Narhjohol was, or that the commodity he traded in was people?

However, one glance at his face was enough to convince me I could expect no help there. He wore the self-satisfied expression of one who has just concluded a profitable business transaction. With a sinking feeling in my stomach I realised I was the merchandise.

"Well," Narhjohol snapped at him. "What you waitin' for?"

"I just wanted to make sure...we did agree fifteen thousand units each—"

"Only if you got 'em both."

"But Narhjohol, even as an ordinary slave, she would fetch four or five times the usual price. Look at her form...her skin, her hair. Is she not different from the common cliff dwellers? It's not my fault I lost the other one. The Gru—"

Narhjohol's expression was one of contempt.

"He was the one I wanted. Save your excuses, you'll get your money when I'm good an' ready. Now leave us."

Jarrok inclined his head slightly and without further argument left the room, closing the door behind him.

I felt desperately alone and helpless. Even though Jarrok had betrayed my trust, he'd treated me well, and with respect. His presence might have tempered whatever unpleasantness Narhjohol might have in store for me.

"Let's be done with this barbaric language. Switch off your translator."

I complied and he immediately changed to *Common Universal.*

"I can see you're surprised to see me," he sneered. "But you don't look too happy."

"I don't understand," I said, my mind whirling. "Our sensors showed nothing—"

"'Course not, my dear. I decided to let you think I'd failed to pick up your trail. I ordered my pilot to stay in stationery orbit beyond the moon, out of detector range. I was just waitin' for Jarrok to contact me."

"But how did you know we were heading for Osind?"

"I have connections. Even a Nifl can be bought if the price is right. It wasn't hard to get the information I wanted."

I didn't think it likely Narhjohol was the type to be easily bluffed, but I had to try something.

"Do you know who I am? "I have contacts on Earth. When the United World Council finds out—"

Narhjohol spat contemptuously, and leaning forward, slowly, almost casually, caught hold of my hair and twisted it between his fingers. He jerked my head back, forcing me to look up into his face.

"Yes, I know who you are...and who you *were.* I also know what happened to you on Phidia, and it ain't very likely Earth will to be sendin' anyone to look for you." He jerked my hair a little harder, making me wince in pain, although I did my best to hide it.

"Even if you could escape from me, you daren't return to Earth. The Global Union ain't kind to those who break their laws. D'you concede the point, *my lady*?" he added, in scornful parody of the way Jarrok had addressed me.

I fought off a sudden feeling of dizziness and unreality. I had no idea how he'd found out about me. I could only assume, as he had indicated, that some Phidians, in common with some Nifls and individuals of all species, have their price.

He let go of my hair and regarded me thoughtfully.

"Remove your garments."

"What?"

You heard." He took a step toward me and waved a heavy blaster in my face as I recoiled.

"Now, or d'you want me to do it myself?"

I complied with shaking hands. There was little choice with his gun trained on me. My stomach knotted with fear and revulsion. Did he intend to rape me? My chances of overcoming him would be small, considering his superior bulk and height, but I would resist with all the strength I possessed. I know a few things about self-defence, and he would not take me without a fight.

Narhjohol laid down the blaster and began exploring my naked body with his rough hands. His long, talon-like fingers travelled slowly over my skin.

Trembling with apprehension, I looked away from his face with its gloating expression. I clenched my teeth defiantly as he turned me this way and that, examining me as though I were some prize animal.

I shuddered. The feel of his cold hands on my body made my flesh crawl. Feeling sick with humiliation and loathing, I glanced at the blaster lying on a shelf just behind the slaver. If I moved swiftly, perhaps I could reach it...

Before I could translate my thoughts into actions, Narhjohol abruptly released his hold on me and stood back. "You may cover yourself again. I'll let you keep your 'maidenhood'...*for now*," he added meaningfully.

I scrambled for my clothes. Slave clothing, I realised, too late. I flung them back on, with as much dignity as I could muster. Stifling a gasp of relief that was almost a sob, I moved as far away from him as I could.

"I take it you *are* still virgin. You an' the Anraatian weren't—?"

"No," I retorted, feeling the colour rise to my face. "We weren't!"

He glowered at me, making it obvious he wasn't too sure whether to believe me or not.

"You'd better be telling me the truth. All slaves undergo a thorough medical examination before they're put up for sale. The methods used are scientific, and very accurate. If I find you've cheated me out of a handsome profit, nothin' you can imagine will come close to what I'll do to you before I sell what's left of you to the highest bidder." He stared at me for a moment, as if in contemplation.

"Jarrok's right. You *will* fetch a good sum. My clients like Terran women...and you're an excellent specimen. There again, I kinda took a fancy to you myself, on Phidia.

Cooperate with me," he went on, with the air of one bestowing a great compliment, "an' I might be persuaded to keep you myself."

"I'd rather die first!" I retorted.

His face twisted in fury, and he slapped me hard across the face with the flat of his hand. I acted instinctively. Before he could strike me again, I caught his arm with my left hand. I pulled forward at the same time, swivelling to the left, and turning my back on him. I bent my knees and, placing my right arm around his waist, straightened up, sending him flying across my left hip to land sprawling a short distance from me.

The element of surprise was on my side. He

obviously wasn't used to slaves fighting back. While he was still dazed I made a dash toward the door. The feeling of dizziness and nausea had increased, and my legs felt weak and reluctant to obey me. As I reached for the iron ring which turned the door catch, my vision blurred and the whole door seemed to fall away from me. At the same time, the floor dissolved beneath my feet. I fell into a black vortex that sucked me in and consigned me to utter darkness.

****

When I opened my eyes again I could see nothing. A wave of panic welled up inside me. I was not in the room Jarrok had assigned me and had no idea where I was.

I turned and, as I focussed my eyes and they grew accustomed to the gloom, saw the faint glimmer of starlight through a small window high up. That reassured me. The darkness had been too much like the blackness of my nightmares. Where was I, though? I reached for my pack to get my wrist flare, then remembered Jarrok still had it, together with my other belongings.

It was just possible to make out the pile of rags on which I lay. They seemed to be all the furnishings my prison contained, not that there was a great deal of space for anything else.

The sound of surf breaking on the rocks below was comforting. At least it meant I was probably still in Jarrok's fortress on the cliff. For a brief, terrifying moment when I woke, I'd been afraid I might already be on board the slave ship. There was still a chance I might escape from Narhjohol.

I tried to rise to my feet and became aware of heavy chains, which loosely shackled my ankles. Using the bare stone wall in front of me as support, I managed to stand, still feeling a little weak and unsteady, although mercifully the feelings of nausea and dizziness had passed.

I tested the door, which as I expected, was bolted on the other side. I looked around in the dim starlight. The window was too high for me to reach, and even if it hadn't been, how would I climb down the smooth walls of the castle, especially with my feet shackled?

Perhaps if I waited for daylight a means of escape might come to me. Miserably I crept back to the rags that made up my bed and eventually fell into a fitful sleep.

Bright sunlight, shafting down through the narrow window, woke me. I opened my eyes, remembering the events of the previous evening, more determined than ever to try to find a means of getting away. I now noticed a curtain drawn across one corner of the room. I dragged myself across and drew the drape aside, with some caution. I found behind it a small washroom with basic facilities and, somewhat to my surprise, running water. Although a prisoner, at least it seemed my needs were not to be entirely neglected.

After a good wash with cold water, I felt something like my normal self again, although I was dismayed to realise my sim-translator was missing. Presumably, the slaver had removed it from my wrist while I was unconscious.

Hunger was beginning to gnaw at my stomach and I wondered if anyone would bring me food, or if Narhjohol in his anger intended to let me starve. Several hours must have elapsed before the sound of the heavy bolts on my door being drawn back answered my question.

One of Jarrok's servants placed a bowl of soup, a hunk of bread and some fruit, together with a goblet of vyrminth, on a ledge by the door. He backed out swiftly, as if I were an animal that might suddenly spring at him.

I moved over to the ledge and tasted the soup cautiously. If there was anything in it, I couldn't tell, but then the drugged milk of the previous evening hadn't tasted in any way unusual, either. Whatever Jarrok had given me must have been in the milk, since I'd eaten very little, except for some pieces of fruit. Abandoning caution, I cleared both the bread, which I dunked in the soup, and the fruit. I didn't touch the vyrminth, although greatly in need of something to raise my spirits.

How long was Narhjohol going to keep me prisoner? He surely wouldn't keep me locked up indefinitely. He must be intending to transport me to his ship. I assumed more food would be brought later in the day. I decided to try to jump whoever brought it, and then hide in the castle until I could make my escape after dark. However, the idea was not without its flaws.

Even if I succeeded in evading Jarrok's guards and Narhjohol's men, my chances of finding my way across the slime pools in the dark with my ankles shackled were slim, to say the least. If the Gru spotted me, I would undoubtedly meet the same fate as poor Dahll. Anything would be better than just abandoning myself to whatever unpleasantness Narhjohol might be contemplating, though. For the moment, however, it seemed there was nothing I could do except wait.

I shuffled up and down, like a wild creature in a cage, vainly searching for some means of escape where there was none. Eventually, after inspecting every corner and examining the walls as far as I could reach, I had to accept there was no way out of my prison. I would do better to conserve my energy.

It seemed a very long time before the bolts were once more drawn back from the door. I flattened myself against the wall adjacent to it, and prepared to spring. To my dismay, it was not one of the guards come to serve me my meal, but Narhjohol.

He entered the room, blaster in hand, closely followed by Jarrok, who, at a word from Narhjohol, stationed himself by the doorway.

I leapt at the slaver, but this time he was ready for me. Seizing my arm in a viselike grip, he threw me heavily to the ground.

I kicked out with both feet, shackled as they were, but he jumped deftly to one side and, leaning down, keeping well out of the way of my feet, rammed his blaster hard against my throat.

"Get up" he snarled. "An' if you try anything like that again, you'll be very sorry."

Scrambling to my feet, I glared at him in contempt.

"You've had enough time to think about it. You'd better have the sense to cooperate with me now."

I didn't reply. He looked around. "Not quite what you're used to, is it?"

"I've slept in worse places," I said stonily. "Much worse."

"An' you might just do so again, if you don't learn some respect," he threatened. "After that stunt you tried to pull last night, you're lucky I didn't have you thrown into the dungeons beneath the castle."

"Why didn't you?"

"Because, my dear, you're too valuable to risk damaging, if it can be avoided."

I shuddered. I hadn't forgotten the future he planned for me. He seated himself on the mattress, causing me to shuffle as far away from him as I could manage. In the confines of the tiny cell, this was not nearly as far as I would have liked.

He laughed, the harsh sound chilling my blood.

"Don't worry, there's no need to be afraid of me, yet. Until I've made up my mind whether to keep you or sell you, I'm not goin' to risk devaluing my investment."

He'd made it obvious that only my value as an "untouched" slave kept him from using me for his own pleasure. I intended to make sure it stayed that way, so I stifled the defiant retort that he flattered himself to think I was afraid of him. I didn't want to tempt him into making me try to prove the point. For the first time I noticed he was holding a small flat object between his fingers. My journal.

"This belongs to you, I believe," he said, changing the subject as he saw me staring at the holocorder.

"You know it does—"

"I might be persuaded to part with it...for a price."

"What price?" I queried suspiciously.

"Just a little information."

"Such as?"

"I'll get to that in a moment. First I'd like to know what you use this for, and why. When I activated it, it appeared to be blank."

"It is blank," I told him truthfully, for I had inserted a fresh data crystal before we left the *Quest*. "It was taken away from me before I had chance to record anything."

"What d'you use it for?"

"Just a personal record. It's of no value to anyone else."

Narhjohol studied me intently. "I ain't sure I believe you, but we'll leave that for now. I'm more interested in the composition of Dahll Tarron's formula."

"Formula?" I asked innocently.

"Yes," Narhjohol snapped. "His formula to counter the effects of hyper-acceleration. If you can't give me the composition, just tell me where it's hidden on the ship."

"I've no idea what you're talking about."

Narhjohol's eyes narrowed dangerously. He

slapped me across the face, twice, so hard I could feel the wheals burning on my skin and knew it would be bruised.

"Don't try to be clever with me, girl. I find it hard to believe he wouldn't have explained the formula to you in case of emergency."

I chose my words carefully, trying to conceal my loathing.

"If Dahll had a secret formula, why should you think he'd trust me with it?"

He smiled nastily. "You were the only person he *could* trust."

"You seem to know a lot about me."

"I do. When I found out you were goin' to be travelling with the Anraatian, I made it my business to find out all about you." He regarded me with some suspicion. "If I hadn't, I might've found it more difficult to believe your relationship with Tarron was as innocent as you made out to Jarrok."

His eyes held an evil glint. He stood and grabbed my arm, twisting it behind my back.

"I'll give you just one more chance to tell me what you know about the formula."

"I don't know...anything," I gasped.

"I don't believe you. You've thrown away your last chance to do it the easy way. Now I'm goin' to have to hurt you."

The note of complacency in his voice made me sure he'd never intended anything else.

He propelled me toward the door, pushing past Jarrok and jerking my arm painfully. I bit back the cry that threatened to force its way past my lips. I tried frantically to think of a way to escape, but it would be difficult with chains around my ankles. Besides, his heavy blaster was in his belt. Although I didn't think he'd risk killing me if he could avoid it, a stunner beam would stop me just as effectively.

He hurried me down a long, winding corridor.

After many twists and turns, we came at last to a part of the castle I'd never seen before. Narhjohol stopped outside a studded, metal door and turned to Jarrok, who'd followed close behind.

"I want this door opened," he ordered brusquely in *Common Universal*, adjusting his translator unit as he did so, and repeating the command.

The Salmaran still gripped my arm tightly. Jarrok glanced uneasily in my direction. He said something to Narhjohol in the Obsidian language. Without my own translator, I couldn't understand the words, but I believe he was attempting to persuade him to be merciful.

"Since when have you shown any concern over the treatment of a slave?" Narhjohol snarled. "Get this door open."

Jarrok complied meekly, almost dropping the antiquated keys in his nervousness, much to Narhjohol's obvious impatience. The slaver pushed me inside and I looked around. I didn't like what I saw. Set into one wall of the room was a control panel, above a sinister metal chair whose sides were fitted with an arrangement of clamps. The back was low and it was obviously not designed with comfort in mind. The rest of the room was bare, the walls plain grey with a metallic sheen, the floor a spotless, sullen white. It had a clean, almost clinical look about it, which was completely out of place in what was, to all outward appearances, a medieval castle.

I'm not sure if I can bring myself to recount what happened next, but if this journal is to serve any useful purpose I must record everything, however distressing and distasteful the memories.

****

I resisted, of course, but Narhjohol was much stronger than I was, and having my feet shackled was a distinct disadvantage. Eventually he forced me to sit in the chair and made the clamps secure so there was no way I could move my arms or legs. Narhjohol touched a control and, for a moment, the room was in total darkness.

Within a few seconds, the blackness seemed to dissolve, the air shimmering in a brief incandescence, before giving way to an eerie, bluish half-light. Narhjohol stood over me holding a shining, short-bladed knife: an evil-looking dagger decorated with strange carvings along the hilt.

"Tell me everythin' you know about the hyper-acceleration potion."

"Even if I knew anything, I wouldn't tell you," I retorted, feeling waves of hot fear flood through me. I took several deep breaths and tried to prepare myself for whatever was to come.

He ripped the flimsy cloak roughly from my shoulders. The knife flashed in his hand. Pain shot through me. Warm blood trickled down my arm.

Again the question. Again the pain...the blood.

I tried to look past him, into the shadows beyond. My eyes were constantly drawn back to that evil blade stained with fresh blood...my blood! After a while, I ceased to think about anything except how to withstand the agonising slashes, which came in relentless repetition across my back, my shoulders, my arms.

I know a little about the formula's composition, and also, of course, where it is stored on board the *Quest*. I did not intend to give Narhjohol the smallest fragment of information. I was glad I knew so little. It was Dahll's formula, not mine, and I owed it to him to make sure it never came into Narhjohol's possession.

There is no point in being anything but frank. Stubbornness and contempt for the slaver, rather than any kind of courage, made me determined he should learn nothing from me. My hatred lent me strength.

Narhjohol became increasingly furious. The pain grew correspondingly more severe. This was no ordinary knife. The burning pain it inflicted was like nothing I had ever known or imagined, even in my nightmares. It seemed to sear through my whole body.

My mind focused on one phrase: "I know nothing about the formula...nothing...nothing..." I repeated it like a mantra, until I believed it myself.

All at once, he took hold of my face with his hand and slowly, deliberately ran the knife down the side of my cheek. I drew in my breath and tried to avoid crying out at the pain of it. He sliced at my skin again with the sharp blade, holding my chin in an iron grip, so I couldn't move.

"It would be a shame to have to spoil your looks. Tell me. Where is the formula?"

I remained silent. Through a haze of pain I wondered if he intended systematically cutting me to pieces if the fear of pain and disfigurement did not induce me to tell him what he wanted to know. I reflected detachedly, as if it were happening to someone else, that it seemed a very strange way to protect his investment.

Suddenly, he loosed his hold on my face and flame appeared in his hand. He moved behind me. Searing heat blistered the skin on my shoulders and upper back so I gasped in shock and pain, then gritted my teeth, angry at my own weakness. I would not let him have the satisfaction of making me cry out like that again.

My hair was damp with sweat, plastered around my face. My arms, shoulders and face ran with blood, obscuring my vision. I saw the Salmaran as if through a red mist. There was blood everywhere. It seemed incredible I could lose so much of it and still remain conscious. Eventually I ceased to equate the pain to any movement on Narhjohol's part, my body racked with waves of burning torment.

At times, I thrashed about, trying to free my arms. The metal bands around my wrists bit into my flesh, adding to my suffering. I clenched my teeth so tightly to avoid crying out my tongue was bleeding. There was the taste of blood in my mouth.

As I grew weaker, I ceased struggling and at last gave up even trying to stifle my own cries. Faintly, Jarrok's voice came to me, raised in protest, then Narhjohol's again, cursing. My eyes kept trying to shut. Painfully I forced them open. To close them would be a sign of weakness. I would not let him know I was weakening. He paused at last, leaning closer to me.

"You can stop this now," he said, his voice taking on a persuasive tone. "You have only to tell me what I want to know an' I'll make the pain stop. I'll have you taken some place where you can have your wounds dressed an' then you can sleep. I'll make sure you have every comfort. You don't have to suffer any more." He paused. "Look, I'll make it easier for you. Just tell me how to get into Tarron's ship. That ain't much to ask is it? All this can stop."

I did not reply, trying to conserve what little strength remained to withstand the torment I knew would resume at any moment. I glared at him through half-shut eyes, with all the defiance I could muster, from the depths of an exhausted spirit that was beginning not to care.

Narhjohol's features distorted with anger, and excruciating pain flooded over me again, leaving me breathless and trembling.

The torment went on and on and on. Narhjohol had the knife in his hand again. The short slashes that cut across my back and shoulders merged to become one long, intense agony.

It occurred to me to try to take hold of the knife, if I could, and put an end to this sadistic torture. But the idea of death by my own hand was not easy to contemplate. While life remained, I somehow still embraced it, clinging to the pitiful hope I would be strong enough to withstand him.

At length the slaver leant over me and loosened the restraints from my right arm. I watched, with a kind of remote fascination, as the blood trickled from across my shoulders, running down my arm in little rivulets. It dripped across my wrist in slow motion, to form spreading circles of crimson on the featureless white floor.

"Such a pretty little hand. You wouldn't want to lose it, would you?" he sneered in honeyed tones. Then his voice changed, making me chill with fear.

"Tell me about the formula...if you want to keep your hand!"

He tightened the bands again, replacing them higher up on my arm. My right wrist was left exposed, although I was still powerless to move it.

"How can I tell you...what I do...not...know?" I moaned weakly.

"You know all right. Tell me!"

"No—" I couldn't take my eyes off the dagger. "Oh, no. Please...no."

"Tell me."

"No...no—"

"Tell...me!"

"No," I gasped weakly, and watched, horrified, the heavy blade, flashing silver in the strange, unreal light. Flashing...descending...rising again.

Narhjohol held it high in both hands, then struck with all his force.

I screamed...

A sound that filled the room—the castle—that echoed and reverberated in my mind.

Searing agony filled my being with the pain and terror of it.

Then, merciful oblivion.

## Chapter Nine

I have no idea how long it was before I awoke, my body trembling with the memory of another nightmare. Sunlight, streaming in through the small window opposite the bed, lit up the room. For a brief, terrifying moment, my mind was blank, except for the remnants of my nightmares. I struggled to make sense of where I was and what had happened to me. Then the events of the previous night flooded vividly through to my consciousness, and I remembered everything. I realised I was in the room I had first occupied when Jarrok brought me to the castle, although I could not recollect how I came to be there.

I felt shaken, weak and exhausted. The inevitable headache that always seems to accompany my nightmares pounded behind my eyes. To my relief it wasn't as severe as some I have experienced. I remembered the events of the previous evening in vivid detail and shuddered as I recalled the agonising torture I'd endured. I was in some pain and ached in every muscle, but strangely the physical pain was not as intense as I would have expected. Perhaps my wounds had been treated with a healing salve to ease the discomfort, if in fact there was any skin left on my back and shoulders at all.

I turned my head slowly and the throbbing increased, making me close my eyes again. I lay there for a long while, unable to move, before sleep claimed me again. I vaguely remember waking and drifting off several times before I was able to think clearly once more.

I still felt incredibly weak, but the pain and

aching had lessened and my head no longer throbbed. What time of day was it? The light had changed, and I was sure several hours must have elapsed since my first awakening.

I remembered every detail of my ordeal with Narhjohol. I went over and over it in my mind. I feared I might have let slip something to enable him to find the information he sought, but I knew in my heart I had not. I'd focussed my mind on just one thing, as Tamarith and Gullin taught me. I'd blocked out everything except the need to keep on repeating that I knew nothing of Dahll's formula.

I relived the moment when the Salmaran struck my wrist with the dagger, slicing through the flesh and bone. Unable to repress a moan of sheer horror, I buried my face in my pillow and tried to blot out the memory.

Eventually I managed to control my visions of the previous night's events and turned back to stare at the window. I was afraid to look anywhere else. I remembered there was a small mirror on the wall to one side of the bed, and I dreaded the reflection I might see in it. After a long, long time I told myself I had to gather what little remained of my courage and face what had happened to me, as I'd done once before, on Phidia.

I pulled back the covers gingerly, steeling myself for what I might see. After a few moments, I forced myself to look at my right wrist. I drew a great, sobbing breath and lay back on the pillows.

The hand was intact, my wrist and arm unharmed except where the heavy metal bands had cut into my skin. But that was as nothing to what I had feared. For some moments, the feeling of enormous relief outweighed every other emotion. I closed my eyes, blinking back the tears, and sent up a silent and fervent prayer of thanks.

It had all been a dream then, a terrifying

extension of my usual nightmare. But no, my body remembered the pain. It had been real. My tongue was raw where I'd bitten into it. I could still taste the blood. My wrists were chaffed and bruised. Besides, the memories were too intense. I'm used to vividly realistic nightmares. Enough to know what happened to me had been no dream.

I eased myself awkwardly out of the bed and dared to look in the mirror. Apart from great dark shadows beneath my eyes and several bruises against the pallor of my skin, the face that looked back at me was as familiar as ever. There was no evidence of the ravages Narhjohol had inflicted with his knife. The rest of me seemed unscathed, too. I crept back to the bed and pulled the silks around me, just as a key sounded in the lock and Narhjohol entered the room.

He looked at me, a smile on his face that wouldn't have fooled a child.

"So my dear, you've come to at last an' find yourself still in one piece. You have Jarrok to thank for being back in such luxury. I'd've thrown you in the dungeons but he persuaded me to bring you back here. His voice held a mocking tone. "My generosity has always been my biggest failing."

"What have you done to me?" I demanded, in a voice that sounded to my own ears, hoarse and weak. "I shouldn't even be alive, after...after—"

He stood silently for a moment, the familiar sneer on his thin lips, obviously enjoying my bewilderment.

"It's quite simple. Everythin' that happened to you last night I projected into your mind, with the aid of some modified holographic techniques, amplified by drugs, which I arranged to be put in your food. You went through the experience of physical torture, but in reality it was all a computer-generated illusion."

"The pain was real enough," I retorted weakly before I could stop myself. Narhjohol smiled superciliously.

"That's the whole point, my dear. I *meant* you to feel the pain. That part of it was real. Only the method by which it was inflicted upon you was an illusion. He laughed harshly. "D'you think I'm such a fool as to disfigure a slave who cost me so much?"

He drew closer. "As it was, I thought I might've gone too far. I was half-afraid your mind might have been affected. I'm glad to see my fears were groundless. A half-witted slave ain't worth much, however attractive."

I sent up another prayer of thanks for Narhjohol's greed. My value as a slave had obviously kept me from far worse sufferings at the hands of the Salmaran.

"What d'you think of the little plaything I had rigged up for Jarrok's amusement?" he went on in his smug voice. "A reward for collecting stock for my clients, an' for kindly allowing me my personal pick of his own choicest slaves whenever I choose."

I turned my head away as he leered lasciviously and went on. "It produces the most delightful fantasies, you know." He laughed without humour. "It also produces fantasies of a quite different nature, as you've had cause to find out."

He stroked his face, as if in contemplation. "Perhaps I was too hasty. I've a feelin' you might've told me what I want to know if I'd been a little more patient."

"How many times do I have to tell you?" I repeated wearily, "I don't know anything."

"An' if you did, nothing I could do would make you tell me." Narhjohol finished for me, sarcastically. "Well, I'll grant you've near enough proved that part of it. I'm almost tempted to believe you. Of course, I could just take you back to my ship an' use the mind-probe to find out if you're lyin', but it would be a pity to lose or damage you if you *are* tellin' the truth. Then I'd have nothing to compensate for your loss, either." He paused, leaning closer to me so that I drew back, as far away from him as I could.

"I've decided to try another way. I don't intend to stay on this primitive little planet any longer than I have to. I'll let you rest for a few days, and then we'll visit the Anraatian's ship an' search for supplies of the formula."

"You might find it a little difficult," I told him candidly.

"I know all about the device to prevent anybody entering the ship," Narhjohol said complacently. "However, you'll render it harmless for me."

I opened my mouth to speak but he interrupted me. "In case you've any ideas about nobly sacrificing yourself, just remember—once the explosive is triggered, my way into the ship will be clear. The sale of the formula will be more than ample compensation for the loss of a slave. But," he continued, a look of great cunning flashing across his face, "I don't really want to lose *you* if I can help it. I've arranged for Jarrok's favourite, the little slave girl he calls Leihdannah, to be chained to you as you work. You may think your own life is worth throwin' away, but from what I've learnt about you, I doubt you'd sacrifice another's life so lightly."

"I'm afraid you'll have to change your plans," I bluffed in desperation. "De-activating the device is a job for an expert, I don't know how—"

Narhjohol's cruel, handsome features twisted into a scowl. "You'll have to do better'n that. I know you held an interstellar space permit on Earth. Such permits are only issued to pilots who are not only capable of handlin' their ships single-handed but of carrying out complex emergency repairs and adjustments. I don't think the disablement of a single explosive device would really be beyond your capabilities."

"Dahll constructed the device," I told him, "and only he could have neutralised it."

"Are you tellin' me he didn't give you the means of gettin' back into the ship?"

"He had no reason to believe we wouldn't be returning to the *Quest* together. He didn't expect to get killed!"

"I can't argue with that," Narhjohol said coldly, "but there's always the risk of sudden death for a spacer. I don't believe the Anraatian would be foolish enough not to make provision for an emergency." He crossed over to the door.

"You've got two days to think about how you're goin' to do it. You're in no condition to be of any use to me until you've regained your strength, so I'm givin' you some time to recover. Make the most of it."

After he'd gone, I lay back in the bed, miserably contemplating a way to outwit him. I knew he was right. I might have considered purposely detonating the device, but I couldn't kill Leihdannah as well as myself. And, as he'd succinctly pointed out, once the explosive was discharged he'd be able to get into the ship, so self-sacrifice would be a little pointless.

My chances of escaping were slight, and it would be infinitely preferably to die here on Osind rather than be taken to Salmar as a slave, but I desperately wanted to prevent him finding the formula. It rightfully belonged to the Anraatians, and I hated to think of Narhjohol getting his hands on it. It wasn't easily accessible, of course, but I'd no doubt Narhjohol would tear the ship apart, if necessary, in order to find it.

I've never felt such intense loathing for anyone as I do for this sadistic, inhuman Salmaran. There had been no necessity for the ordeal he'd put me through the previous night. His objective would have been achieved just as well by forcing me to help him to board the *Quest* and show him where it was hidden in the first place. He knew his threat to Leihdannah would ensure my cooperation. He'd made it quite plain, however, he'd derived real pleasure from seeing me suffer, and from tearing my flesh to imaginary ribbons.

I could understand why Dahll hated him so much. For his sake, I had to find some way of destroying the formula before Narhjohol could lay his hands on it.

****

To my relief, Narhjohol kept away from me for the rest of that and the next day, and I saw nothing of Jarrok. My food was brought to me as before, and my door was always kept locked. At least my chains were gone, removed, presumably, while I was still unconscious, so I could move around freely. Also, fresh clothes had been left for me. They were still a slave's attire, although, if anything, even more richly encrusted with precious stones, but it was better than the torn and sweat-stained outfit I was wearing when I regained consciousness.

There was nothing for me to do but try to rest and recover my strength, and make ready to seize the slightest opportunity to escape. Rest I did, but I could not sleep. My mind was too full. I tossed and turned sleeplessly both nights. A plan began to form in my head. If I failed to escape from Narhjohol, once I gained access to the *Quest*, no doubt he would board her and force me to show him where Dahll had hidden the formula. He'd probably insist I download its encrypted composition from the computer. If I could make sure he left Leihdannah outside the *Quest*, I could surreptitiously set the ship's self-destruct mechanism on a short countdown. I was past caring about my own survival, and there was no way I'd allow Narhjohol to take me on board his ship. Besides, I owed it to Dahll's memory to make sure the Salmaran never had the chance to use the formula for his own purposes. If I had to die, at least I'd make sure I took Narhjohol with me.

Early the following morning, when it was barely light, I heard the sound of hooves in the courtyard, and a great deal of noise and commotion. I ran to the window. The room in which I was imprisoned was high up and although I could see figures running frantically back and forth, and others riding shanya, I still could not make out exactly what was happening in the confusion below. For what must have been several hours, I listened to the sounds of fighting. The castle was apparently being attacked, but by whom? No one brought me food that morning, but I was too anxious to know what was going on to feel much hunger.

When at last I heard someone approach and the door was unlocked, it wasn't Narhjohol, as I expected, but Jarrok who entered the room, holding a small bundle.

He held out my communicator bracelet and indicated I should activate it.

When I'd done so, and Jarrok's words once more made sense, he caught hold of my arm. "We must go swiftly, my lady, before Narhjohol comes for you."

I backed away from him suspiciously. "I don't know what you're up to, Jarrok. You surely don't expect me to trust you after—"

A look of acute anxiety crossed Jarrok's face, something that might have been fear. He glanced back over his shoulder. "My lady, *please*. The castle is besieged. We must hurry."

I still wasn't sure if he was trying to trick me for his own purposes. I stalled for time, calculating my chances of overcoming him and escaping.

"Why have you suddenly decided to help me get

away?"

"The way he treated you, it was not right," Jarrok almost whimpered. "I never intended him to hurt you. Besides, he cheated me on the price and it is not for the first time." He glanced nervously at the door. "I'm ahead of Narhjohol this time. He knows not that I have a second set of keys."

He pushed the bundle into my hands. It was my survival pack, together with my blaster, and my boots, which I pulled on gratefully. The sandals I was wearing were less than practical.

"The castle has many underground passages. Narhjohol intends to get away through one of them, taking you with him, but I know of another way—"

He never finished the sentence. A figure clad in light armour burst into the room. Jarrok had his back to him.

"Jarrok, *look out!*"

He half turned...too late. A look of anguished disbelief spread across his pallid features as he fell to the ground, his skull cloven from the blow delivered by his assassin's sword.

Seeing me standing, almost stupefied with shock, the man hesitated a moment, raising the visor of his helmet. That was my chance. I already had the blaster in my hand. I aimed it at his temple and fired.

As he fell, I stepped as respectfully as I could over Jarrok's dead, bloody body, and into the corridor. Which way? I had to decide quickly. My blaster was set on stun. The man I'd shot would recover soon. I heard footsteps running, and voices, one of which was unmistakably Narhjohol's.

I fled along the passage in front of me and down some steep, winding steps. When I reached the bottom, I found myself in another passage, which was just as unfamiliar. I wasn't the only one fleeing blindly. Jarrok's servants were running in terror, some of them screaming hysterically. Who or what they were running from wasn't immediately obvious, but I joined them on the principle of there being safety in numbers.

In the general confusion, I doubt if I was even noticed. I realised how conspicuous I would look by comparison with the olive-skinned, fair-haired slave girls, though, should I have the misfortune to run into any of Narhjohol's men.

I cursed silently for not having the foresight to use one of the sleeping silks from my bed to cover my head and shoulders, but it was too late now. We'd reached the main part of the castle, the ground littered with corpses and wounded men. I heard the sound of voices, steel against steel...and blaster fire. Here in this dark castle everyone was my enemy. Somehow, I had to try to find a way out. If only I could find one of the underground passages Jarrok had spoken of.

I turned, only to find my way barred by another of the armoured men, his back turned toward me. This one wasn't holding anything so primitive as the steel sword that had killed Jarrok. He had his fingers closed around the butt of a blaster.

I didn't have time to ponder this anomaly. I spoke softly and, when he whirled round, let him have the stunner blast in his chest. His armour absorbed some of the stun beam, but he fell to his knees, his weapon clattering to the ground. I kicked it out of the way, and as he struggled to rise I kicked out again, aiming at his head, and he fell back, unconscious.

Hearing running footsteps, I darted behind a stone pillar and found myself in front of a narrow opening in the wall, at the head of another flight of steps. I had no idea where they led, but they seemed deserted. Hurriedly descending them, I stopped at the bottom. The passage at their foot ran straight ahead, illuminated from torches in sconces on the stone walls.

The torches became fewer the further I went, and gave out only a dim light, casting monstrous shadows. At every turn in the passage, I expected one of Narhjohol's men to confront me, but I seemed to be alone in the underground labyrinth. The light was now so dim I could scarcely see at all. The air grew steadily danker and colder and eventually the niche lights ceased altogether. I was hopelessly lost, but the passage had to lead somewhere. At least I could hide down here until everything was quiet and perhaps try to make my escape from the castle later, when the fighting ceased.

Rounding a bend I almost fell over something bulky lying in my path. My heart thudded uncomfortably against my ribs, my flesh crawling at the thought of what I might find. I delved into my survival pack until I found my wrist flare. Strapping it on, I gazed around in its comforting glow.

The object on the ground in front of me, in a pool of half-congealed blood, was a body. One of Jarrok's men, judging by his clothing. I seemed to be in the part of the castle housing the dungeons Narhjohol had described. The doors to all the cells stood open, the inmates apparently having been released by whomever, or whatever, had killed the man at my feet. Presumably he'd been one of the prison guards.

Well, now I knew I wasn't in one of the tunnels leading outside the castle. I stood for a moment, undecided whether to go on or turn back. To go on might be dangerous. The killers of Jarrok's guard might be in the passages ahead. To turn back could be to risk running straight into Narhjohol.

I was about to dim my wrist flare, as a precautionary measure, when I heard footsteps behind me, approaching fast, and another sound, heavy...lumbering. The decision made for me, I ran as silently as I could. I reduced the illumination from the flare as I went, until it gave out the merest sliver of light, just enough to enable me to see where I was going.

To my despair, after running for several minutes, I found my way barred by a wall of stone. This was apparently as far as the passage went. I turned slowly, prepared to fight for my life, to find myself confronted by a tall, slender man in the armour of the castle's attackers. Behind him, a short distance away, stood two of the Gru and several other figures in armour.

The man's flare, at full intensity, swept over me, dazzling me, as he stepped closer. I flung my arm across my face to shield my eyes from the glare, at the same instant, drawing my blaster from my belt. I raised the weapon to fire, and a hand shot out. Strong fingers gripped my wrist, even as I tried to activate the trigger.

"Would you shoot your rescuers? Don't you know me?"

My finger slackened on the trigger button and I dropped my arm from in front of my eyes. I recognised the voice, even before he raised the visor of his helm, revealing a face I'd given up hope of ever seeing again.

## Chapter Ten

"Dahll!" I cried incredulously. Impossible, crazy explanations flashed through my mind, sending it whirling in confusion. "Dahll, I don't think I've ever been so glad to see anyone in my whole life. I...I was told you were dead." I was almost sobbing in my amazement and relief. I leaned back against the wall for support, feeling suddenly very weak, both from lack of food and the shock of seeing him again, alive.

"I'm no ghost, I assure you," he said, gently disengaging the blaster from my nerveless fingers and lowering his flare away from my face, while I gazed at him in bewilderment. I took a step toward him, and swayed as my knees suddenly gave way. He took hold of my hands to steady me and frowned as the flare showed up the red wheals and scars on my wrists.

His distinctive grey eyes narrowed in concern. "What's been happening to you?" He gripped my hands more firmly and I leant against him gratefully, until the dizziness faded and my strength returned. Then, still holding on to my hands, he held me at arm's length, as if I were a small child, studying me closely.

"You're as pale as death and your face is bruised. You look as if you haven't slept properly for days—"

"Thanks, you certainly know how to make a person feel good about themselves," I retorted with a feeble attempt at levity.

"I'm serious. What're you trying to hide from me?"

"Nothing, Dahll. I'm all right now, we can talk later." I peered past him. The passage behind him was empty. Neither the armoured men nor the Gru were visible in the light cast by Dahll's flare.

"There were a couple of Gru in the passage a moment ago."

"Yes, they were with me. I sent them off to check the castle for any of Narhjohol's men who might not have been able to escape."

This confirmed what I had been beginning to suspect. It was becoming apparent that almost everything Jarrok had told me had been a lie. And I had been foolish enough to let myself be taken in by him.

"Jarrok—he was the Lord of the Castle—he told me the Gru were killers. He said they killed for the pleasure of it."

"Don't let them hear you say that. They have very sensitive feelings. Without their help I doubt if we'd have been able to get into the castle at all."

I returned my wrist flare to full beam and we started back along the corridor, keeping a wary eye open for any of Jarrok's men who might still be around. As we walked, Dahll told me about the Gru. Far from being the mindless, merciless killers Jarrok had made them out to be, they were the planet's ruling species, and highly intelligent. Nekhotex, the Gru who had taken him that first day, had been trying to save us both from Jarrok.

"I tried several times to contact you on the communicator, but I couldn't get through."

"It was on 'translate' until it was taken from me," I explained. "Dahll, what's been happening? How did you find me?"

"I was beginning to think I never would," Dahll said grimly. "We searched everywhere. We tried the dungeons several hours ago, but you weren't among the prisoners. Then two of my men reported they'd been knocked unconscious by a stunner beam aimed at them by a young woman." He looked at me with the glimmer of a smile. "A mad woman with a blaster? I decided it had to be you."

"Thanks again, but what d'you mean, your men?"

"The cliff people. They've been planning an attack on this castle for a long time, but they needed a leader, someone who could give them weapons and show them how to use them." He smiled again, but without much humour. "I had to raid the *Quest*'s arsenal of hand-weapons. I just hope they'll be prepared to give some of them back."

"But I don't understand. The computer scans indicated only two intelligent races indigenous to Osind."

"That's right." Dahll replied paradoxically. I wanted to question him further but we'd reached the steps leading to the upper levels of the castle, where we came upon a group of several of the cliff people in armour. Dahll conversed with them briefly, then turned to me.

"The fortress is now under our complete control. Everyone connected with the castle, except for the slaves and the prisoners, who have been set free, is either dead or has surrendered and been taken captive. Unfortunately Narhjohol seems to have escaped, leaving several of his men to bear the brunt of the attack while he got away."

"Dahll, he was here this morning, when you attacked. You could have gone after him, instead of looking for me."

Dahll favoured me with one of his mysterious looks.

"Is that what you reckon I should have done?"

"I just don't like to think you lost him because of me."

"In the first place, I haven't lost him. He wants

to catch up with me just as much as I want my revenge on him. We'll find each other, sooner or later. In the second place, I don't desert my friends." He grinned. "Besides, you're my first charter passenger. It wouldn't do much for my reputation if I had to admit I'd left you imprisoned on a strange planet while I pursued my own personal vendetta!"

I followed him up the rough steps to the upper floors and we made our way out of that castle of death. It was good to be in the open again.

As I breathed in the tangy salt air, I seemed to revive, as if my imprisonment in that dank and musty fortress had been slowly sapping my will and my strength. Sea birds wheeled and screamed overhead, and a warm breeze tugged at my hair and caressed my face. I felt alive again.

We walked carefully down the steps leading from the castle. They were slippery with blood and littered with the bodies of friend and foe alike. There had obviously been a bloody battle and casualties had been heavy on both sides. I could see the heavy metal gate on the other side of the stone bridge, before the tortuous path leading down to the beach. It lay smashed and twisted, like the carcass of a grotesque, gigantic insect.

We stepped onto the bridge, also strewn with dead and badly wounded men. We had to tread carefully. One lay right across it, dressed in the Salmaran style, obviously one of Narhjohol's men. I was a little way ahead of Dahll at the time. As we reached the motionless figure, I saw the wide-open, staring eyes still had some life in them. I threw myself to the ground, just as a bolt of energy whanged past me.

I felt an excruciating pain in my shoulder and, for the third time since my arrival on Osind, lapsed into unconsciousness.

****

I awoke to the appetising aroma of something cooking over a campfire. I sat up. It was not yet dark, although one or two early stars glowed out on the horizon. We were on the beach beneath the cliff. I had a warm blanket around me and someone had dressed my shoulder and wrists. Several of the cliff people sat around the fire nearby, and Dahll tended a steaming pot.

I hadn't eaten since the previous evening, and hunger pangs began to gnaw insistently at my stomach.

I called softly and Dahll looked across, then ladled some of the contents of the pot into a bowl and came over to me with it.

"Here, drink this. The nights on Osind are cold, it'll help warm you. Afterward I'll bring you some baked fish."

I drank the soup eagerly. "Thanks. I'm so hungry."

"We can soon cure that, but how're you feeling otherwise?"

"Fine, except my shoulder feels a bit stiff and sore. What happened? I remember the Salmaran—"

"You were caught in the heat of his blaster as he fired. You dived out of the way or it would have been much worse, but you knocked yourself unconscious when you hit the ground. Your shoulder's blaster-burned, but it's not serious. I used some of the Phidian salve from my survival pack, and it's healing nicely...along with the bruises on your face. I also gave you a shot to make you sleep for an hour. You looked as though you needed it." He frowned. "You were lucky. That...garment..." He hesitated over the word, as if not sure whether the term was quite accurate. "That garment you have on is so flimsy and covers so little of you it's a wonder you weren't burned more severely."

"Yes, well, it's not exactly what I'd have chosen

myself," I said defensively. "I didn't have much choice in the matter."

"I wasn't criticising. In fact, it's rather fetching."

I drew the blanket more closely around my shoulders and smiled self-consciously.

"Knowing you, I suppose you're going to tell me I should have been more careful. First I allow myself to be captured, and then I get shot."

"It was hardly your fault. With so many bodies lying around, we were just unlucky to come across one that was still alive. As for being captured, I have to admit Jarrok did look a more attractive proposition than the Gru."

I sighed. "I shan't be sorry to leave this planet. I'm tired of being rendered senseless and then waking up in a strange place."

Dahll gave me a swift, searching look. "What's been happening to you?" he asked again. "And who bound you so tightly your wrists were rubbed raw?"

"It's a long story, Dahll. I'll tell you about it later. How about some of that fish you promised? If you only knew how hungry I am—"

Dahll smiled slowly, and his voice had a slight trace of amusement in it. "Since we first met, I don't think I can recall a time when you didn't seem to be hungry," he teased.

"I haven't eaten since yesterday."

He was immediately contrite, and his expression became serious again.

"Sorry, I'll fetch some for you now, but I still want to know what's been going on up there." He nodded in the direction of the castle, gaunt and forbidding on the cliff top.

I suppose I'll have to tell him something, but I don't want him to know about my encounter with Narhjohol if I can help it. He already has too much hatred for the Salmaran, and knowing about the way Narhjohol tortured me to try to get the formula would only make that hatred stronger.

I was so ravenous I couldn't help but enjoy my meal, despite my normal aversion to eating the flesh of living creatures. Afterward, I remembered something.

"Dahll, my survival pack, where is it?"

Don't worry, I have it here." Dahll handed it to me and I rummaged through it anxiously. I heaved a sigh of relief when my groping fingers found what I was seeking.

"My holocorder, Jarrok took it when I first arrived at the castle."

"It's important?"

"Only to myself. It's a sort of diary, a personal log. I don't know why, but I feel it's important to keep one. I've done so since before we left Phidia."

A thought crept into my mind. "How did I get down here when I was unconscious?" I asked, although I had a feeling I knew the answer.

Dahll smiled. "Nekhotex and I took it in turns to carry you. The path was steep, but you weren't exactly heavy. Are you feeling up to going back to the ship in a little while?"

"Of course," I agreed, slightly surprised, "but I thought we'd be camping here for the night."

He gave me one of his mysterious looks. "Ah, well, there's something I haven't had a chance to tell you yet. I know where the *Destiny*'s headed."

"What? Oh, Dahll, don't keep me in suspense, tell me!"

"They're on their way to a planet in the Pleiades system, called Brend-Igon. Apparently we only missed them by a few hours, so the sooner we take off after them, the more likely we are to catch them before they leave for somewhere else."

He helped me to my feet and placed the blanket around my shoulders. "I'd like you to come over to the fire and meet some of the cliff people, and afterward I'll introduce you to Nekhotex and Janwi. They're waiting just by the water's edge, and I know they want to meet you."

There is little more to tell about our sojourn on Osind.

The cliff people were hospitable and friendly, once they'd overcome their initial reticence, although of course I didn't really have enough time to get to know them as well as Dahll does.

I wish I could have had the opportunity to learn to communicate with the Gru. I greatly regret the way I misjudged them. Their voice patterns are quite unlike ours, but Dahll worked out a complicated sort of sign language with them, interspersed with the occasional native Osindian word from him and high-pitched whistles and plaintive sounding calls from them. Still, I was not sorry to leave that treacherous planet, where nothing appears to be as it seems. It was good to return to the familiarity and safety of the *Quest*.

As soon as I could, after the ship lifted off Osind, I washed myself in the cleansing mist and slipped into fresh overalls. I took the slave's garments I'd been obliged to wear in Jarrok's castle and prepared to throw them into the ship's dematerialisation unit, much to Dahll's obvious disgust.

"Just think what they're worth. Those gemstones look real and there's all that gold and silver embroidery..."

"I don't care if it's worth a fortune," I retorted, defiantly giving the appropriate command to the computer. "I don't want anything to remind me of my incarceration on Osind."

"You could've sold them."

"I'm not that desperate for money. Just having them on board would remind me of Jarrok. Although," I admitted, "I can't help feeling rather sorry about what happened to him. He didn't deserve to die the way he did. Your man needn't have been so brutal."

Dahll glanced at me, almost pityingly.

"What?"

"Oh, nothing," he replied, shaking his head slowly. "I just don't think I'll ever figure you out. From the look of you, I don't imagine he gave you a pleasant time."

"Oh, let's forget about him," I urged. "I want to know about Nekhotex and his people, and what you were up to when I was a prisoner in the castle."

Dahll told me as much as he'd been able to learn about the Gru and their relationship with the cliff people. It seems the two species appeared on Osind at about the same time but had evolved along completely different lines. If it's true life on all planets originally came from the sea, then somewhere in the evolution of the Gru they must have decided to go back to it. Slow and cumbrous on land, they are quite at home in the water. From his "conversations" with them, Dahll believes they have a highly advanced sub-aquatic civilisation as well as a complicated social structure.

For centuries, he told me, the two species had existed independently of each other, without any attempt at communication. The cliff people split into small groups with specific territories and over time had built clifftop communities all along the coast. These were nearly all presided over by fortresses like the one in which I'd been imprisoned. Evidently they were built to protect the various domains against any of the other groups who might have ideas about expanding their own territories.

"Apart from occasional skirmishes with neighbouring communities," Dahll went on, "their lives were relatively peaceful and undisturbed. Then, about a hundred and fifty years ago, according to their calendar, a large starship crash-landed on

Osind. Where in the galaxy it came from is a mystery, but her passengers and crew soon took full advantage of their technical superiority over the cliff people. They drove them out of their forts and villages, capturing many of them and enslaving them."

I muttered something about advanced species invariably taking advantage of more primitive ones.

"True," Dahll said, and continued his story. "Over successive generations they interbred with the cliff people, both races being enervated while retaining some of their individual physical characteristics. The invaders forced the native Osindians to add to the castles and villages, and they were obliged to build smaller, less comfortable dwellings in the cliffside for themselves." He glanced across at me. "This confirms our earlier observations about the cliff-dwellers' prowess as builders and masons. The invaders had complete mastery over them, swords and armour being little defence against the superiority of blasters.

"They apparently made no attempt to contact or communicate with the Gru, believing them to be nothing more than aquatic reptiles. Occasionally they hunted them for sport, and realising early on that the Gru's tough scales deflected blaster-fire, cannibalised their ships' weaponry systems to build laser-cannons to use against them. They also learned to tame and ride the native shanya and discovered that, due to their awkwardness on land, the Gru were virtually defenceless against a rider with a blaster."

"Yes, Jarrok told me as much."

"When we landed, the cliff people at first assumed we belonged to the same race as their oppressors. That's why they were reluctant show themselves. The Gru, having also observed our arrival on the planet, and noting we were not armed heavily enough to be dangerous, decided to make contact, but Jarrok spotted us at the same time."

As Dahll continued his story, he told me the Gru had indicated their willingness to help him rescue me, but he'd needed to gain the trust of the cliff people in order to enlist their help, as well. This he had achieved, thanks to his promise of modern weapons from the *Quest* and, I suspect, a certain aura of honesty and trustworthiness he tends to project. An aura enhanced by his casual charm and good looks and quiet, confident manner.

The appearance of the *Quest* in the heavens, before we landed, had not gone unnoticed. Rumours began to spread that Dahll was an emissary sent from the stars to free them and overcome the tyrants who ruled over them. They vowed to follow him to the death, if necessary, in an attempt to storm the castle. Contrary to what Jarrok had intimated to me, they are a courageous people whose only reason for not trying to overthrow the castle lords before was the inferiority of their weapons. After all, courage is merely suicide if not tempered by intelligent forethought, and the cliff people are not naturally suicidal or stupid.

"What I'd like to know," I said, after he'd finished explaining all this, "is how you managed to take the castle. After all, the quantity of hand weapons on board the *Quest* was never intended to be sufficient to supply an army."

"True," Dahll agreed, "although I was able to manufacture several more using the synthe-unit. And of course I didn't have a great deal of time in which to select and train those who were to use them. I had to choose the ablest and most courageous, so the force was not all that large. However, others of the cliff people chose to join us, using whatever weapons they already had." He paused for a moment.

"The castle-holders have become complacent, and we had the advantage of surprise. The last thing they were expecting was a revolt. Several of the Gru diverted the attention of the guards operating the laser-cannon, while Nekhotex, Janwi and myself, together with the volunteers from the cliff people, worked our way up the cliff and across the fields behind the castle. We were able to enter the courtyard and overcome the rest of the guards before putting the cannon out of operation."

"You make it sound easy," I commented, wondering how much he'd left out.

He smiled. "Not for the Gru, it wasn't. It's only because Janwi and Nekhotex are young and not yet fully-grown they were able to make it to the castle at all. Their presence caught the guards unaware and made it that much easier for us to overcome them. We didn't come through entirely unscathed, and once we were in the castle itself, our casualties were pretty high, although thankfully most of the injuries were fairly minor."

He glanced at me impishly. "It wasn't made any easier by you shooting the people who were trying to rescue you." I made a face at him and he continued.

"All things considered, we came out of it pretty well. And of course," he said, "we were able to add the weapons of the men we'd overcome to the ones from the *Quest*'s arsenal."

"I wonder if we were right to leave them with the means of destroying each other," I mused, half to myself.

"Well, it's always a risk to introduce modern technological weapons to a relatively primitive society," Dahll said. "But they'll need them if they're to overcome the other castle-holders, and there are apparently several of *them* further along the coast. Besides, the Gru are highly intelligent and now that the two species have learnt to cooperate, it would probably have been only a matter of time before they started manufacturing their own weapons to defend themselves anyway." His reasoning was grimly logical.

"Why d'you think they never tried to communicate with each other before?"

"It seems the Gru often tried to help the cliff people in their fight against the castle lords, but they were regarded as just large, friendly animals. Ridiculous, isn't it?"

"I'm afraid I've heard that story before," I said. "On Earth the seas used to be inhabited by huge, gentle and intelligent creatures, the dolphins and their kind. Only we didn't just ignore them, we exterminated them out of greed and ignorance, and my people never knew what they'd done until it was too late."

Dahll nodded sympathetically. "I suppose there are parallels on most planets inhabited by humanoid civilisations. Anraat can't claim to be entirely innocent of such crimes, either."

"I thought my last moment had come when I turned round and saw you in that absurd armour," I admitted, deciding it was time to lighten the conversation. "What was the idea? It couldn't have been much protection against a laser."

"No," Dahll agreed, "but it's some defence against blaster fire. Besides, it served to confuse the enemy. They couldn't be sure how many of us there actually were, when we all looked the same."

"You confused more than the enemy," I said. I paused. I needed to know something.

"Dahll...there was a room in the castle, some kind of holo-chamber. Did you find it?"

Dahll looked at me astutely. "Yes, the equipment was so obviously Salmaran. I gave orders for it to be destroyed, together with its power source. Why, what d'you know about it?"

"Oh, nothing, I just heard some rumours, that's all." From the look on his face when I said it, I don't think he believed me. I hate deceiving him, but I can't bring myself to tell him the truth, not yet, anyway. It may be cowardly of me, but I just want to forget my experiences on Osind.

"Are you quite sure—" He broke off in mid-sentence.

"What's up?"

"There's something coming through on the scanners."

We were sitting in the recreation area, waiting for the hyper-acceleration serum to take effect preparatory to entering hyperspace. I turned to look at the visual output screen. The object moving rapidly away from us was obviously a ship. On the small screen, with no accompanying data, how big it was, or at what distance wasn't immediately obvious. Presumably, the *Quest* had only just come within scanner range of her.

We raced to the flight deck and Dahll seated himself at the control panel.

"Can we have her on full magnification?" I asked.

Dahll touched a control and she came into close-up. I took a deep breath and clutched at Dahll's arm with trembling fingers.

"That's her. That's the *Destiny*," I told him, almost afraid to take my eyes away from the scanner. A mass of data appeared on the output screens—mass, velocity, distance, size and class. The ship was rapidly accelerating, and since we were already cruising at just under light speed ourselves, there was nothing we could do to decrease the distance between the two ships.

Dahll looked at me, then turned back to the screen. "You were right, she certainly *is* some ship!" An edge of excitement tinged his voice. "If only we can make contact with her. Quickly, open a frequency while we're still within hailing distance."

I was already trying to establish a communication link, but even as he spoke, the outline of the *Destiny* became indistinct and strangely incandescent, glowing at the edges with the colours of the spectrum. As we watched, there was a brilliant flash and she disappeared, leaving nothing but empty space.

## Chapter Eleven

Dahll and I looked at each other, too stunned to speak.

"Why?" I asked at last. "Why couldn't she have waited just a little longer?"

Dahll's fingers flicked rapidly over the control pads, as if he could somehow make her reappear again, although we both knew there was no point and the computer's scanners were registering accurately. He turned to me, looking almost as disappointed and shocked as I was.

I suppose," he said, in his matter-of-fact manner, "she saw us on her scanners and decided not to wait around to see if we were hostile."

I shook my head. "I don't think so, Dahll. A ship like the *Destiny* could destroy the *Quest*, without the slightest risk to herself, and she could have hailed us to find out our intentions if she wanted to. Besides, we're so small by comparison we probably hadn't even registered on her sensors yet."

"Then she must've already calculated her next jump into hyperspace at this point. It's just unfortunate we didn't catch up with her sooner."

"Just bad luck," I said bitterly. "What I don't understand is how she came to be in this sector of space at all."

Dahll considered for a moment. "Well, since one of Osind's neighbouring planets apparently has some interesting plant and animal life, I reckon they must've stopped off to take a look."

"Yes," I agreed thoughtfully. "And if you're right, she must only have left the Hvelgelmir constellation a short while before we did."

I turned away disconsolately. "To be so close, and then to lose them."

"Why don't you go to your cabin and rest? I'll try to recalculate our next entry into hyperspace. We'll need to extrapolate the *Destiny*'s course and speed very accurately but it doesn't need two of us."

He was right about one thing. The accuracy of the calculations was vital. In the nothingness of hyperspace, we would be flying blind and there was a very real danger we might run straight into the *Destiny* if the coordinates were not worked out very carefully.

"She normally cruises at standard plus nine," I said flatly, not moving.

Dahll whistled softly. "You call that cruising?"

"The *Quest* can match it," I responded defensively, as if she were *my* ship.

"Yes, at almost top speed. Still, with that information and the data we already have, the computer should be able to come up with the *Destiny*'s present speed and trajectory."

He was again fingering the control pads and scanning the information on the read-out screen.

"Why don't you go and rest," he repeated. "You've been through a lot, and you need—"

All I could think of was how much I longed to find the *Destiny* again. Every minute wasted was a loss we couldn't afford. In my frustration, I lashed out at the only person available. "Rest is the last thing I need. Why are you always so patronising?"

Dahll flinched, almost as if I'd hit him. "Is that what you think?" he asked softly, without looking at me.

"Ever since we left Phidia you've treated me like I was your kid sister. Well it may surprise you to know I've been taking care of myself for a long time. I'm a qualified hyper-pilot, I don't *need* looking after."

I don't know why I spoke to Dahll like that. I regretted the words as soon as they were out of my mouth. It is Dahll's ship. Strictly speaking, he has every right to give me whatever instructions he thinks necessary.

"I'm sorry," he said quietly. "I didn't mean anything by it. I can't help it if I feel concerned for you."

I knew I'd hurt his feelings, but I couldn't take it back. Miserably I stood behind him and laid both hands lightly on his shoulders.

"Dahll, I'm sorry. I didn't mean what I just said. I'm on edge, but I had no right to take it out on you." I groped uncertainly for the right words. "You're such a good friend, I owe you so much. If it wasn't for you I'd still be in the clutches of N—of Jarrok."

He turned his head to look at me. It's not always easy to tell what he's thinking, but if he noticed my slip, he gave no sign.

"It's all right. I understand how you must be feeling. Anyway, you're probably right. I reckon it must seem to you I'm being patronising, but I feel responsible for you since you're a passenger on my ship..."

I sighed, suddenly realising how exhausted I was. "I think I *will* take your advice and go to my cabin for a while, if you're sure there's nothing I can do here."

"Nothing." He waved a casual hand toward the computer console. "The computer won't take long to produce the necessary data. Don't worry," he added, "We'll find her again. It's not as if we don't know where she's headed."

He was right, and his words should have made me feel better, but they didn't. When I reached my cabin I knew that, however tired, I was too tense and anxious to sleep. It's the first time Dahll and I have come anywhere near to quarrelling, and I feel ashamed and guilty at my unprovoked outburst of temper.

I watched the stars through the viewport for a while. The sheer beauty and immensity of deep space always helps me to put things in perspective. When at last the tension began to leave me, I sat on the edge of my bunk and reached for my holocorder. I've recorded everything that happened since our landing on Osind.

I've just finished in time, for Dahll has appeared on the communicator screen to ask me to return to the flight deck for the jump into hyperspace.

****

158-04.06

At first there was nothing but blackness. I could feel it all around me, liquid and terrifying. Terrifying? Why should it be? I have no fear of the dark. But this was different from any kind of darkness I'd experienced before.

There was nothing. No sound, not the faintest pinpoint of light, just the darkness, stifling, all encompassing...and I could not escape. I drifted for a long while before I realised the blackness was no longer all-pervasive. At the far end a light was spreading. The sun bathed the lake in brightness. The lake! So that's where I was, bathing in the lake in one of the few areas of Earth not affected by radiation or pollution. I'd been instructed to make certain I had an anti-radiation shot first, just in case, but I knew I was safe. There were un-mutated fish in the water, and healthy, normal plants growing on the shore.

I floated lazily for a while. Voices...strange voices. I'd thought I was alone. I opened my eyes. I could see no one. The voices continued, but the light was changing. Something was happening to the water. Yes, the light had changed again, red...red...blood red. But it wasn't the light, it was the water. The water was turning into blood! I struggled frantically to escape.

Somehow the lake had hold of me and would not let me go, growing more viscous every second, like some hideous, living quicksand. The more I struggled the deeper I sank.

I cried out for someone to save me. *There must be someone who will help me.*

Darkness again, impenetrable darkness. Voices...strange, soothing. Then I was running through endless, unlit corridors. Something pursued me through the blackness. Things, slimy and snakelike reached out, grasping.

I realised I was no longer running. I couldn't be, for my feet refused to move any more. I was paralysed and helpless, and whatever was pursuing me was coming closer. If only I could see, if only it weren't so dark...if I weren't so consumed by this feeling of terror and complete helplessness.

*Someone, please help me.*

Another voice. Excruciating, agonizing pain. Blackness...myriad impossible, garish colours, flashing in small explosions before my eyes. Then that voice again.

I opened my eyes. I lay in a white bed, in a white room. The light was not bright, but such a contrast to the previous darkness it hurt my eyes. A face close to me—oval, purple eyes gazed solicitously into my own. Bewildered, I tried to ask who he was, where we were, but somehow I could not speak, could not even move.

Then, abruptly, I was back in the castle on Osind, strapped in that hateful chair of torture, with Narhjohol standing over me, brandishing a knife. The feeling of terror, which had hold of me all this time, was still there, but it was not Narhjohol I feared.

I watched in horrified fascination as he raised the knife slowly, oh, so slowly...

"Quickly, she's coming round."

That soothing voice again, soft, reassuring. I looked trustingly into the purple eyes. His name, he told me, was Yan Kloor. I was quite safe. I must not be frightened. As he spoke, the terror in my mind faded. I relaxed. His eyes were so gentle, so kind. Yet as I watched, they seemed to lose their soft purple colour and become crimson, until they were like red, glowing embers. The person before me changed until he no longer bore any resemblance to a humanoid being. He grew in height, his face and body changing until he took on the appearance of a monstrous spectre, a creature of indescribable evil. I realised he held a scalpel in his fingers. I lay helpless and petrified with fear. This was my pursuer, the thing I feared more than anything else.

He ran his thumb along the edge of the scalpel, enjoying my fear, and I screamed as he struck, and warm, bright blood stained the whiteness all about me.

I sat bolt upright, trembling from head to foot. My heart's violent pounding brought me back to my senses. I requested the computer to increase the lighting until I could see clearly the few familiar personal objects in my cabin. My skin felt cold and clammy, although my bunk is programmed to activate and maintain a constant, computer-controlled temperature whenever it is used. My nightmares always follow the same pattern and I awake cold and terrified.

A dull throbbing pounded behind my eyes. This is also consistent with my nightmares. I could vaguely remember throwing myself down on my bunk after we entered hyperspace, completely exhausted.

I checked the time. I'd only been asleep for about

four hours and still felt terribly tired and drained. Perhaps Dahll was still on the flight deck. I'd be very grateful for his company. His cabin is at the other end of the living quarters, some way away from the passenger section. He'd told me he would get some sleep himself, leaving the ship under the control of the main computer, but knowing Dahll, he could well still be working.

The pain in my head grew worse and my vision began to blur. I was still shivering, my mind full of the horrors of my dream. I forced myself to get up, to pull on my clothes, and made my way shakily to the sick bay. After I'd given myself the medication, I sat on one of the soft, padded couches in the main area.

The remedy encourages the brain to produce a natural painkilling substance and takes a little time to work. I drew my feet up onto the couch and rested my head on my arms, suddenly overcome by the memory of my dream and a heavy feeling of loneliness and self-pity. I couldn't get that hideous face out of my mind. What is it? Why am I so afraid of it? Is it merely a fragment from my distorted, confused nightmares, or does it really exist? I feel the answer lies in my past. Why can't I remember? Will I ever be free of my nightmares, or will I have to endure them for the rest of my life? So many questions.

I know, deep down, what I really fear is that one day I will find I'm not dreaming. That whatever it is that threatens me in my dreams, the thing with eyes like a creature from Hell, will still be there when I wake.

I blinked back the tears filling my eyes, angry at a fate that seemed to throw obstacles in front of me at every turn. Angry with myself for my weakness. Tears weren't going to accomplish anything. I'm not a child. But my loneliness when I thought of the *Destiny,* and the man I love, threatened to engulf me. Will I ever find him?

I haven't for a moment revealed to Dahll how full of doubt I am. Space is so vast. I could spend the rest of eternity one step behind the *Destiny*, always just missing her.

I felt a gentle hand on my shoulder and started violently, almost crying out in alarm. I'd been so wrapped up in myself I hadn't even heard the soft whine of the hatch opening.

Dahll sat down close to me. "It's only me. Who...or what were you expecting?" After a moment he said, "The computer registered that you were here, and I wanted to check you were all right. Hey," he went on, placing a brotherly arm around me as I grasped at him in my relief at hearing his familiar voice, burying my head in the comforting warmth of his shoulder. "What is it? Tell me."

"I...I'm sorry," I said in confusion. I drew away from him, struggling to regain my composure. "I had a nightmare, that's all. I'm still not quite sure what's real and what isn't."

"Don't you think you could tell me the rest?"

"The rest?"

He regarded me candidly. "We've been friends too long to play games with each other. You didn't need to come here because of a nightmare."

"No," I admitted, "I had a headache, a migraine. Yan Kloor gave me something for when it gets bad."

"You've had them before, then?"

"Yes, but not often since I've been on board the *Quest*. I'm all right so long as I give myself the medication when I feel it coming on."

"You should've told me."

"I didn't want to worry you with my problems. You have your own, and there was nothing you could do."

He gave me one of his looks. "I'd still prefer to know. Anyway, what was this nightmare you had?"

I shook my head. "I'd really rather not talk about it. I'm too tired now, I just want to sleep."

"Listen," Dahll said persuasively. "I know we agreed, you and I, right at the beginning, our arrangement was to be strictly business. No entanglements, no complications, and a mutual respect for each other's privacy." He looked at me again in that direct way he has. "I think you'll agree I've kept to that agreement. But," he hesitated, almost shyly, "two people can't travel and work together on the same ship for as long as we have and remain strangers to each other. Every time I look at you, I see the sadness in your eyes. Why don't you tell me why finding the *Destiny* is so important to you?"

I needed to talk to someone, and I owed it to Dahll to tell him about myself. I started, hesitantly at first, but he was such a sympathetic listener I soon stopped holding back.

I told him of my work before I met the crew of the *Destiny*, about my time on board her, and how my feelings for one of them had gradually deepened into love.

The circumstances in which I was parted from him and the rest of the crew are still a blank. I had to rely mainly on what Yan Kloor and Yett Sitta had told me, which was not a great deal. Telling him about the 'treatment' I'd undergone was the hardest. When I'd finished I looked at Dahll intently, waiting for his expression to turn to one of horror, or worse, pity, but his face showed neither.

"Aren't you shocked?" I asked tremulously. "Now that you know don't you find me...abhorrent?"

"Why should I?" His tone suggested amazement that I could even consider the possibility of such a thing. He put his hand on my arm, and his eyes were very serious as they met mine. "How could you think something that wasn't your fault, which was quite out of your control, would make me feel any differently toward you? If I can accept it, why can't you?"

It was difficult to argue with his logic. I wondered if all Anraatians were as practical as Dahll.

"I'm so afraid that *they* won't understand. What will I do if *he* can't accept it? If we ever find the *Destiny* again, that is."

"We'll find her," he promised firmly. "Of course we will." He paused. "I'm glad you told me. I knew there must be someone on board that ship. Someone you cared for. You must love him very much to search for him across the galaxy. If he cares as much about you, what you've just told me won't change anything."

"I hope you're right, Dahll."

"I am, trust me. About those nightmares of yours, though. D'you reckon they're connected with what happened to you on Phidia?"

"They must be. I'd never had them before."

"And the headaches are obviously connected with the dreams?"

I nodded. "It must be partly psychological. The nightmares seem to occur when I've been worried or upset. It always follows the same pattern, although the actual dreams themselves may be different. I end up running from something, something I'm terribly afraid of. I run and run, but I always come face to face with it...him. The most frightening thing is I feel he really exists. That I should know who he is, if only I could remember."

"Perhaps that's because you've had the same dream so often."

"It's possible," I agreed, "but I don't think so."

He was silent for several seconds, watching my face, as if not sure whether to say what was on his mind.

"What exactly happened to you in that fortress? Was it Jarrok who hit you?"

My hand went to my face, although I knew the bruising had subsided and was now barely noticeable, thanks to the salve. Another Phidian medication whose composition is a mystery to me, although I believe it contains similar healing substances to those found naturally in the bodies of all living creatures.

"No, in fact Jarrok treated me like a guest rather than a slave. He even called me his lady, as if I were somehow different from the other..."

I paused. He suddenly looked startled, as if I'd said something of considerable significance. After a moment, he shook his head and smiled that slow smile of his.

"For a moment I thought—it's just that—well that phrase has a rather special meaning on Anraat." Before I could ask him to explain, his expression grew very serious. "So it was Narhjohol, then. Perhaps I shouldn't ask. I realise you mightn't want to tell me. But...did he use torture on you when you were held at the castle?"

I hesitated before answering. "What makes you think that?"

"You almost told me yourself. And I know Narhjohol and his methods. The equipment in the castle was similar to that which he used on my family. Only he didn't stop until he'd killed them. Besides, when you asked me about the room where he'd installed his holographic horrors, I reckoned you must know more about it than you let on."

"I had to know if the equipment still existed. I was hoping you'd say it had been destroyed."

"Along with quite a lot of the rest of the castle and several of Narhjohol's men," Dahll said, with evident satisfaction. Then his eyes darkened, and he looked at me in the same way he did when he had first told me about his father and sister's death at the hands of the Salmaran. "I know Narhjohol," he repeated. "To him, the men and women he takes as slaves are just merchandise or playthings—" he broke off, clenching his fists fiercely, and looked away from me. It was obvious what was going through his mind.

"It's all right, Dahll," I said gently. "He limited himself to torture. He was hoping to get a good price for me and didn't want to devalue the goods. Anyway, I'm far more capable of defending myself than you give me credit for."

I told him briefly of my experiences as a prisoner. I didn't mention the humiliation Narhjohol had put me through on our first encounter in the castle, and left out as much of his treatment of me as I thought I could get away with. Dahll tried to draw me on this, but I think he could see the memory of it was painful to me, so he did not press too hard.

He smiled, for the first time since I'd started my narrative concerning Narhjohol, when I told him how I'd managed to overcome the slaver at our first confrontation.

"I wish I'd been there," he said, "I'd've enjoyed seeing that."

I stifled a yawn. Lack of sleep was catching up with me. "It didn't improve his temper any," I admitted. "And unfortunately I didn't get a chance to try it on him again."

"So now we both have something to hate Narhjohol for. I'm sorry. If I'd believed you'd be in any danger from him, I wouldn't have agreed to take you along in the first place. I'll drop you off at the nearest planet with interstellar technology, and somehow I'll find the money to pay for your passage to Brend-Igon. I should still have enough credits—"

"Don't even think of it," I said, flashing him a look I hoped would tell him I wasn't prepared to argue about it. "I'm as keen as you are to see Narhjohol killed, now. If you think I'm willing to let you go after him without me, you're very much mistaken. There's nothing to reproach yourself for," I added quickly. "I was only too glad to find a ship and a pilot I could trust."

"You should've let him have the formula."

"Dahll, how could you even suggest it? The formula belongs to you and your people, and I'm sure he'd have treated me exactly the same way whether I'd told him or not. He made no secret of the fact he enjoys seeing people suffer."

"You're probably right, but I'll make him pay for it, and for the death of my family, I swear it." The words were spoken quietly, but with such determination I felt a chill run through me. I hadn't forgotten Tamarith's warning, and all at once a grim sense of foreboding stole over me.

I said nothing. I still felt incredibly weary. Dahll spoke softly to me, but I don't remember what he said, although I vaguely felt him put a pillow beneath my head and place a thermal cover over me. I must have fallen asleep then, because when I awoke it was several hours later and I was alone in the sick bay.

****

158-18.10

We re-entered normal space as we approached the Hyades system. Nothing of consequence had occurred, and we expected to re-engage the hyperdrive once we were safely past the last star in the system and the only planet that circles it, on course for the Pleiades system. We were still working on the extrapolations Dahll had made, in conjunction with the data downloaded from the computer.

However, as we approached the planet, identified as Lyrrh, we picked up a signal the main computer interpreted as being a distress call coming from the surface.

"I don't like it," Dahll said, looking serious. "All the data we have indicates Lyrrh is completely uninhabited. The surface temperature is a little too hot for comfort in many of its regions, it's subject to violent storms, and the surface cools down rapidly at night. There's also an unexplained warning about primitive life forms. It doesn't seem to be the ideal place to start a colony."

"Which means the call most likely came from someone who crash-landed on the planet and is hoping to be picked up," I suggested.

"Yes, but according to the computer, the signal's coming from a ship so small she could only be a ferry. Since it's coming through in Universal code it must be a humanoid species..."

"And there's no sign of the mother ship," I finished for him, beginning to follow his drift.

"That's what's worrying me," Dahll admitted. "If she'd been attacked by another ship we'd have felt the shock waves, and even if she'd been completely destroyed there'd be debris and our scanners would've picked up the radiation signature."

"Well we can't just ignore the call," I protested.

"We could lose the *Destiny* if we answer it."

"Dahll, apart from directly contravening Universal Law if we do nothing, whoever is sending those signals may be hurt. They could die if we don't follow it up."

"I reckon you're right." Dahll turned back to the control panel and began feeding instructions to the navigation computer. "I'll try and get a bearing on the signal. Once we've established the area from which it originates, we'll land a few miles away, just in case."

I nodded. It was unthinkable not to investigate a distress call, but as I record this in my cabin before preparing for our landing on Lyrrh, I can't help wondering if perhaps I have now lost all chance of ever catching up with the *Destiny*.

# Chapter Twelve

"What about an inflatable?"

We were deciding what to take with us in our survival packs, besides the standard food and medical supplies.

I looked up from my task of folding Sitta's cloak to fit into the smallest possible space. It's amazing how something so light and compressible can be so warm. The thermal suits are not the most convenient items of clothing to carry around. I preferred to do without mine when I could, although Dahll was taking his, just in case the nights proved as chilly as the computer predicted. "Well, the scanners are showing a large area of swampland near where the signal seems to be coming from. It might be advisable," I said.

"On the other hand," Dahll mused, "We don't want to carry anything more than is absolutely necessary in the hopper, and if we should need a raft we can always cut down a few small trees and make one."

Having perversely answered his own question, he strapped on his blaster and handed one to me. I checked it was fully charged, then stuck it in my belt.

"Ready?" he asked.

"As ready as I'll ever be."

We entered the airlock and stepped out onto the surface of Lyrrh. The sun filtered reluctantly through the sulphur-coloured clouds. The ground was a dull, brownish yellow and the rocks that littered it were dark brown and shiny, like glass. In the distance, a few tall, straggly trees and other vegetation bordered the swampland, which stretched an interminable distance. From it rose a thick, steamy vapour.

Dahll checked the dial of a small instrument he held in the palm of his hand.

"The signal's coming in strongly, about six kilometres due east...toward the swamp, then." We looked at each other and sniffed the air deprecatingly. There was a heavy, fetid smell about the area, as if something unpleasant had died there recently.

"We'd best find that ship and see if there's anyone still alive, then we can get back without wasting any more time," Dahll said, fiercely practical as usual.

While I guided down the hopper and settled myself at the controls, he set about rigging his "safety device" to the *Quest.* The planet might appear to be deserted, but there was no point in taking any chances, especially in the present, rather suspect circumstances.

As soon as he'd finished and seated himself beside me, I started the vehicle and we headed in the direction of the swamp. We'd only travelled something like five Terran minutes, when we heard a dull explosion. From the general direction of the swamp, a plume of smoke rose black against the sky.

I increased the hopper's velocity to maximum and we sped toward the swampland. The smoke, which had seemed so close, was in fact much farther away than it appeared. Small boulders strewed the ground before us, as well as the many mounds of dead and rotting vegetation that lay like seaweed washed up on the shore by the tide. I was glad we had the hopper and could hover above the ground, or the terrain would have severely hampered our progress.

As we neared the swamp, the landscape softened. In front of us increasingly numerous pockets of thick, bubbling ooze appeared, from which rose jets of hissing steam. The vegetation was encroaching swiftly. It spread everywhere, in hideous shades of sickly yellow, red and ochre. Not a trace of healthy, photosynthesising green in sight. Even the leaves on the spindly trees in the distance were a dull, reddish brown. Oxygen-producing plants had to exist for the atmosphere of Lyrrh to be breathable, but they seemed noticeably scarce in this particular region.

The smoking black hulk of the wreck lay on the very edge of the swamp. The fire, which must have swiftly consumed the small ship, had been contained by the swamp itself. Two bodies lay sprawled some distance away.

We landed the hopper gently, and Dahll held out his hand.

"May I have your blaster for a moment?"

I was slightly puzzled, but Dahll rarely does anything without a reason. I handed it to him, wordlessly.

He took it from me, and after inspecting it cursorily, made an adjustment and handed it back to me.

"I'm sorry," he said, with a wry smile. "It's not that I don't respect your abhorrence of killing, but—" he nodded toward the remains of the ferry, "if that's not what it seems, then someone's gone to an awful lot of bother setting it up to lure us here. If there's trouble, I don't fancy being shot in the back by someone who's just recovered from one of your stun-beams."

I shrugged and pursed my lips a little. "You might have trusted me to calibrate it myself," I muttered, but I knew Dahll was right. I might not like the situation, and the thought of shooting to kill *is* abhorrent to me, but, as he'd hinted, if we were heading into a trap, my being squeamish would probably get us both killed.

We reached the bodies, and I turned the nearest one over gently. The horrifying injury he'd sustained had nothing to do with what had happened to the ship. Someone had shot him at close range, with a blaster. I shuddered, although it wasn't the first time I'd seen the damage that such a weapon could inflict.

The garments he wore were black and anonymously styled. There was no identifying badge of any kind that I could see. They were typical of the style, though not the colour, worn by most spacers from the Allied Planets.

"Mine's dead!" Dahll said in low tones.

"Mine, too. He's been shot."

Dahll hurried over to me. "Both of them the same." He ripped away what was left of the man's rough shirt and pointed to a mark on the shoulder. "See that brand? These were Salmaran crew members."

I stared at the markings, meaningless to me, burned into the skin. I moved back from the body and saw fronds of yellow vegetation had somehow become wrapped around his leg. Cautiously I plucked at one of them with curious fingers and sprang back with a sharp cry as it removed itself from the body and coiled around my wrist, creeping slowly up my arm. The thing was alive...sentient. From the blood on the man's leg, which also covered its tentacles, it appeared it had been feeding off him. Now it was about to suck the blood from me as well.

I reached for my gun with my other hand, but before my fingers could make contact, Dahll aimed a thin blast of energy at the main stem. Immediately the tentacles loosened their grip on my arm, falling writhing to the ground.

Without speaking, Dahll rolled up my sleeve and inspected my wrist and arm. The sleeve of my tunic had protected most of my arm, but on my wrist the impression of the small oval suckers showed up as angry red wheals on my skin. Dahll delved into his pack and busied himself applying salve. "We can only hope that thing's not venomous. Perhaps I'd better give you a general anti-toxin shot, just in case."

After he'd finished his ministrations, Dahll rose quickly to his feet, gun in hand. He nodded toward a lone rock, which stood a short distance away, its appearance rather like a roughly-hewn clenched fist.

"There're two more bodies by that peculiar-looking rock over there. I'm going to investigate."

"I'll come with you."

"Be careful, there's something very wrong about this whole setup." He made for the strangely-shaped rock standing apart from an outcrop of smaller rocks and boulders. I slipped behind one of the largest, blaster at the ready, as Dahll reached the first body, lying face downward. I could see the other, a short distance away.

Dahll knelt down guardedly, and the figure suddenly exploded into life, twisting onto his back and kicking out with heavy-booted feet so that Dahll went sprawling backward. As he fell, he fired his blaster, but the bolt went wild. It slammed into a clump of vegetation, which immediately shrivelled into a black, smoking mass, emitting a pungent smell. As it burned, it let out a piercing shriek, which was almost like an animal scream.

I fired at Dahll's assailant as he went for his own weapon. I didn't do more than inflict a flesh wound, but by this time Dahll had scrambled to his feet and launched himself at the man. At the same time he fired at the other "body" that was also on his feet now and in the act of going for his gun. Number

Two went down with a hoarse yell, catching the full force of Dahll's blast.

Dahll was struggling with his opponent, trying to take his gun from him before he could draw it from his belt. Another figure sprang out from beyond the rocks and aimed his weapon at Dahll's back.

Even at that distance, I had no trouble recognising him as Narhjohol. I held my breath and fired. Perhaps in my anxiety to prevent him from shooting Dahll I fired too quickly, or perhaps he moved just as my blaster discharged. Whatever the cause, the blast just missed the slaver and hit his weapon instead, sending it spinning from his hand, to fall some distance away in the undergrowth.

He crawled stealthily toward it and I fired again, forcing him to dive for cover. I tried to see what was happening to Dahll, without risking being hit myself.

The Salmaran was thickset and heavy in comparison to Dahll, who while tall is slim and wiry. So although it was fairly easy for Dahll to keep out of his way, it was not so easy for him to land a blow that would be likely to disable his opponent.

I kept firing in Narhjohol's direction. He was clever, dodging my fire and making use of every possible cover. At least my fire was preventing him from getting back to his weapon, and he was moving further and further away from it. Bending low, I sprinted forward a short distance, flattened myself behind another rock, and took aim at Narhjohol again. For a moment I thought I'd hit him, but then he ducked out of sight once more.

I flung an anxious look at Dahll. To my relief, he seemed to have the upper hand. A right-handed blow to the Salmaran's jaw sent him spinning. As he reeled forward, his fingers closed around Dahll's blaster, but it was the last mistake that Salmaran would ever make, for Dahll's aim was unerring and fatal. The force of the impact lifted the Salmaran off his feet. With a sickening screech, he fell, lifeless, to the ground. I loosed another shot at Narhjohol, trying to aim ahead of him and cause him to break cover.

Dahll raced over to where the slaver's weapon had fallen and retrieved it from the scrub. As he did so, I noticed a slight movement in the bushes behind. Another of Narhjohol's men appeared, his weapon trained on Dahll, out of my range.

"Dahll," I yelled. "Dahll, behind you!"

He whirled round and his blaster sent home its flaming bolt of death. I turned back to where Narhjohol had been. He was no longer there.

A slight rustle in the undergrowth alerted me to danger behind me. I spun around and fired. A cry of pain told me my aim had hit home, but my would-be assailant could not have sustained more than superficial burns, because I saw him race away in the distance.

Dahll fired after him, but by now he was too far away for his aim to be effective and he turned to me anxiously. "You all right?"

"Yes, of course. Sorry, Dahll, I tried to stop Narhjohol from getting away but—"

"Don't worry about it. You couldn't be looking in two directions at once. We'll get another chance at him...and you did divest him of this."

He examined Narhjohol's strange weapon, regarding it with distaste. He set his mouth in a hard line as he examined the butt of the weapon. "Not a mark on it, and it must have absorbed the whole blast. I'll bet Narhjohol's hand wasn't even scorched."

"What is it?" I asked curiously. The large, rather bulky weapon was like nothing I'd ever seen before.

"A molecular scrambler," he said in disgust, "outlawed by the Union and all the civilised planets for the last fifty years. Only someone as twisted as Narhjohol would even consider using it." He threw it a long way out into the swamp.

"I've never seen one before."

"Its effects are not confined to its immediate target," Dahll informed me. "The ray's diffusion kills everything in range, as well as horribly mutating it. As for anyone who received the main force—" he paused meaningfully, warming to his subject.

"Yes, I can imagine what it does, and I don't think I want to talk about it. You'd better get cleaned up," I said, changing the subject. "Your face is bleeding and your lip's cut." I don't think he'd noticed his injuries, which were thankfully only superficial.

"Just lucky, I reckon," he said lightly, when I mentioned he might have been more seriously injured. "It appears Narhjohol's not worried about killing me any more." He looked at me apologetically. "He probably thinks he'll have another go at getting the formula from you, if I'm dead."

I said nothing, having promised myself when we left Osind that I would never let the Salmaran capture me alive again. When I'd cleansed and dressed Dahll's minor lacerations, he looked once more toward the swamp, in the direction Narhjohol had taken.

"We should've brought the inflatable after all," he mused. "Still, it shouldn't take long to build a raft. Those trees over there should be ideal, provided they don't have the same habits as that monster which had hold of you!"

The trees were, in fact, quite ordinary, thin-trunked and easy to fell. Dahll cut them with his sonic cutter and I lashed them together with strands of creeper twisted into a rope. When the body of the raft was completed, we went back to the *Quest*. We decided to sacrifice some of the ship's lightweight food and water containers, securing them at each end of the raft to help keep it afloat. It was hard work and we didn't pause to rest or eat for many hours. However, the resultant craft was small, light and floated beautifully.

We stood back and admired our handiwork.

"With that," Dahll said, "I should be able to catch up with Narhjohol without too much trouble. I doubt if he has the brains to think of making a raft. He's probably hacking down the vegetation and going overland."

"Perhaps he'll get eaten by some of it," I suggested hopefully.

"I'm not sure that's a subject we should joke about," Dahll said. "I'm not at all happy about those things."

"Anyway," I went on, the significance of what he had said earlier suddenly hitting me. "What d'you mean, *you'll* be able to catch up with him? We're in this together, remember?"

"No, Dahll said firmly. "I'm going after him alone. It's my guess he sent his ship into hyperspace so we wouldn't be able to detect her on the *Quest*'s scanners. He's probably waiting for her to come back and contact him so he can arrange to be picked up." He paused significantly. "If I'm not back within three days, or if Narhjohol lands a ferry anywhere near the *Quest*, take off, fast."

"Aren't you forgetting something?" I asked, giving him my sweetest smile. "You're so good at ordering me to stay put, while you have all the action. If you recall, I have a score to settle with Narhjohol myself, now. I'm coming with you."

Dahll gave me a disparaging look, and then grinned suddenly.

"All right, we go together. I reckon we don't have time to argue about it, if we're not to lose him."

We covered the hopper with the discarded branches of the trees we'd used to construct our raft, and Dahll set up a smaller version of the explosive devise he'd rigged to the *Quest*. After carrying the raft between us for some distance, we found a suitable place and launched it into the murky waters of the swamp.

We made fair progress. Dahll had constructed a rough paddle, which served us very well when the raft came to a standstill in the sluggish by-waters, or drifted into the clumps of reed-like vegetation. This not only grew all around but in the torpid water itself, impeding our progress so much there were times we had to use the blasters to cut our way through.

When it began to grow dark, we pulled the raft up onto the bank and built a fire. We were both hungry and made a meal from our survival rations. None of the vegetable matter in the area looked either safe or inviting to eat, so we didn't bother with any tests. There seem to be several species of primitive fish-like creatures living in the waters of the swamp. Tomorrow we'll try to catch some and find out if they are edible.

Having eaten, we constructed a shelter for the night from the small saplings and bushes growing close to the water, careful to avoid anything that looked even vaguely carnivorous.

****

It is now only a few hours before dawn, and I've taken advantage of the privacy of my turn on watch to bring my journal up to date. Two things occurred which are worthy of mention. One was the appearance of several glowing, reddish lights, which appeared to be some distance away. The other was a stealthy rustling noise close by, then an unearthly scream, followed by a low moaning, wailing sound, almost like an animal in pain. After that, I kept the fire well stocked up with the wood we'd gathered earlier while it was still light. However, I neither saw nor heard anything further.

I hope we find Narhjohol soon, for Dahll's sake, since I know he won't rest until he fulfills his vow of vengeance. For myself, however, I feel a deep sense of dread. I want to get back to the *Quest* and leave Lyrrh. There is an atmosphere about this planet, something evil...sinister. It's difficult to rationalise, but I feel we are not welcome here. It's a feeling I have rarely experienced before, and it fills me with foreboding.

## Chapter Thirteen

158-22.10

I don't know if I will be able to finish this entry. Dahll is sleeping now, so I must try to bring my journal up to date.

When I awoke after our first night on Lyrrh, I thought at first what I was looking at must be a trick of the light. Then, as the sun rose higher in the sky, I could see it was no illusion.

Dahll had taken the last watch and apparently did not experience any of the strange lights or the sounds I saw and heard earlier. Now we stood together and stared in disbelief. The whole landscape seemed to have changed overnight. The stretch of swamp near where we were camped was now almost clear of vegetation. However, the shoreline was covered in a tangled mass of plants and creepers, which had not been there the previous night. We'd no sooner recovered from this rather disturbing discovery than we came upon the remains of a large plant lying on the ground a short distance away from our shelter. It sprawled untidily, shrivelled and torn, a little brownish sap still oozing from the broken stems. Next to it was another plant, crimson in colour and presumably of the same species, but quite different in the intensity of colour and the strength and crispness of its stems and leaves, if, in fact, the long, tentacle-like appendages could accurately be described as leaves.

The main stem itself looked plump and bloated, and I realised the disturbances I'd heard in the night had probably been this plant making a meal of its comrade. It didn't explain the strange lights I'd seen, though.

"Delightful wildlife they have around here," Dahll remarked dryly. "It's lucky for us the carnivorous types seem to be so luridly coloured. I think we can be reasonably confident anything that's not is likely to be normal vegetation."

"We'd better not take any chances, all the same," I cautioned. "I don't think I'd have been so happy to sleep in the shelter if I'd known the relatives of the branches we used to construct it were apt to go hunting at night for their food."

"Only the woody plants we used for the shelter can hardly be said to bear much relation to these brutes." Dahll gave the dead plant a cautious prod with his boot.

We examined it curiously, taking care to avoid contact with the living one, which lay as if basking in the morning sun, no doubt satiated by its recent meal. The remains of what appeared to be roots were, in reality, fleshy limbs, or more accurately tentacles, covered with suckers to facilitate movement across the ground.

I shuddered, at once fascinated and repelled. "I wonder if the *Destiny*'s ever visited Lyrrh. Laitha, her biologist, would have enjoyed herself no end trying to classify these carnivorous plants."

"There don't seem to be any animals as such, unless we count the fishy creatures in the swamp, and I've seen one or two large, rather ugly lizards. Nothing else, though."

I nodded. The predatory plants appeared to be an evolutionary attempt to amalgamate fauna and flora, although in reality they seemed more inclined toward fauna, reminding me of gigantic Terran sea anemones.

We made a hasty breakfast, deciding not to waste time trying to catch any of the finny life in the swamp. Dahll was anxious to return to our search for Narhjohol. We decided to ration what was left of the food we had brought with us. If we were careful, it should last another three days before we were forced to sample the dubious delights of the swamp fish.

"I wonder how far ahead of us Narhjohol is," I mused as we set off on the raft once more.

"Well, unless he's been travelling all night, which I doubt, he can't be all that far ahead of us. He must've calculated when we'd be likely to land on Lyrrh and based the return of his ship on that, so it's my guess he'll wait out there somewhere until she comes back into planetary orbit and he can contact her."

"Meantime, he's probably setting another trap for us."

"There's no telling. Anyone who could kill two of his own men and destroy a ferry to use as bait for us is capable of anything."

I had to agree. "Why d'you think he killed his own men, though? Surely killing slaves would make more sense—"

Dahll shook his head. "Haven't you realised yet how ruthless, not to mention greedy, he is? His crew's expendable, slaves are worth money."

"Of course." I cringed at Narhjohol's complete disregard for life. "Since his ferry probably wouldn't hold more than six or seven Salmarans comfortably, it doesn't seem likely there are any more of his men running around now."

"I wouldn't count on it," Dahll cautioned. "As I said, he's capable of anything."

It was late that afternoon when we finally came upon the Salmarans again. We'd known we were close. The tracks, which they'd not attempted to hide, grew ever plainer and easier to follow. Obviously we were meant to find him, which made us doubly cautious.

We beached the raft and trailed them to their camp with no difficulty. We approached, under cover of what trees and scrub there were, aware it had been a little too easy and we could be playing right into the slaver's hands. However, there appeared to be only two of them, and we had the advantage of surprise.

We watched them, through a gap in the trees, seated around a small campfire. Narhjohol sat on one side of the fire with the other Salmaran, my adversary of the previous day, opposite him. They seemed about to share a meal.

We approached from the direction of the swamp. Dahll turned and gestured to me to stay where I was. I opened my mouth to protest and thought better of it. Dahll had the right to challenge Narhjohol himself. He'd pursued the slaver longer than I had, and I would be of more use to him, should he get into difficulties, if it appeared we had separated.

I flattened myself behind one of the scrawny trees, making sure there were no carnivorous plants in the vicinity, and kept a wary eye open for possible danger.

I had an uneasy feeling. It seemed odd, even suspicious, that the Salmaran had not posted the other man to guard while he ate. I felt a sudden chill as I wondered if we'd underestimated the capacity of the ferry and were even now being observed.

The thought no sooner entered my mind than a figure leapt out from the top of a high rock that overlooked the clearing, and knocked Dahll to the ground.

I aimed my blaster, measuring the distance to see if I was close enough to do any significant damage to Dahll's assailant without hitting Dahll. However, both were now on their feet, and I realised the Salmaran was armed only with a knife. He lunged at Dahll's gun arm, trying to grab the weapon, but Dahll dodged him deftly, kicking out and sending the knife spinning from his hand. After a brief scuffle, Dahll hit him on the back of the head with the butt of his gun. He whirled round as a streak of green fire missed him by no more than an ice cat's whisker.

Narhjohol! I spotted a sudden movement through the trees, but it was like shooting at shadows. Where was the other Salmaran? A twig cracked to my right. As I turned and fired my blaster, a knife embedded itself in the tree I sheltered behind. It pinned the loose-fitting sleeve of my tunic to the bark, making my shot go wild.

I struggled to free myself as the man strode toward me, a leer on his face which made me struggle all the harder.

"Let's have a little fun," he hissed, "while our friends are occupied!"

"Let's not," I said, through gritted teeth. I turned the barrel of my gun toward him, but he seized hold of my hand and twisted it sharply before I could activate the trigger, forcing me to drop the weapon. He grabbed hold of me, ripping the front of my tunic. I was still pinned to the tree by my sleeve and could do nothing to protect myself, for he had the muzzle of my own blaster against my breast.

As he stepped even closer, moving the blaster and using it to jerk my head up to look at him, I kicked out hard, but he sidestepped neatly. Laughing unpleasantly, he almost casually hooked his leg around mine so I couldn't try it again.

I cried out involuntarily, and, unable to move my head, strained my eyes to look past him, toward Dahll. Following my gaze, the man half turned...and caught the full force of the energy blast from Dahll's weapon. He crumpled to the ground, where he lay moaning and writhing, bleeding profusely, his chest and abdomen ripped open.

Dahll's reactions were lightning fast and, as he shot the Salmaran, he threw himself to the ground. Almost in the same instant, he rolled over to avoid the slaver's fire, at the same time firing his blaster into the bushes where Narhjohol lurked.

I quickly freed myself, bringing together the torn pieces of my tunic and securing them with my belt. I slipped the knife that had held me to the tree into my boot. I never *did* get my own back from Jarrok. The Salmaran Dahll had stunned rose from the ground and launched himself at me. I kicked out, and he swerved and rolled over, springing up again and reaching for my arm. I fought frantically, bringing into force all the methods of unarmed combat I could muster. He was obviously not used to this method of fighting and was unprepared as I kicked out again, knocking him off his feet. He crumpled to the ground and I whirled round, aiming a strategically placed chop to the back of his neck. He fell awkwardly, hitting his head.

I knelt down and examined him carefully. He would live, even if he did wake up with a headache. After making sure he had no other weapons on his person, I retrieved my blaster from the ground where it had fallen and looked to see what was happening to Dahll.

Narhjohol had drawn closer to Dahll's cover. He aimed his blaster, then threw it down with an oath. I could only assume it had either malfunctioned or exhausted its power. Coming out into the open, Dahll trained his weapon on the slaver, but a fourth Salmaran appeared from behind a clump of rocks, firing wildly. Dahll ducked back down under cover, firing at his new assailant, but his weapon, too, needed recharging by now. I groaned inwardly. It must have been obvious to Narhjohol, as well as to me, that the blaster's power was nearly spent.

I held my own weapon in both hands and fired, seeing a figure go down, not knowing if I'd killed him or not. My concern for Dahll at that moment overcame my aversion to taking a life. Dahll re-emerged, holstering his weapon and glancing across at me as he prepared to launch himself at the slaver.

All at once, Narhjohol brandished a knife. Presumably, he'd had it hidden, strapped to his arm. It was a weapon I recognised by its shape and the strangely carved hilt. It—or its image—was the one he'd used on me in the torture room on Osind.

Narhjohol's lips curled in a sneer of triumph, and I bent down swiftly to throw Dahll the Salmaran knife from my boot. I knew he had no other weapon. The sonic cutter and laser were with our packs on the raft and were tools, rather than weapons.

As he caught it, my attention was drawn to the Salmaran he'd shot earlier. A moaning cry escaped his lips, ending in a bout of coughing and gasping. A bloody froth covered his face. He was choking on his own blood.

I gazed down at him, and could not help feeling pity. It was incredible anyone could have such a horrific wound and still be alive, let alone conscious. He had only a short time left to live. His eyes were open, and I seemed to see a silent plea in them. Remembering the look on his face just a few minutes earlier, I felt myself harden. Then I acknowledged that he was, after all, still an intelligent being. A man, even if he was of an alien race. Whatever he was, or had been, he did not deserve to die in such pain and indignity. I could at least ensure his death was quick.

I slipped behind him, so he could not see me, adjusted my blaster to a moderate but lethal energy level, and fired at his head. As his body became suddenly still, I turned away, sickened. I've seen men, both Terran and alien, die before. This was different. This was the first time, to my knowledge, I have ever deliberately killed, let alone in cold blood.

I tried to console myself with the thought that it had been an act of mercy and I would have done as much for any creature dying in agony. But what, came the unthinkable thought, if it had been Dahll?

I pushed the thought aside and forced myself to turn back to the two combatants. Both had sustained injuries, although neither appeared to be seriously hurt. Dahll's sleeve was soaked with blood, and the Salmaran was bleeding from several minor wounds.

They seemed to have forgotten about me, as each dodged the knife thrusts of the other. Dahll's agility gave him an advantage over Narhjohol's bulk and brute cunning. He seemed to be holding his own, avoiding the savage slashes of the slaver's blade. Narhjohol, though, appeared to be growing careless, incautious in his efforts to inflict a mortal injury on the young Anraatian.

Narhjohol was backing off now, toward the swamp. All at once he closed in again, lunging at Dahll's throat with the long blade. Dahll dodged him adroitly, inflicting a deadly wound in the slaver's side as he did so.

I saw Narhjohol draw back sharply. They were now very close to the swamp's edge. He seemed to stagger, and touched the ground with his hand, as if to recover his balance. He straightened up, and flung a handful of grit and sand in Dahll's face. Half blinded though he must have been, Dahll seemed instinctively to dodge to one side to avoid the thrust of Narhjohol's knife. At the same time, he brought up his knee and knocked the Salmaran backward into the muddy waters of the swamp. He plunged in after him, ducking fleetingly beneath the surface. The slaver floundered to his feet and closed in to grapple with him once more.

I was standing well back, trying to keep out of Dahll's way. By the time I reached the water's edge, it was nearly over. Narhjohol, already badly wounded where Dahll's knife had sliced into his side, lunged recklessly at Dahll, obviously intent on delivering a final and fatal blow.

Dahll dodged out of the way. Turning back and striking out with his own knife, he buried the blade up to the hilt in the Salmaran's chest. Narhjohol's dying scream rang out over the swamp, then ceased abruptly, ending in a horrible, wheezing sort of gasp. Dahll wrenched the knife away, allowing the slaver's body to fall back into the swamp. It sank out of sight in the murky water, which now ran red with blood.

After washing the blade in the swamp water, Dahll wiped it carefully on his shirt and stuck it in his belt. His eyes met mine and I read in his face no triumph, only a great weariness and sense of inevitability. Abruptly his expression changed to one of pain and horror. He overbalanced and fell, desperately reaching once more for the knife and vainly trying to shake off the monster that had hold of his leg.

The water boiled and frothed and now I could see a huge mass of purplish-black tentacles. I aimed my blaster and fired into the middle of the brute, taking care to avoid hitting Dahll. I fired repeatedly, until at last the charge of my weapon was exhausted. The blackened, shattered thing floated on the surface, tentacles spread out limply in all directions. I assumed it was another of the predatory 'plants.' Whatever it was, or had been, it was now quite dead.

I waded into the water and helped Dahll onto the bank.

He leant wearily against a rock. "You all right?"

I shook my head in amazement.

"Dahll, you're incredible! You're the one who's hurt, and you're asking me if *I'm* all right?"

He grinned weakly. "Habit, I reckon." He winced and looked away from me, obviously in a great deal of pain.

"Let's have a look at that leg," I ordered, and he sat down obediently for me to inspect his injuries.

There were a number of long purple spines, like needles, embedded in the flesh, just above his boot, which had probably saved him from being more seriously injured by the vicious spines. I removed the boot, ripped the leg of his slacks and removed the spines one at a time, as gently as I could. Even so, it must have hurt—a lot. I placed a few of the spines in an isolation cube from my pack, for later examination. I was worried in case they might contain venom. If I had samples, it might make it easier to find an antidote.

I sterilised the knife and made incisions at the site of each wound in the form of a cross. I allowed the blood to flow for a while before bathing it with an acidic solution from my medical pack. Since the small bio regenerator was still on board the raft with our main supplies, I applied some Phidian healing salve.

I gave him a general antitoxin shot, hoping it would be sufficient until I could reach the rest of the medical supplies on the raft.

He bore my ministrations without flinching. When I'd dealt with his leg, I turned my attention to his other injuries. He'd sustained several knife wounds, the worst one being in his left shoulder, and had obviously lost a lot of blood. I always carry a tiny Phidian bio-scanner, and I ran it over Dahll's body to make sure there were no internal injuries, but the readings came back clear.

"D'you think you can make it to the raft after you've rested for a while? I've only a small emergency medical kit with me. The rest of the equipment is on the raft, and some of those lacerations are pretty deep—"

"I'll be fine," he said, in a voice beginning to shake a little. "Of course I can make it to the raft...I just feel a bit...weak. I'll be...all right."

He closed his eyes, and I busied myself trying to staunch the flow of blood from the wound in his shoulder and smearing salve on the less serious ones. I knew he needed to rest, but I was anxious to get back to the raft and treat his wounds properly. Besides, the light was rapidly waning, and I didn't want darkness to fall before we pitched camp for the night. First, however, there was something I needed to attend to.

The Salmaran lay where he had fallen, close to his dead companion. He opened his eyes as I bent over him. I made a careful adjustment and fired my blaster. There'd been enough killing. The stun beam should be enough to render him unconscious for several more hours, long enough for us to get away from this place. I hoped he'd be so grateful to find himself still alive when he awoke he would not feel tempted to follow us, but I removed his blaster, just in case. I assumed Narhjohol's ship would pick him up eventually, by which time, with luck, we would be far away.

The fourth Salmaran, the one I'd shot at, was also dead. I did not dwell on the question of which of us, Dahll or myself, had fired the fatal shot, knowing I'd done the only thing possible under the circumstances.

We started back to the raft when Dahll had recovered enough to make the short journey. As soon as we reached it, I made him as comfortable as I could and dressed his wounds. I spread some more of the salve on the ones that were only superficial and used the bio-regenerator on the more serious ones, some of which were very deep. I gave him another antitoxin shot and broad-based antibiotic shots. There was nothing more I could do for him except give him a general analgesic to ease the pain.

We made slow progress along the swamp and eventually found a suitable place to rest for the night.

Despite obviously being in pain, Dahll insisted on helping me to construct a rough shelter, overruling all my protests. And he's the one who seems to think *I'm* stubborn and self-willed!

Soon after I started my evening watch there was a terrific electrical storm. Rain lashed down in torrents, extinguishing our fire and turning the earth around our shelter into a quagmire. We'd dragged our little raft ashore and built the shelter around it, so at least our supplies were quite safe.

The lightning flashed, blue and vivid, lighting up the surrounding countryside and making the branches of the trees stand silhouetted like monstrous, demonic hands, claws extended. It grew very cold and I was grateful for the warmth of Sitta's cloak. The small light-globes we'd brought with us, placed at strategic points around our shelter, gave out a comforting glow.

I went over to where Dahll lay at the back of the shelter. He'd managed to change into his warm thermal suit, and I was glad to see he was sleeping. I'd given him a mild sleeping draft after our evening meal, guessing he was probably in more pain than he would admit.

I covered him with a light thermal blanket from our emergency pack. Despite the night's coldness, his skin was warm and he seemed comfortable. I went back to the entrance of our shelter to watch the storm.

It took several hours to abate. I was about to see if I could resurrect the fire when Dahll moaned softly. I crept over to where he lay. I placed my hand on his brow. He burned with fever. He moaned again and flung off the blanket. I examined his leg by the light of my flare. It was swollen and discoloured. I had obviously been right to fear that the spines might be venomous or carry an infection. It would be several hours before I could give him another antitoxin shot, so I used the small regenerator again to try to speed up the healing process.

I examined his knife wounds. They were clean and miraculously had already begun to close and heal. The minor ones already had a layer of healthy new skin, thanks to the salve.

I replaced the old dressings with fresh ones and laid a cloth moistened with cold water on his forehead. His eyes flickered open.

"Are you thirsty?"

He nodded weakly. I helped him to some water and went back to tend to the fire. He called my name softly.

"Please...don't leave me."

"It's all right. I'm still here. The rain's stopped now, but the fire's gone out. I'm going to try to relight it," I said, moving back to where he lay.

"Don't leave me," he repeated, grasping at my cloak when I once more tried to move away.

"Dahll, are you in pain? Shall I give you something for it?"

"No, just stay...with...me."

I seated myself beside him, cradling his head in my lap. He looked so pale and vulnerable. I felt he must, in reality, be older than he looked. He certainly had more than his fair share of strength and courage and determination. "It's going to be all right," I said softly. "Try to get some rest."

I loosened the fastenings of my long cloak and arranged it so it covered us both. After a while, he grew still, and I sensed he was sleeping again. I tried not to move for fear of disturbing him.

I began to grow very tired. It was a few hours before dawn, and I'd had no sleep since the previous evening. I slowly eased my aching limbs into a more comfortable position. As I did so, my eyes caught a flicker of light moving toward the entrance of the shelter.

I stiffened, suddenly alert again. Tiny, glowing tongues of flame danced in the darkness, writhing and twisting around themselves like miniature whirlpools of living fire.

At first, I thought it was a trick of my eyes, caused by fatigue. After a while I decided it was just marsh gas, but as I watched I became aware that the 'flames' were orderly. They moved in groups of threes and fours, gliding in straight lines and then circling to retrace their steps in what seemed to be a methodical fashion, as no Will o' the Wisp ever did. I began to feel I was in the presence of something malevolent...evil.

Then I heard the voices. Strange, unearthly voices, which had nothing to do with flesh and blood.

"Take the male," they hissed, "while he yet lives. Before the life-force within him dies and is of no use to us."

"Wait. The female is stronger," came another voice. "Stay until she sleeps. Then will be our chance, and we can take them both."

I reached for my blaster, by now fully charged, and fired a steady beam in the direction of the 'flames.' When I laid down the gun there was nothing, only the darkness.

Had the voices been in my imagination, or was it a dream? But I knew I had not slept. Trying to recall the experience, as I record this, I realise they did not speak in words at all. Yet I had understood, like that time on Niflheim, with Gullin.

I've always loved the night, the beauty of the

darkened, star-filled skies. Here, however, on this forsaken and perilous planet, it is menacing, with the sense of something lurking, lying in wait. Much as I dislike the idea, I have resorted to using a Phidian stimulant to stay awake. For Dahll's sake as well as my own, I can't allow myself to sleep until we're once more on board the *Quest*.

## Chapter Fourteen

518-25.10

It took the following day and half of the next to reach a place where we could beach the raft and continue on foot to the wreck where we'd left the hover-hopper. I discarded all unnecessary supplies and put the rest into one supply pack so I could carry it and still help Dahll stay on his feet.

The swamp appeared to have receded and the landscape changed again, so we had further to walk. The air was very hot, although the sun's rays seemed to have difficulty in actually penetrating the heavy yellow clouds. It would have been easier if we'd travelled by night, when it was cold, but I had decided the journey was too dangerous to undertake in the dark. Although I also felt the presence of the 'flames' during the day, it seemed they were stronger and more active at night.

Dahll showed no improvement. I encouraged him to take frequent sips of water, and tried to keep him as cool as possible, using some of the water to sponge his face and arms. I tied my hair back in a thick braid and changed out of my torn tunic, wearing only shorts and a light sleeveless chemise, but even that clung to me in the humidity.

Even with my support, Dahll could only move a short distance at a time without having to stop and rest. I hated to have to ask him to move at all, knowing every step must be causing him untold agony. He grew weaker all the time, and I was afraid if we did not return to the ship soon he might not make it at all.

On one of our frequent stops to rest, he begged me to go back to the *Quest* and take off after the *Destiny* alone. "I'll just slow you down. If you leave me now, you might be able to catch her."

"Dahll, do you really think I could leave you here?"

"I have to face facts," he said softly, in subdued tones. "I'm not going to make it. Reckon my luck finally ran out," he added, with a ghost of his former grin.

"Dahll, stop it!" I was frightened by the resignation in his voice. "Don't you dare talk like that. You can't just give in, of course you'll make it. You'll be fine once we reach the ship." He didn't reply and I wished I could be as confident of his recovery as I tried to sound.

His knife wounds seemed to bother him very little, and even the bad one in his shoulder was almost completely healed. The wounds in his legs were what worried me. The antitoxin and antibiotic shots didn't seem to be having much effect, although possibly they may have slowed down the progress of the poison in his system.

I began to think we would never make it to the wreck, but then, at last, I saw it up ahead. A mass of dead metal in the middle of the clearing, and beyond it our hover-hopper.

It took a little while to remove the branches that covered it and disable Dahll's safety device. I managed to help him into the little vehicle and settled myself behind the controls.

A mercifully short time later the *Quest* came into view, as we'd left her. My feeling of relief at seeing her standing apparently undisturbed was only equalled by my anxiety to leave Lyrrh. I landed the hopper and helped Dahll out of the machine and into the shade of the *Quest*'s shadow. His anti-intrusion device was still intact when I checked it carefully for any sign of tampering. It wasn't easy to deactivate, even knowing the correct disarming sequences, and I forced myself to take my time over the task. It would be ironic to make it this far, only to blow us both sky high with our own safety precautions!

I'd just finished the final sequence, and glanced across to where Dahll sat, when I heard a slight rustle behind me. Turning, I came face to face with the Salmaran I'd left unconscious on our last encounter. He leapt at me, catching me off balance.

I staggered to my feet and tried to fight him off, but he was very strong, and I was not at my best, having deprived myself of sleep for so long. I reached for my blaster, at the same time trying to kick out at him. He aimed a punch at me, and I went sprawling a second time. He bent over me, grasping my throat with both his hands. I kicked out again, trying to reach up to tear his hands away with one hand and attempting to unholster my gun with the other. His face was close to mine, his harsh breath almost suffocating. I turned my head away, with difficulty.

Suddenly I was half blinded by blaster fire, and the Salmaran yelled, releasing his grip and falling across me. With an effort, I managed to extricate myself from beneath him. Scrambling to my feet, coughing and gasping for air, I looked down at my assailant. He was quite dead.

I walked slowly over to Dahll and sank down beside him, clasping his arm with both hands. His face was deathly pale; his blaster hung limply from his fingers, but he was still conscious.

"Thanks," I said wearily. "Let's get back on board the *Quest* and off this wretched planet!"

Dahll was now in a very weak condition. I managed to get him to the sick bay, bathed his face and hands, cleaned and redressed his wounds and left him resting in the hyper-acceleration chamber.

This is a similar facility to the ones built into the pilot seats on the flight deck. I knew he'd be comfortable there for both take-off and acceleration to light speed. At least while unconscious during acceleration he would be free from pain.

The sense of foreboding that had been with me all the time we were on Lyrrh evaporated once we were on board. By now it was dark outside, though, and I seemed to sense the 'flames' around the ship, waiting. The ship's external sensors and the observation panel confirmed this, registering a vast number of unknown energy sources.

I lifted off the planet as soon as it was practical to do so and, when we were safely in deep space, initiated hyper-acceleration procedure. Once we reached standard hyper-speed and I was satisfied the control systems were stable, I returned to the sick bay to check on Dahll.

He was conscious, the chamber's anaesthetic having been dispelled once acceleration into hyperspace was accomplished. He drank a little water but would eat nothing. I talked to him reassuringly until I saw he was sleeping again. I made sure the sensors monitoring his life-processes were functioning correctly and instructed the computer to inform me immediately if there was any change.

I went to my cabin, where I stripped off my clothes and stepped into the shower chamber. I revelled in the cleansing mist, removing the dust and grime of Lyrrh from my body. Then I collapsed onto my bunk and drifted into a deep sleep.

****

I'd allowed myself eight hours to catch up on my lost sleep...and it was enough. Before the light in my cabin once more brightened to full intensity and the computer politely informed me my self-allocated sleep quota had expired, I was awake, trembling from hideous dreams. This time there was no one to comfort me. My only consolation was I seemed to be spared the blinding headache that usually accompanies such nightmares. I forced myself to shut out the image of the fiend who haunts me, as I headed for the sick bay, having paid the price for my sleepless nights on Lyrrh.

Dahll's respiration rate has fallen a little, although the instruments registered no immediate cause for alarm and had therefore not alerted me. He is so weak, though. It seems his life is gradually slipping away, and I can do nothing more to help him. I changed the dressings and applied fresh salve, wishing I had greater medical experience and skill. My work at the medical centre on Phidia had mainly involved dealing with minor accidents and was purely routine. I know little about alien viruses and noxious predatory plants.

He doesn't even seem aware of my presence now and is slipping deeper into unconsciousness. I tried putting one of the spines in the computer's analysis unit to see if it could come up with a possible antidote. Unfortunately there is nothing in the database that comes even close.

I am updating my journal here, in the sick bay, while our journey back to the *Quest* is still fresh in my mind. I don't want to leave him, and I am too worried about him to sleep.

****

158-29.10

I've been sitting with Dahll almost continuously since we left Lyrrh, afraid to leave him, snatching a few hours sleep on one of the couches. He can't die...I won't let him.

Oh, Dahll, what a strange relationship ours is...never lovers, yet somehow, surely, more than friends.

I feel so helpless. Do I have to just sit here and

watch him slowly lose his grip on life? Even if I had the knowledge, I haven't the facilities to produce a serum to counteract whatever was in the spines of that plant.

The Phidians would know. I'm certain they could help him. But Phidia is so far away, he might not survive the journey. Anraat is closer, and the *Quest*'s autopilot is programmed to take us there, leaving me free for most of the time to tend to Dahll. I've slowed down his life processes as much as I can, short of complete cryogenic-suspension, in the hope of delaying the progress of the poison in his system.

I pray the Anraatians will be able to find a cure. If not, it seems only fitting that Dahll should die on his home planet, among his own people.

****

159-35.02

It seemed the *Quest* knew she was going home. I pushed her to the limit, asking more of her than I have ever, to my knowledge, asked of any ship before. The gallant little craft responded in a way that made her seem almost sentient, as if she were aware that Dahll's life depended on her speed. I have speculated sometimes on whether the bio-neural repair and regeneration systems incorporated in most starships might, somehow, imbue the ship with some kind of awareness. I know scientific opinion states categorically this is impossible, but I can't help wondering.

I was taking risks. I instructed the autopilot to maintain a constant speed of standard by twelve, a speed a small craft like the *Quest* is normally only able to withstand for short periods at a time. However, none of the instrument readings indicated any sign of stress in the drive or the ship itself. I only began to reduce speed when the star system to which Anraat belongs showed up on the scanner.

I suppose an Anraatian ship, piloted by an alien,

presented something of an anomaly to the Control Officers at Anraat's major spaceport, which lies just outside the city of Henira. After confirming my identity, they acknowledged my request for permission to land, in tones that suggested surprise, if not outright suspicion. After some delay, permission was duly granted.

I'd no sooner touched down than I received an official request from the head of Control for permission to come on board. I had no choice but to agree, but I emphasised the *Quest*'s rightful pilot was in urgent need of medical attention. I activated the lift and eventually an elegant, white-haired Anraatian, with a distinguished air about her, stepped from the airlock.

"My name is Krian Beldron. I am the officer responsible for overseeing the arrival and departure of all aliens to and from this planet." She held up a silencing hand as I started to speak. "Yes, I know your ship is registered as Anraatian and was built and designed on this planet. However, our data banks indicate you are not Anraatian." Her attitude and demeanour suggested she was not a person to be fooled easily and intended to get some answers.

"I'm not trying to hide anything," I assured her. "I'll tell you whatever you want to know, after this ship's pilot has been taken to one of your hospitals. The only reason I brought the ship here was because he'll die without medical help."

The head of Control eyed me sharply, and although she made no threatening moves, I was aware of the weapon at her hip, and knew she did not entirely trust me.

"Show me your Anraatian pilot."

I took her to the sick bay. There was no change in Dahll's condition. I bent over him, checking the instruments anxiously.

"He's been badly hurt and he's lost a lot of blood.

He'll probably need a transfusion. Also—" I unclipped a container from the rack. It held the three spines I'd taken from Dahll's leg. "He was attacked by a form of predatory plant life on the planet Lyrrh. I believe these spines carry some sort of viral infection, and possibly venom."

She looked at me, her expression no longer suspicious.

"You've been nursing him yourself?"

"There's no one else on board," I said irritably, for I was tired, and worried we were wasting precious time. "It's all in the ship's log. Can't these questions wait? Please help him, before it's too late."

Officer Beldron nodded curtly. I suppose she'd formulated her own opinion of my relationship with Dahll. "I will make immediate arrangements for him to be admitted to our nearest Medical Unit for treatment."

She spoke into a small communicator on her wrist. After a brief conversation, she turned to me again.

"There will be someone here shortly to take him to the Medical Unit. Now, you will please tell me his name and your own, and your planet of origin."

Wearily I gave her the details, without elaboration. She will, no doubt, examine the ship's log, which I've kept up to date since we left Lyrrh. I'm afraid I was deliberately mendacious about my origins, making it appear I was a citizen of Phidia. I don't like deceiving Dahll's people, but I remembered my promise to Yan Kloor, and until I know them better it seems wiser not to let the Anraatians know I come from Earth.

I was required to produce my Spacer's Permit, issued on Phidia, before I could leave. Happily, it is the standard interstellar issue and gives only my name and authorisation number and code, with the usual personal details. I suppose Krian Beldron could trace my home planet from this if she checked it out thoroughly, but she gave it only a perfunctory glance before handing it back.

I was spared any more awkward questions, for the moment, by the announcement that the transport vehicle had arrived to take Dahll. I wanted to go with him, but they wouldn't let me.

Accommodation had been arranged for me, I was told, where I could rest and refresh myself before answering a few more questions. I hadn't expected to be letting myself in for a series of interrogatory sessions when I headed for Anraat. Krian Beldron, although outwardly pleasant and polite, seems to be something of a martinet.

I asked if I might attend to certain matters on board the *Quest*, such as checking the systems I need to leave running, and closing down the others. When approval was forthcoming, I made the check as quickly and effectively as I could.

While the Officer was occupied removing the log, I surreptitiously instructed the computer to seal off the sick bay. Doubtless, this will provoke more questions if they decide to search the ship after I've left, but she is, after all, a private craft and Officer Beldron has already been inside the sick bay once. The formula is well hidden, but I don't want to take the risk of anyone knowing about it, even his own people, until Dahll has recovered enough to be able to handle negotiations himself.

****

159-02.03

It's been three days. Still they will not let me see Dahll. I have a comfortable suite in a building just outside the spaceport and am being treated with the greatest respect and consideration. I'm able to come and go as I please. The *Quest* is still in the landing bay and so far, to my knowledge, has not been searched by the Anraatian authorities.

As soon as I had a meal and a short rest on the day of our landing, I was taken to another building and subjected to yet more questions by another official. He seemed very interested in knowing my connection with Dahll.

There was no point in being evasive, as it was all in the ship's Log anyway. I answered his questions as accurately as I could, including the fact that I was trying to track the *Destiny*, a Terran ship of which I had once been a crew member.

When they finally allowed me go back to my quarters, I slept until the early hours of the next morning. I'd only just showered and dressed when I received another visit from Krian Beldron. She was less formal than on the previous day. Perhaps she'd been studying the Log and satisfied herself that the particulars recorded there coincided with the story I'd given her.

In response to my anxious questions, she assured me Dahll was being well cared for and responding to treatment. Apparently, the venom contained in the spines was analysed at the Medical Unit. The analysis found it to be almost identical to that of a similar plant species indigenous to a remote, uninhabited planet rich in minerals, on which they have exclusive mining rights. The serum developed against this species appears to be having the desired effect in Dahll's case. His fever has broken, and although he is still very weak, they expect him to make a full recovery. I'll be allowed to visit him in a few days when he's stronger.

Meantime, she said, I was to consider myself a guest in the city. If there was anything I needed, I had only to ask.

I thanked her and assured her my only concern is for Dahll's recovery, and as soon as he's well again we'll be leaving to resume our search for the *Destiny*.

In the back of my mind is the knowledge that

my chances of finding her grow slimmer with each day that passes. Krian has promised to make enquiries of every ship that arrives on Anraat. It seems there is nothing else I can do now but wait.

****

Anraat is obviously a highly commercialised planet, bustling with activity, if Henira is typical. The Anraatian women are of a very striking appearance...and an extremely haughty demeanour. I suppose this is hardly surprising, since they are accorded the greatest adulation and regard by the males of this planet. It is not, strictly speaking, a matriarchal society, but I have yet to see a woman perform even the lightest task if there's a man around to do it. Very few women do any menial work and many hold supervisory positions of great responsibility. They appear to be well content with their status and show no indication of wishing to change it.

A thriving, busy city, Henira is frequently visited by the inhabitants of numerous other planets. I couldn't help an involuntary shudder when I spotted a woman and two men who, from their appearance and colouring, were obviously Salmaran. I shall never be able to look at a Salmaran again without thinking of Narhjohol and his brutal companions.

I know I shouldn't allow myself to be prejudiced in this way, but it's difficult not to be when I think of my treatment on Osind and Narhjohol's complete disregard for life.

I wish they would let me see Dahll. They keep telling me he's improving steadily, but I shan't be happy until I see him for myself.

****

159-05.03

I've been on Anraat for six days and have just returned from my first visit to Dahll since our arrival. Krian Beldron herself escorted me to the Medical Unit. She seems to have taken on the role of my personal guide, having obviously decided I didn't have any sinister motive for arriving on Anraat in Dahll's ship. The building was large, square and white. Inside, the long, shining corridors had the same antiseptic smell of hospitals the galaxy over.

She attracted the attention of an orderly and, after a brief discussion with him, led me along another corridor and stopped in front of a plain metal door. She indicated I should enter, and as I knocked tentatively and it slid open, she withdrew tactfully.

The room was small without being cramped. At first, I thought three sides of the room were glass, looking onto rolling fields and deep blue Anraatian skies. Then I realised it was, in fact, a computer controlled holographic projection.

Although in reality the Medical Unit is in the middle of the city, fields and flowers are much more restful to look at than buildings and jostling crowds. The illusion was completed by a warm draft of air, which wafted across the room, bringing with it the scents of exotic flowers and grassy meadows.

Dahll was lying on a long, low couch facing the projection. He turned as he heard me enter the room. At once his face broke into that boyish grin which is so familiar. Apart from being very pale, he looked almost like himself again, but as I drew close I could see the strain of what he had been through had not left him entirely unmarked. He seemed thinner, and to have lost some of his youthfulness.

"I asked for you, but I was beginning to think you weren't coming."

"I've been trying to see you for nearly a week," I said, seating myself on a comfortably padded chair near him and placing a friendly hand on his shoulder. "You're certainly looking a lot better than when I last saw you."

He looked at me with a very serious expression in his gold-flecked eyes.

"I wouldn't be alive at all if it wasn't for you."

"Nonsense. I didn't do any more than you'd have done for me."

"You killed that monster on Lyrrh, fixed my wounds and took care of me...and risked losing the *Destiny* in order to bring me back here."

"Was that any different from you risking Narhjohol getting away while you rescued me from the fortress on Osind?"

He shrugged. "I reckon we've both been through too much together to start counting up favours, but thanks. I know what it must've cost you to turn back—"

"Forget it, Dahll. I wasn't going to just leave you to die."

His expression didn't alter. "How are you feeling?" I asked, changing tactics. "Is there anything you need, something I can bring you?"

He shook his head. "No, thanks, I've everything I need. What about you? Are you being treated all right?"

"Exactly as I'd expect to be treated by your people. I'm being overwhelmed by consideration for my welfare. Although I have to say they did seem a bit over-security-conscious to start with. I think they suspected I was planning a single-handed invasion. And Officer Krian Beldron—she's the Head of Control for Alien Immigration at the Spaceport—"

Dahll nodded. "Yes, I know, she's been to see me—"

"Oh, I see." I felt a little annoyed at the information she'd been allowed to see Dahll before me. Why should officialdom come before friendship? "Well," I went on, "she's promised to help us trace the *Destiny*. There seems a good chance someone from Anraat might know something about her." Perhaps by the time you're well again we'll have some news of her whereabouts—"

"I hope you will." There was something in Dahll's voice that should have prepared me for what he was about to say before the words were spoken. "But you must go on without me. I shan't be going with you."

## Chapter Fifteen

I looked at Dahll in dismay, stunned by his sudden pronouncement. Until then it had not occurred to me he would ever go back on our agreement.

"It's going to be a long time before I'm able to go back into space. Too long for you to wait."

"I'd rather wait until you're well again, however long it takes, than hire a stranger," I said, with some feeling.

Dahll shook his head. "Come now, you're not thinking straight. You know as well as I do, if you don't leave immediately when you hear news of the *Destiny,* you'll probably never find her again. You can't afford to wait around until I'm fit to pilot the *Quest*. Besides..."

He hesitated for a long moment, looking at me in that strange way he has sometimes. "It's better that we go our separate ways now. You don't need me. You never did, just my ship."

"Dahll, that's not true," I protested, surprised and hurt by his words and puzzled by the expression in his eyes. "I couldn't have come this far without you. And what would have happened to me on Osind if it hadn't been for you? I'd probably still be languishing in a cell...or dead, because I would have found some way to kill myself rather then let myself be taken on board Narhjohol's slave ship."

"If it hadn't been for me, you wouldn't have been in any danger from Narhjohol in the first place," Dahll said softly. "You know I'm right. You may have lost too much time already." He placed his hand lightly on mine.

"You don't think I like the prospect of never seeing you again, do you?" His tone was casual and the words spoken lightly, but his eyes still had that strange expression in them. "Nothing's changed, has it?" he went on gently. "You've never once stopped thinking about him, and you won't rest until you've found him again."

He was right, of course, but there was something about the way he said it...how could I have been so blind? I swallowed hard. "I'm sorry, Dahll," I said after a moment. "I'll start looking for another ship." I forced a smile, desperately trying to get our relationship back on its former easy footing. "There must be someone on Anraat who's willing to take this 'mad, self-willed Earth woman' halfway across the galaxy on what might turn out to be a wild goose chase."

"You misunderstand," Dahll said slowly. "I don't want you to have to look for another ship. I'm giving you the *Quest*."

I looked at him incredulously. "But you can't. She's *your* ship. I couldn't take her—"

"We have a contract, remember? I don't intend to break it."

"The contract was for two years, and it's almost that now. You have every right to call our agreement settled."

"Only if there was no sign of the *Destiny*. That's not the case. You're so close now. Our agreement still stands."

"I release you from our contract. I can't let you do this."

Dahll shook his head. "There's no going back on an Anraatian contract. I've had plenty of time to think about it. You hired my ship in order to find the *Destiny*. There was no specification I had to go along, too."

"But she's worth far more than I paid you."

"Central Administration pays well for scientific discoveries. With what I'll get for the formula, even allowing for the percentage I promised the Phidians, I'll probably be able to buy a small fleet of ships just like her."

"I'd almost forgotten about that," I admitted. "I've been too worried, wondering what was happening to you. I sealed off the sick bay in case the Authorities decided to search the ship. I haven't said anything to anyone about it."

Dahll smiled, dispelling that strange, sad expression from his eyes. "I knew I could rely on you to keep my secret safe. Even on Lyrrh, when I thought I'd never see Anraat again, I knew you wouldn't let it fall into the wrong hands. As soon as I can get out of this place I'll start making arrangements to have it patented and distributed." He paused. "And if you won't accept the *Quest* as a gift, then think of it as being your share of the profits. You're entitled to something."

"I don't see it that way. She's your ship, she belonged to your father."

"Have you forgotten," Dahll murmured, "Anraatians are notoriously unsentimental. And you did save my life. Nothing I could give you could repay that."

"There's nothing to repay," I insisted. "You'd have done the same if our positions were reversed." But I could see he was resolute. "All right," I relented, "I *will* take the *Quest*, but if I can ever find a way of bringing her back to you, I will."

"Good," Dahll said, looking relieved. "I knew you'd see sense in the end. I'll have her overhauled and refurbished."

"There's no need—"

"Yes, there is. She's been in space a long time." He gave a ghost of his former grin. "And you gave her a bit of a battering to get me here, from what I can gather. She's probably in need of some maintenance and attention by now. Even the bio-repair systems need a little help now and then. And you have to admit she's designed to be functional rather than for home comforts."

"You're surely not thinking of fitting her with flowery pink wall hangings and lacy drapes?" I suggested facetiously.

He laughed softly. "I wouldn't have thought that was quite your style, but if it's your fancy you can have her fitted out any way you choose."

"I rather like her the way she is. I wish I knew how to thank you."

Again, his fingers closed over mine for a moment. "You know there's no need for thanks. I'm just glad you've agreed to take her."

He lay back, looking suddenly very tired.

I realised I'd stayed longer than I had intended. It was surprising some protective medic hadn't ventured in to drive me out. Dahll is still weak, and it is going to take him a long time to recover fully. "I think I'd better leave now," I said softly. "I'll see you again tomorrow, if they'll let me. Try to get some rest. You need to build up your strength."

He regarded me quizzically. "Rest? That's all I've done since I've been here." His eyes glinted with their old humour. "I hope you're not going to start trying to treat me like you're my nurse, just because I'm helpless."

I kissed him lightly on the forehead and made for the door. "You...helpless? That'll be the day!" Still, I knew how he must feel. He's always been so strong and independent. It must be very frustrating for him, having to just lie there. He looked so alone as I glanced back at him. I don't think he has anyone at all left on Anraat. From what he told me, Narhjohol was responsible for the deaths of his entire family.

They told me after my visit he'd been very ill and it had not been at all certain he would live through the night of our arrival. The virus has taken its toll and left him weak and liable to tire very easily. However, he is young and strong. He will, they assured me, recover fully, with no lasting after effects.

I have been in something of a daze since returning to my suite, my mind reeling with the bombshell Dahll delivered.

As I record this, I can't help but wonder if I should have resisted more strongly when Dahll offered me the *Quest*. He must know I would never have held him to the balance outstanding on our contract, although I'm not quite sure how I would have managed to pay for my passage on another ship.

Too late now for self-doubt. I know him well enough to be sure that if I tell him I can't take her after all, he will be deeply hurt. I won't inflict that on him, on top of everything else. I won't easily forget what I saw in his eyes...the words, unformed, which he would not allow himself to speak.

Tamarith was right. Right about the danger we were both in and also about the closeness of the bond that's grown between Dahll and me. But now that bond of friendship must be broken, and I have to go on alone. However tired I am of searching, something deep within me compels me to go on. As Dahll so astutely observed, I can never rest until I find the *Destiny* again.

****

159-10.03

For the last five days I have been too busy to add any more to my journal. There has been so much to do on board the *Quest,* and I've been to see Dahll every day. Outwardly, at least, he seems cheerful, and happy to be supervising the maintenance operations and conversions to the *Quest*, even though such supervision has to be from the Medical Centre, since they will not allow him to leave yet.

He seems to have a small army of engineers at his command, and I can't begin to imagine what the total cost is likely to be. I keep insisting that there is no need for any great changes. He just grins and says she is in need of refurbishing and the cost will be minimal when set against the profits of the formula.

The formula...ah, yes, Krian Beldron was not too pleased when she discovered I'd kept it a secret from her. I think Dahll managed to smooth things over and convince her I acted from the best motives. At any rate, no action has been taken against me, and I continue to be treated with the greatest courtesy.

There is just one innovation I would like to have incorporated into the *Quest*. I asked if it was possible to have a visual computer image in addition to the vocal output facility on the computer. I don't relish the prospect of incalculable time in space without seeing another face, artificial though it might be. My request, as it turned out, posed no great problem. Although most Anraatians would find it too distracting, their technology is more than capable of such a contrivance.

I spent several hours looking at computer-generated images until I found one I thought would be good company. Male and white-haired, he was more a grandfather figure than a father figure, but he will help combat the solitude on what may be a long voyage.

I notice every time I visit Dahll that the holo-projection has changed. Yesterday it was a vista of vast, reddish brown desert. In the foreground, waving gently in the soft, warm breeze, a clump of the most beautiful iridescent blue flowers I've ever seen. They reminded me of large, Terran roses.

Dahll told me they grow only in the Kantachturian desert on Anraat and are very rare. They spring up after a rainfall, which may not occur for several years at a time, and if cut while in full bloom never fade or die. Even the delicate perfume remains, he said. While the projection could give me some idea of their beauty and an indication of their scent, I found myself wishing I could see and smell the actual flower. Sadly, they are so rare that even if I were to go to Kantachturia I might still never come across one.

When I saw him this morning, Dahll seemed to be acting a little strangely, by turns, mysterious and slightly morose.

"I haven't heard anything from Krian," I ventured, by way of conversation. "She promised to let me know if she had any news of the *Destiny*."

"I asked her to tell me first," Dahll said, with the merest hint of a smile.

"Oh, did you?" I queried, more sharply than I intended. "You must be feeling better. You're starting to take charge again."

"I thought," he said quietly, "if the news was discouraging, it might come a little easier from me."

"Oh." My resentment dispelled at once. I should understand by now that Dahll usually has a reason for his actions.

"As it happens, the news is good."

"What? Oh, Dahll, you mean—"

"She arranged for messages to be sent to all Anraatian ships in the Pleiades sector. We just received reports from two of those ships. One of them was actually in contact with the *Destiny*."

"And?" I prompted breathlessly.

"Our message reached them after they'd spoken with her crew. She seems to be following the same flight pattern we've already extrapolated on the charts. Krian has the details." He paused. "Of course, the exchange between the two ships was brief and purely routine, but there was nothing to indicate conditions on board the *Destiny* were anything other than normal."

I sat down quickly. I'd been standing facing the holo-image, today a tranquil lakeside scene with low mountains in the background. Strikingly marked horse-like animals cropped the grass, while tiny, colourful birds skimmed low over the water to catch insects.

"It seems they're likely to spend some time in that sector of space," Dahll went on. "The planets in the system are devoid of intelligent life but abound in animal and plant life of a diversity apparently not expected. If you leave at once, you might be able to reach them before they leave..."

"But the *Quest* isn't ready," I said, trying to retain some semblance of an equanimity I did not actually feel.

"She will be," Dahll stated confidently. "It'll take no more than two days to have her ready for liftoff. She's not as fast as the *Destiny*, of course, no ship I know of is, but she can match most ships many times her size. You'll catch up with them."

"And what about you, Dahll?" I asked softly. "What're you going to do?"

He smiled slowly. "Once I've finished here, and found a ship that suits me, I'll sort the Phidian's share of the profit from the formula. Then I've a fancy to go back to Niflheim. There's nothing left for me on Anraat now, and I find the idea of Niflheim rather attractive."

"I can think of at least one person there who will be more than pleased to see you."

"I would like to see Tamarith again," he said, catching my meaning. "But now you'd better start making arrangements for your departure. You don't have a lot of time."

****

159-12.03

After two of the most hectic days since our arrival on Anraat, the *Quest* and I were finally ready for liftoff this morning. I would never have believed, a few days ago, so much could be accomplished so quickly. Comfortable as the ship was before, the various changes and innovations Dahll has now incorporated make conditions on board practically sumptuous.

He has stocked the library with holo-discs recording the best in Anraatian art, music and literature, so my leisure hours will be pleasantly filled. Also included are some discs recounting the history and customs of the Southern Continent of Anraat, since I'm curious to learn more about this part of Dahll's home world.

The computer has been enhanced, as specified. As well as the other additions to ensure my comfort and well-being, the whole ship has been renovated and her interior gleams with subtle colours and shining metalwork. Even the name I gave her, the *Quest*, now appears on her hull, beneath the statutory Anraatian identification symbols.

I was on board, completing the final checks before going to the Medical Unit to say goodbye to Dahll, when a familiar voice requested permission to come aboard.

"Since when do you need permission to board the *Quest*?" I asked him. "She's still your ship."

Dahll stepped from the airlock, looking around critically. "Not bad," he said mildly. "You happy with the improvements?"

"They're fine, and thank you. I still can't quite believe it. But what are you doing here? I thought you were supposed to be resting."

"I've rested enough! I managed to persuade

them to let me come to see you off. And," he admitted, wandering around the flight deck and looking toward the main console, "I wanted to take a look at the *Quest* now that the modifications are completed."

"You don't fool me," I told him softly, putting myself in his place and imagining how I would feel if the *Quest* were mine and I was giving her to someone else. "So much for Anraatian lack of sentiment. Don't worry. I'll bring her back to you one day, I swear it."

We were both stalling, trying to put off the moment when we would have to say our farewells.

"D'you mind if I look around?"

"Of course not. As I said, she's still your ship. Help yourself."

Dahll spent a long time inspecting the *Quest* in minute detail, from the flight deck to the living quarters, while I informed Krian Beldron that I would be ready for liftoff as soon as he left. However, now the moment was nearly here, I realised how difficult it would be to say goodbye to him.

At last he appeared to be satisfied and wandered back to where I stood.

"There's enough of the hyper-acceleration serum on board to last you for however long you may need it. Have you everything else you need?"

"Thank you, yes. I've seen Krian and my clearance papers are all in order. I'm just waiting for official permission to lift off. "And you, Dahll," I added. "Will you be all right?"

"The patient will live, and should…eventually make a complete recovery."

"I didn't just mean the virus you picked up off that thing on Lyrrh."

He smiled that slow smile of his. "I know. Neither did I."

He took my hand and raised it to his lips, in the

same gesture he made when we first met on Phidia.

"Goodbye. Take care of yourself and travel safely. I know you'll find him. Anyone who wants something as much as you do is bound to find it in the end."

I reached up and kissed him lightly on the lips, hugging him to me for a moment, hating the thought of having to leave without him.

"Goodbye," I said reluctantly. "Remember me to Tamarith and Gullin. We *will* meet again one day, I promise."

"I hope you're right," he said softly.

"Of course I am. I have to return the *Quest* to you, remember?"

As he re-entered the airlock and I prepared for liftoff, I realised just how much I'm going to miss him. I had little time to dwell on the matter before the moment was broken by Krian Beldron's voice as she appeared on the main communicator, informing me I had clearance for takeoff...and wishing me luck!

I fixed my eyes on the main observation panel, determined to get one last glimpse of Dahll and his home planet before initialising the liftoff sequence. The last memory I have of Dahll is of him standing tall and pale, the early morning sun turning his fair hair to gold. He looked like a young Viking god from the ancient Nordic legends of Earth. I like the analogy and it seems appropriate that he intends to return to Niflheim.

****

I've given myself the necessary dose of the formula and am recording this in the pilot's cabin—that used to be Dahll's—while the ship is still cruising at sub-light speed. The proximity of the pilot's cabin to the flight deck makes it expedient to sleep here rather than in my old cabin in the passengers' quarters.

When I first entered the cabin after liftoff, I

noticed at once a sweet, delicate scent, which filled the air. On my pillow, I found a single perfect Kantachturian desert rose. I smiled softly to myself as I picked it up and gently fingered the lustrous, waxy blue petals.

No need to wonder who placed it there.

****

159-15.03

Anraat seems scarcely more than a memory to me now, although I miss Dahll's company even more than I'd imagined. The *Quest* is on course for the Pleiades system. This will probably be the last entry I will make in my journal for some time, since the routine occurrences on board the ship will be recorded in the ship's log.

I feel my search must be nearly over. I know I can't give up, whatever happens and however long it takes. If the *Destiny* has left the Pleiades by the time I reach there, I will carry on. I must—no, I *will*—find her.

# Part III

## Chapter One

*The starship Destiny, mantled in the darkness of eternal night that was deep space, glided through the gaps between the stars at a speed fractionally below that of light. Ahead of her, seven parsecs distant, lay a small but brilliant sun and its planets, still unexplored. They were now at a safe enough distance to prepare for entry into hyperspace without endangering the planetary system they had just left. On the flight deck, however, there was an aura of perplexity as the ship's commander and second-in-command studied the panel before them. A single blue 'blip' pulsed persistently where there should have been nothing but empty space. The two men exchanged looks, each struck by the memory of a similar occurrence nearly four years earlier when they had gone to the rescue of a small ship, and the woman who piloted her.*

****

"Are we sure it is a ship?" Jon queried, not taking his eyes off the 'blip' on the panel, although there was nothing else it was likely to be.

Kerry Marchant ran his hand through his dark hair, his expression more than usually brooding.

"That's what the sensors indicate...and a small one at that. As soon as she is close enough for *Metisa* to scan, I will let you have the data," he observed, busy once more with his calculations.

Jon nodded and left the flight deck, aware his second-in-command was more than capable of assessing the potential of their unexpected companion in this uncharted sector of space. It might be wise to leave him alone to contemplate.

Kerry dismissed the thought running through his mind. Could it be their last leap through hyperspace had accidentally sent them back too far in time? He frowned. Logic told him that was impossible.

All chronos and instruments were registering normal, and there had been no distress beacon. Besides, the complex multiple fail-safe devices, built into the stabilising system developed to overcome the time-dilation effect resulting from faster-than-light travel, were designed to the most stringent standards. They were linked to the main computer, which would have given immediate pre-warning of a possible malfunction in any part of the system. The type of accident that had killed Jess's father could never happen to the *Destiny*. Moreover, her course appeared to be stable, and she was behind them, not ahead of them.

It had to be a coincidence, this strange little ship, if ship it was, suddenly appearing on their trajectory. Just coincidence...

He turned back to the instrumentation panel, checking and rechecking. Memories crowded in, memories he'd banished from his waking hours, although not from his dreams...never from his dreams.

He shook his head impatiently and tried to shut out those memories and concentrate on analysing the data before him. *She* belonged to his past, a very private part of him he could never let go, or share with anyone else.

Several hours passed before the stranger was close enough to be visible on the main scanner. The crew of the starship stared, fascinated, at the alien craft. Although essentially different from terrestrial ships, her design a little unusual, the small craft was perfectly proportioned with an intrinsic beauty and grace.

"What information is available so far?" Jon asked.

"She's apparently a non-terrestrially-designed hyperspeedster with a very sophisticated and efficient ion-drive; nitro-oxygen atmosphere, so presumably from an Earth-type planet, and carrying a humanoid crew of one," Kerry stated, keeping his tone expressionless. "She's also extremely fast for her size. Sensor readings indicate she has followed us since we left the Pleiades system, although at a distance too great for her to register on the scanners until now."

"Let's see what she looks like on full magnification."

Kerry gave the command to the computer, and the ship grew in size until she almost filled the screen and they could read the name on her hull, immediately below her alien identification symbols.

"Well, one thing is obvious. Whoever she is, her crew appears to speak *Common Universal*," Kerry remarked, reading the name aloud.

"You've tried hailing her, of course."

"Naturally," Kerry replied pragmatically. "She's probably still too far away to pick up our signal, but I'll keep trying until she answers."

Exactly fifty-three minutes later, Kerry made contact with the small ship. He felt the colour drain slowly from his face, and switched on the ship's general address system. The voice coming across from the small craft was a woman's, and one they all remembered. She requested permission to transfer from her ship to the *Destiny* and identified herself as Jestine Darnell.

****

At the sound of Jess's voice, the rest of the crew

made for the flight deck. Stunned, they seemed unable to take their eyes away from the main scanner and the small ship, which hung like a gemstone in the velvet darkness of the void.

Eventually they looked at each other in disbelief. That Jess was dead was an indisputable fact. They'd all seen her body, cold and lifeless. So how could that soft, husky voice, so familiar to all of them, possibly belong to her? Frustratingly, there was no visual image to go with the voice. Either the ship did not possess visual image transmitting facilities or Jess, if that was really who she was, did not wish to show herself.

Jon broke the silence. "Kerry, we all saw Jess's escape module destroyed. You set the charge yourself. Whoever—or whatever—that is out there, it couldn't be Jess."

Kerry turned fiercely. "If it's not Jess, how do you explain her voice and the fact she knew our names? You all heard her."

"There could be several possible explanations. Perhaps she's a telepath—"

"If that is the case, we had better ask Delian and Ragin to look into her mind," Kerry said coldly.

Delian looked directly at Kerry, although he was speaking to them all.

"You know we can't do that, it would be against our laws to do such a thing even if we wished. However, she 'feels' like Jess, and we can detect nothing evil or alien about her from the emanations reaching us—"

"Then I'll take Ferry Three and transfer across to the ship myself. That way none of you will be in danger. I will maintain audio-visual contact, and at the first hint of trouble you can take the *Destiny* out of here."

Jon put a restraining hand on his second-in-command's shoulder. "And leave you? Kerry, you're not making sense. I'm sure I speak for everyone on board when I say we were all fond of Jess and wish by some miracle it could be her in that little ship, but it's impossible. If you board that craft, you'll probably be walking straight into a trap."

Kerry shrugged him off with a violent movement. His hand went to his blaster.

"I warn you, Jon, I intend to go, with or without your approval. Do you think I wouldn't know Jess's voice?"

"Voices can be imitated, as well as individuals. Have you forgotten the shape-shifters of Andromeda? There's no way that could really be Jess!" He lowered his voice until it was only audible to his second in command. "Kerry, you were always the logical one. You had no time for sentiment. However hard, you have to accept that Jess is dead."

Jon's patient reasoning won through at last. Abruptly the desperation, the temporary insanity even, which had almost made him lose control, faded from his mind. When he spoke again, Kerry's voice held a tone of utter resignation.

"You're right, of course, Jon. Whoever she is, she has to be an impostor, though why—"

"Perhaps she wants the *Destiny* and this is a trick to put us off guard," Berne suggested softly. "After all, there are many people on Earth, as well as alien civilisations, who would pay handsomely for the capture of a ship like this."

"Yes," Kerry agreed. He kept his expression once more calm and devoid of emotion, allowing no sign of the inner conflict which moments before had threatened to rob him of his reason. "Thank you for reminding me. All right, Jon. What do you suggest we do?"

"Are you sure the sensors indicate no other life forms on board?"

"None."

"Then we'll accede to her request and allow her to transfer across. I guess there are enough of us to overpower her, should she prove dangerous."

****

Calmly, almost autonomously, Kerry re-opened the communication channel and instructed the ship's pilot to confirm she had a small transit or repair vehicle. When this confirmation was forthcoming, he activated the main airlock and watched on the scanner as she skilfully manoeuvred the *Quest* to a flight trajectory synchronous with the ship that dwarfed her.

After a few minutes, a panel in the *Quest*'s hull slid open and ejected the tiny transit vehicle. As soon as their computer confirmed the vehicle was safely on board, Kerry closed the entry hatch, and he and Jon made their way to the launch bay. Their visitor stepped from the module as they arrived.

Kerry had mentally prepared himself for this confrontation, but the slender, strikingly lovely young woman who stood before them was so much the living image of Jess he was unable to tear his gaze away from her.

The silky, red-gold hair which fell in waves over her shoulders and past her slender waist. The creamy whiteness of her flawless skin. The perfectly shaped, firm, high breasts and softly rounded hips—the way she carried herself—the subtle but distinctive fragrance she used, all this was imprinted vividly in his memory. Even the clinging garment she wore, tightly belted and sweeping into soft folds around her feet was the same rich green colour Jess had loved to wear. And her eyes. Surely, such eyes could only belong to Jess?

He watched as those beautiful emerald green eyes glanced at the weapons both he and Jon had drawn, and then looked at him with an expression of bewilderment in their depths.

With an effort, he suppressed the wave of longing which swept over him. He reminded himself sharply that Jess was dead. There had not been a day when he had not thought of her, lived again the desperate moment on Phidia when she had saved his life at the cost of her own. He would give up everything he held dear, including his own life, even the *Destiny* itself, if he could only believe this was really the woman he still loved, the woman who had died to save him.

Reason told him there was no way this could be Jess.

He'd placed her lifeless body in the escape capsule himself and watched it destroyed. This alien creature, masquerading as his dead love, had to be an impostor. Perhaps the vision he was seeing was an illusion, a hypnotically-induced fantasy fabricated by the being from his own memories. If so, it must be a mass hallucination, for he could tell by the expressions on the faces of the rest of the crew, who had now joined him and Jon, that they, too, were seeing Jess.

"Kerry," she said softly. "Kerry, I've been searching for you for so long. Why did you leave me?"

"Who *are* you?" Kerry ground out the words between clenched teeth.

The expression of bewilderment turned to one of anguish, and all colour left her face.

"You ask that...have I changed so much?" She seemed to have eyes only for him. The rest of the crew might as well not have existed.

"No, that's the strange thing," Kerry replied acrimoniously. "You look exactly as Jess did the first time I saw her, and after nearly four years that's a little hard to take."

She smiled slightly, although her eyes were still bewildered. "You haven't changed much, either, Kerry, except for that scar on your face."

His fingers went involuntarily to the left side of his face, where he knew the scar, though faint, still showed against his skin. Disbelief began to make way for anger—anger that anyone, especially an alien being, should masquerade as his beloved Jess.

"Clever, but you don't trick me that easily. You may look like Jess, you may know things she knew, but however closely you resemble her I know you're an impostor." He paused for a long moment.

When he spoke again, it was with an effort. "You could not possibly be Jess," he said very quietly, "because she is dead. She was killed by a mutant known as Ayandos, when she stepped in front of a laser meant for me."

****

Jess swayed unsteadily, overcome by a feeling of terror. Now she remembered! As soon as she had stepped on board the *Destiny*, the missing pieces of her memory had started to return. Now the thing that eluded her since she woke up in the Medical Centre on Phidia revealed itself at last. The memories came flooding back.

*Ayandos!* He was the fiend who walked her nightmares. The fiery red eyes, unnatural white skin and hair belonged to the alien Ayandos. Her mind reeling, she was swept back in time, living again that moment on Phidia.

She felt fear, like a titanium band, tighten around her heart as she saw the tiny gun in the albino's hand. He was pointing it at Kerry. She wrenched herself free from the alien's rough grasp. A streak of brilliant white light...a sudden acrid smell of burning flesh—blood—and pain more intense than anything she'd ever known.

She cried out, and crumpled, senseless, to the ground.

****

She came to in the *Destiny*'s sick bay. Her

dreams had been hideous, but no longer terrifying. When full consciousness returned, she understood her dreams. She felt her nightmares would not bother her again. Like everything one fears, now that she knew the thing that had so terrified her, and had faced up to it, the reality was not as horrific as the fevered imaginings of her subconscious mind.

Her dreams held no terrors for her now, but she felt stunned and empty. She ached with the physical pain of unshed tears, but was unable to weep to relieve the gnawing feeling of desolation deep within her. The emptiness weighed her down and threatened to overwhelm her.

It was ironic. Kerry was convinced she was dead. Obviously, the Phidians had kept the truth about her survival from the ship's crew. She had prepared herself for Kerry's possible rejection, and his revulsion at what had happened to her, but she'd had no reason to think he wouldn't believe who she was.

Her mind was a jumbled confusion of bewilderment and self-recrimination. She'd never felt so alone, not even that day on Phidia when she'd had to face the reality of the medical procedure she'd been subjected to.

Kerry believed her to be an impostor. She'd thought she could return to the *Destiny* and take up the threads of her old life where she left off. Now she realised it was not so simple. Life did not stand still. One could not just go back!

That was not all. A sudden realisation shocked her and left her mind reeling in despair. She sat up and rested her head despondently in her hands, asking herself, not for the first time, how she could have been so blind.

Perhaps, she mused dejectedly, it would have been better if the Phidians had allowed her to die, after all. At last she accepted what they had done to save her, but life without the man she loved, to share it with, had no meaning. Where once she had relished being alone in the vast beauty of space, now the thought of being alone filled her with despair.

What a fool she'd been. How could she not have realised... But no, that line of thinking led only to madness.

She closed her eyes and prayed silently for guidance. She did not ask for a miracle, just direction. There had to be a purpose to her life, otherwise why should she not have died on Phidia? Nor did she ask for an immediate revelation of that purpose, for was she not possessed of free will, a mind of her own? But she could not believe a Divine Creator, who had formed the myriad planets, and the stars she loved, would have returned her life to her without a reason.

Perhaps she was not meant to spend the rest of her existence with one person, after all. Perhaps there was work for her to do that would take all of her commitment and love, and it would be enough. If she was patient, she would no doubt discover the answer. For now, all she could feel was the pain and heartache of what she had lost.

Yan Kloor had said when she faced the reality of her nightmares she would have no more reason to fear them. That, at least was true. She tried to understand why he had not told her of her "death" at the hands of Ayandos. Perhaps it had something to do with the fact that the emotion of love between a man and a woman, as she knew it, did not exist on their planet. The concept of anyone being willing to sacrifice their own life to save that of the one they loved must be completely alien to the Phidians.

Perhaps, also, Yan Kloor was ashamed to admit they'd deceived the *Destiny*'s crew.

She had the last piece of the puzzle. As the wise physician had said, she'd needed to find it for herself. He'd told her nothing about the albino. The Phidians must have erased all evidence of Ayandos's occupation, so fearful were they of even the notion of violence. The only information they had given her was how she was instrumental in bringing the *Destiny*'s crew to Phidia to defeat an invader. That and the steps they had taken to save her when her body was damaged beyond repair.

If she'd known the truth then, that the *Destiny*'s crew believed she was dead, would she have had the strength to accept it? Now she had to. The expression in Kerry's eyes had told her that as far as the crew of the *Destiny* was concerned, Jestine Darnell no longer existed.

It had been imperative for her to find them, to remember for herself, to piece together the severed remnants of her memory. However, it was a mistake to think she could go back to how things were. All she'd succeeded in doing was to re-open old wounds for Kerry. She knew him to be a man who did not love often or lightly. There had been sorrow and loneliness in his eyes, as well as suspicion, when he looked at her. Yes, she'd had to find them, but—she came to an abrupt decision and purposefully squared her shoulders—now she must leave. She no longer had any place on the *Destiny*.

She stood and approached the hatch. Before she reached it, however, it slid open and Laitha entered.

"I said I'd check to see if you were awake yet...Zeldra gave you a mild sedative."

Jess looked at the other women intently. Could she trust her? They had always enjoyed each other's company, and Jess considered Laitha to be her friend.

She decided to take a chance. "Laitha, will you help me get back to my ship?"

"Without the others knowing?" Laitha demanded, somewhat dubiously.

Jess nodded slowly. "It shouldn't be too difficult. Where are they?"

"They're in Jon's quarters, trying to work out whether or not you could possibly be Jess, or if you're some kind of shape-shifter."

"Why didn't they just take a DNA sample while I was unconscious?"

"Because you—I mean Jess—never had any reason to record her DNA sequence on the *Destiny*'s medical computers, so we have nothing to compare it with."

"Of course. I hadn't thought of that."

"Besides," Laitha said, "if you could copy Jess's looks, you could probably copy her DNA, as well."

"Do *you* believe I'm an impostor, a shape-shifter?"

Laitha looked doubtful. "I don't know. I don't see how you could be Jess, and if you were, why would you want to return to your ship?"

"Because—because I'm not—I'm not who I say I am. It's all right," she added hastily as Laitha's hand went to her blaster. "I don't wish you or anyone on board the *Destiny* any harm."

"Then why pretend to be someone you're not?"

"It's a long story. Too long to go into now. I didn't know that...that the real Jess was dead. Kerry saw through me. I have failed. I must leave."

Laitha's hand did not leave her gun.

"I swear I mean no harm. I only want to leave peacefully, to get back to my ship. Listen," Jess pleaded. "Do you really think, if I was planning to harm any of you, or the *Destiny*, I'd have come on board like this, alone and unarmed?"

Laitha hesitated, uncertainly. "Wouldn't make much sense," she admitted. "But then, neither does the fact you're standing here looking like the twin sister of someone I know to be dead."

"Trust me, please. Go back to the others, tell

them I'm still sleeping. Just give me a chance to get away."

"How do I know you're telling the truth? How do I know you won't attack us as soon as you're on board your own ship?"

"I could have done that before, without risking my own safety by transferring to the *Destiny*," Jess said reasonably. "All I can do is give you my word that if you help me to get back to my ship I'll leave at once, and you'll never see me again. You can watch me leave on the scanner. The *Destiny*'s computers will register any powering up of my weapons array once I reach my ship, and all it would take would be a word from you and you could destroy me. My ship wouldn't stand a chance against the *Destiny*'s weaponry."

Laitha nodded, very slowly. "All right, I'm not sure why I should believe you, but I'll do it. I'll instruct *Metisa* to open the hatch and allow you to leave. There's no one on the flight deck just now. Soon as you take your ship out of here, I'll get back to the others and make up some story about you overpowering me." She glanced at Jess, her expression guarded. "I'm very good at pretending."

Jess looked at her questioningly.

Laitha looked uneasy, and lowered her gaze for a moment. "I'm not doing this for your sake," she said, "I'm doing it for him. I don't want him hurt any more." She looked directly at Jess again. "I don't know if you're telling me the truth or not, and I don't really care. I liked Jess. I couldn't blame Kerry for falling in love with her. And he's never so much as looked at another woman since she died. I don't think he ever will. It's taken a long time, but he was starting to get over her death, to come to terms with it, and now you've stirred up the memories again. The sooner you're off this ship, the better it will be for us all."

Jess studied her shrewdly for a moment. They had been good friends, and she'd enjoyed the times they'd shared together on board the *Destiny*. She'd thought they knew each other well, but now she realised there was a side of Laitha she had never even guessed at.

"Then I should go now—before the others make up their minds about me, one way or another."

Laitha ushered Jess out of the sick bay, still keeping the gun trained on her, and together they made their way to the airlock, where Jess's ferry waited.

"Remember," the other woman told her as she climbed into the tiny transit vehicle, "I'll be watching on the scanner."

"I'll remember," Jess said, wishing she could tell her the truth. But it was better this way. Better now for Kerry to go on believing she'd died on Phidia. As the little vehicle headed toward the *Quest*, Jess took one last, long look through the rear viewport at the beautiful, gigantic ship and then looked resolutely away.

## Chapter Two

It seemed to Jess she wandered aimlessly in space for countless millennia, without purpose or direction, enveloped in a hopeless melancholia that sapped her strength and her will.

In reality, it was only hours since she had left the *Destiny*. She had allowed the *Quest*'s control and auto-navigation systems to take over, under the direction of the main computer. Seated numbly by the observation panel on the *Quest*'s flight deck, she stared, unmoved and almost unfeeling, at the stars that had once filled her with wonder.

She was shocked out of her mood of utter dejection by a sudden meteoroid shower. The computer's insistent alarm brought her to her senses, forcing her to take action, more for the ship she had grown to love than for herself. A meteorite, mercifully a small one, grazed the side of the ship, the force of the impact slamming her across the flight deck. She struggled to her feet and lunged unsteadily across to the control panel.

The ship began to spiral as she reached the controls. Somehow, she managed to stand upright. Desperately she noted the data on the control screen. It took all her skill to bring the ship back under control as she engaged the manual controls to correct the spin. Under her experienced fingers, the powerful engines responded with corresponding side thrusts until the *Quest* gradually righted herself and the lights across the panel once more returned to green.

She breathed a sigh of relief, but the struggle

was not over. For twenty or more ship's minutes, she battled her way through the field. Her fingers flashed over the command pads as she plotted a course to avoid the largest of the rocks. When at last she passed through the shower and returned control to the ship's electronic brains, her mind was once more clear. She checked the damage, then confirmed initialisation of the auto-repair systems and knew she needed to make a decision.

Niflheim was calling her, but she could not go there. Not yet, although she'd made a promise and she intended to keep it. One thing was certain, she could not drift aimlessly in space. There were many options open to her, and any one of a number of planets where she might settle and find a worthwhile occupation. There was only one, however, that seemed right. A purposeful expression in her eyes, she began to feed the coordinates into the *Quest*'s navigation computer.

****

The pale twin moons were barely risen over the jagged contours of the Phidian landscape, lying enshrouded in purple twilight, when the *Quest* made planetfall. Jess activated the main external scanner and looked out over the outlines of the well-loved distant mountains. For the first time since she had left the *Destiny* behind, her mind was at peace.

Phidia. It had seemed to her the only place left to go. She knew she would be welcome here. Perhaps on Phidia she could forget. She would try to find work at the Medical Centre again, and by immersing herself in the daily routine, the aching remorse and emptiness within her might lessen, the loneliness become a little more bearable.

There were several other ships in the Mirrahn spaceport, she noted. Most were small, private hyperspeedsters like her own, together with the usual contingent of commercial freighters and passenger liners. She informed Spaceport Control of her identity, as was required by all craft visiting the planet. Her instruments confirmed the Phidians had scanned and classified the ship as soon as it entered the planet's atmosphere. Even so, she was obliged to quote, in detail, all the relevant authorisation codes and identification sequences.

The lengthy initial formalities completed, she allowed herself a few hours rest before preparing to leave the ship. She knew when she disembarked she would have to endure further questioning to satisfy the stringent Phidian security regulations.

****

Jess ate a light meal, then showered and changed into a long, simple but elegant dress of a lightweight material, suitable for the fashions and warm climate on that part of Phidia. She was about to make an official request for permission to disembark when she received a request over the ship's communicator to activate the lift for a visitor.

Scarcely believing her ears, she complied. He did not identify himself, but she would know his voice anywhere, despite the time that had elapsed since they had last seen each other. The visual confirmed it, but still she could not believe it. He couldn't be here, on Phidia!

She waited, in mingled anticipation and apprehension, and after a few moments, a young man, tall and good-looking, stepped from the airlock. His clothes were immaculately cut and obviously expensive, although there was nothing flamboyant or ostentatious about them. His shirt, fashionably split down the front, was of a fine material, as were the matching, stylish pants and boots.

The air of quiet self-confidence he always radiated was even more apparent. He looked older, more mature, but his smile, when his eyes met hers, was just as she remembered.

For a moment, they stared at each other in mutual disbelief and pleasure, then hugged each other tightly, as old friends.

"Dahll," she breathed, standing back and gazing at him, her mind racing in a confusion of disordered thoughts and emotions. "Dahll, it's so good to see you. But I thought you were going back to Niflheim. What are you doing on Phidia?"

"I was about to ask you the same question," he said, giving her that mysterious, inscrutable look, which after all this time she still found vaguely disturbing. "I couldn't believe it when I saw the *Quest*. I thought you must've sold her, but when I made enquiries, I discovered she was still registered in your name."

"You should know I'd never sell her. She wasn't mine to sell anyway, and I promised to bring her back to you, didn't I?" But you still haven't told me what you're doing here."

He smiled enigmatically. "I told you I was coming to Phidia to negotiate their share of the profits from the formula."

She shook her head. "No, or if you did, it didn't register. So much happened during those last few days on Anraat."

"Yes. It seems a long time ago, it *is* well over a year, ship's time. I've been on Phidia for a while now." He grinned. "It's almost become my second home. I keep my new speedster docked here, which is how I came to spot the *Quest*."

She studied him astutely, and led him to the recreation area, where she gestured to him to be seated.

"How are you?" she said lightly, as she handed him a glass of his favourite fruit wine and sipped at one herself. "You...you look different somehow." Or was it perhaps her perception of him that had changed?

He laughed softly. “No, I’m still the same...a little wealthier. I did well out of the formula.” The difference went somewhat deeper than that, but she let it pass. She realised he was looking at her with the same expression of grave solicitude on his face she had seen so many times in the past.

“What brings you here, Jess, what happened? Did you lose the *Destiny*’s trail? Didn’t you find them after all?”

“Oh, yes, I found them,” she said, looking down at her glass and running her fingers abstractedly around its rim. “I found them.”

He watched her, unspoken questions in his eyes.

After a moment, she went on. “I shouldn’t have tried to go back. It was a mistake.”

“What happened?” he asked again, softly.

“He’s in love with a memory,” she told him simply. She hesitated for a moment, before going on. “When he saw me again, he thought I was an impostor, a shape-shifter. Oh, it wasn’t his fault,” she said hastily. “It was the only way they could explain my reappearance. You see, I didn’t know it, but they were told I was dead. The Phidians are so afraid of violence they wanted to be rid of them and the weapons they brought as soon as possible. So obviously they didn’t explain what they were doing to keep me alive.”

She put down her glass and stood a few paces away, half-turning toward him.

“I understand now. Yan Kloor made no secret of the fact they were glad to see the *Destiny* leave, even though they helped save the planet. He didn’t tell me they’d deliberately misled her crew, though.”

“But surely,” Dahll said gently, “surely you could have made Kerry understand. If you’d told him what you’ve told me, about how they saved your life, you could have made him believe you.” His expression showed he found it inconceivable Kerry could possibly have doubted the evidence of his own eyes.

"Yes," she agreed. "I could have made him believe me. I could have told him what...what the Phidians did to save me. And there are things I know that no one else could possibly know. Things we talked about together in private. Or I could have opened my mind to Delian and Ragin. They would have known I was telling the truth. But—" she looked away. "I suddenly realised—" she hesitated, unsure of herself...of him. Aware something between them had changed and would never be the same again.

"Yes?" He stood and stared at her wordlessly, compelling her to look at him once more.

"I'm not fickle, Dahll, really I'm not. I...I don't understand, myself. I did love him—very much. Part of me probably always will. He's not a man one could easily forget. But as soon as I was on board the *Destiny*, I knew I didn't belong there any more. I realised how little we really knew each other." She hesitated again. "Not...not like you and I know each other."

There was a long pause, as Dahll's face registered disbelief, followed by the gradual dawning of understanding.

She smiled gently. "We almost know what the other is thinking now, don't we? Without the words even being spoken." She looked at him appealingly, but he did not attempt to make it any easier for her.

"What is it you're trying to tell me, Jess?" he demanded softly.

"I don't really need to tell you, do I, Dahll?"

"Yes, I'm afraid you do." He no longer even tried to hide the love in his eyes. "You see, if you don't, I might not be able to believe it. *Tell* me," he whispered fiercely. "I need to hear the words."

She stepped close to him, putting her hands on

his arms. She looked deep into his eyes and spoke the words she'd been afraid to say, because for so long she was reluctant to admit it, even to herself.

"I...I couldn't stay with him because...I suddenly realised all the time I was searching for the *Destiny* and Kerry, I was growing to love *you*...and I couldn't see it."

He put his arms around her then, holding her very close. He looked at her with an expression that told her that to him she was the most precious thing in the Universe. He sighed deeply. "Jess, I've waited a long time, and travelled an awful lot of light years, longing to hear you say that. I never really believed I would."

"Yet all the time we were on board this ship together, you never told me how you felt."

Dahll looked surprised. "We had an agreement. I gave you my word...and I wouldn't have tried to come between you and another man."

She reached up to meet his kiss, a kiss as different from the burning passion she'd felt with Kerry as it was from the gentle, almost brotherly embrace she had shared with Dahll on Anraat. An exhilarating sensation of happiness welled deep within her, a sense of utter contentment. She knew now, beyond any doubt, she belonged with Dahll. Nothing...nothing would ever part them again. "I've missed you so," she told him huskily, when at last his lips released hers. "I never thought I could be so lonely without you."

"I've missed you, too," he said tenderly. "You know, I've loved you almost from the first time we met. I think I knew it that first day on this ship when I found you hadn't used your shield. He paused. "For a moment I thought you mightn't recover, and I knew then the fear I felt for you was more than just concern for a passenger."

"And yet you gave me the *Quest* to search for

Kerry."

"I had to," he said candidly. "Letting you go was the hardest thing I've ever done, but if you'd stayed on Anraat, and lost the *Destiny*, you'd always have wondered if you could have found her if you were able to go on. You might have grown to resent me. I couldn't handle that."

She looked wonderingly at this man she'd thought a boy, remembering his gentleness with her when she'd first told him about Kerry, his hatred of Narhjohol and his ruthless determination to kill him. She recalled how he'd single-handedly trained and organised an efficient fighting force from a band of primitive cliff dwellers. She remembered also his vulnerability and courage, his strength and his sensitivity. And he loved her. Loved her enough to let her go!

"I won't ever leave you again," she murmured.

He held her away from him a little. "Are you quite sure this is what you want? If there's the slightest doubt in your mind...you found the *Destiny* once, you could find her again."

"No, Dahll. If I hadn't been injured on Phidia, things would be different. But...nothing's the same any more. It's not Kerry who changed, it's me. We've been together too long and been through too much, you and I. We belong with each other. I love you," she said again. "*I love you.* How could I not?"

He took both her hands in his, looking at her with a proud, gently possessive expression in his eyes.

"Then, under Anraatian law, and with your consent, I take you, Jess, for my Lady, my only Love. And I give myself, all that I am and all that I have, to you alone for all eternity."

Jess had not wasted her time alone on board the *Quest*. She'd learnt much of the Anraatian customs from the holo-discs on board, and understood the response that was required.

"In the presence of the Universal Spirit, the one true God, I take you for my Life Companion. All that I have, and all that I am, I give you, Dahll, and you alone, to be your Lady, your only Love, for the rest of time," she said softly.

She twined her arms around his neck, lips slightly parted to meet his once more, in a slow, searching kiss that seemed as if it would last forever. A kiss which grew in its intensity until he gathered her up and set her down on her feet near the sleeping couch in the pilot's cabin.

He cupped her face in his hands and kissed her once more. "I understand on your world there are certain formalities and ceremonies which must be completed," he said, his eyes never leaving hers, "but although the commitment is no less permanent, things are simpler on Anraat."

"I know." Slowly she untied the front of her garment, letting it slip down over her shoulders as she reached out to him.

He took her in his arms and she slid her hand beneath his shirt, stroking his skin lightly with her fingertips. She pressed her cheek against his chest for a moment, before looking up into his face again. His lips caressed her mouth, her throat, the curve of her breasts. His hands moved lovingly, almost reverently, over the contours of her body, and she knew beyond any doubt it was meant to be. It seemed as though she'd been away for a long time and had now, finally, come home. The thought occurred to her that sometimes a miracle might be granted even if it had not actually been requested.

They lay together at last, naked in each other's arms. She held herself close against him, loving his warmth, the smell and feel of his skin against hers. She revelled in his kisses and the soft words of love he whispered, wanting to hold him like this forever.

It felt like the most natural thing in creation, as if they had always been in love. Dahll was the gentle and considerate lover she would have expected. As they gave themselves to each other, it seemed nothing existed except the two of them.

The last link with her past was severed forever. As they came together in that most precious of human contacts, the *Destiny* faded to a distant memory, as if something from another time, another existence. After a while she ceased even to think. Her spirit soared, her soul taking flight, joining irrevocably with his, one and indivisible. She seemed to touch the stars themselves, as they exploded in shimmering light around her, in a rapturous sunburst of shared joy and love.

****

Later, when the universe stopped spinning and the stars settled, more or less, into their former positions in the heavens, she lay in his arms, her fingers clasped in his, almost afraid to speak. Afraid to break the spell in case she was dreaming and found herself alone once more, with only her memories.

"Now you are truly my Lady and no one can ever part us," Dahll whispered. She sighed softly, trembling at the thought of how she had almost lost him, feeling his arms tighten protectively about her.

In the subdued light of the cabin, he regarded her with so much love and concern it almost took her breath away. "You all right, Jess?"

"Yes," she murmured at last, a soft smile playing around her lips. How often had he asked her that? "Yes, of course. But...Control will be wondering why I haven't left the ship!"

To her consternation, he laughed softly. "The Chief Controller saw me come on board. He knows you have a visitor. Presumably you went through all the necessary preliminary security checks, so there's no particular hurry for you to disembark."

She could not argue with his logic, but thought of the Phidians made her remember what for so long she had wished she could forget. She drew away from him a little, scanning his face anxiously in the dim light. Her voice trembled with a fear she could not suppress. "Can you really love me, knowing what they did to me? Can you...can you love a freak?"

He held her to him again. "Jess, have you still not accepted it? The Phidians cloned a new body for you when you were so badly injured they couldn't have saved you any other way. That doesn't make you a freak."

"No? Then what does it make me?" She pressed her face against his shoulder, shuddering as she imagined her brain kept alive in fluid suspension. The brain patterns, her complete psyche, mind and soul, then being transferred into a cloned replica of herself. A cloned replica which Yan Kloor had told her took about six weeks to grow to maturity. They apparently considered it wasteful to allow a clone replacement to develop beyond a point corresponding to approximately twenty years' growth. Hardly surprising Kerry was so sceptical upon seeing a woman whom he not only believed to be dead, but who seemingly had not aged at all in the four years since he had last seen her.

Isolated scraps of nightmare memories floated before her eyes. No, she reflected grimly, they had not all been dreams. She tried to push the memories of those nightmares to one side, but they would not be repressed. "It's unnatural...immoral."

He held her even closer, until gradually the tenseness left her. "This body is your own," he said, his voice softening as he kissed her face, "grown from your own original cell. It's no more unnatural or immoral than organ transplants...which were once looked upon with great suspicion on my world, as perhaps they were on yours?"

She did not answer, and he went on persuasively. "The Phidians presumably use the same technique themselves to prolong their own lives. You didn't consider them freaks, did you?"

"I...I suppose not," she murmured doubtfully.

"No one as lovely as you could ever be called a freak. I've told you before, if it doesn't matter to me, why should it to you?"

"I suppose I've been conditioned to think of it as being wrong, by the teachings of the Union," she admitted.

His voice was very gentle. "Forget the Union, that's all in the past. It's the future you must think of now." He paused before mentioning curiously, "You still haven't told me what you're doing on Phidia. Did you intend to rejoin the Mission and carry on with your ministry here?"

"No," she said sadly. "I don't think I'm fit to be a missionary any longer. I've lied and deceived...and killed." She tried to shut out the vision of the dead Salmaran on Lyrrh.

He kissed her hair. "I think the Universal Spirit would forgive you. "You've always acted with the best of intentions."

"Besides," she went on, "The Mission would have informed Earth of my 'death.' My resurrection would be a little hard to explain. I was hoping to find work at one of the Medical Centres here, once I'd sorted out the rather hurried way I left this planet with you."

"Would it have made you happy, working here?"

"I'd have felt I was being useful. It seemed like the right thing to do. I knew the Phidians would accept me, and I'd nowhere else to go. I can never return to Earth."

"Why not?"

"Cloning is illegal there," she explained. "The

Union outlawed the process to prevent overpopulation in the days before FTL travel made it possible to colonise the stars. The law was never rescinded. They ruled it was unethical and an affront to the commands of the Universal Spirit. It's a crime punishable by death to perform or collaborate in such a procedure."

Dahll whistled softly. "Not exactly known for their compassion, your Earth Union, are they?"

"The Phidians fear war and violence more than anything. They knew I came from Earth and about the cloning of humans being illegal there. They were afraid if news were to reach Earth of what they'd done, it might spark off an interstellar incident." She paused for a moment. "On the other hand, they apparently felt they couldn't allow me to die when they had the means of saving my life. Only those who were actually concerned with my treatment at the Medical Centre—Yan Kloor and his associates—knew who I was and where I come from. They kept it a secret from the rest of Phidia and made sure the *Destiny*'s crew left without any suspicion of what they were doing to save me."

"You are my Lady," Dahll said slowly. "As such, when we register our commitment to each other with the Anraatian Authorities, you'll be eligible for Citizenship immediately rather than needing to fulfil the statutory three year residency requirements. It means returning to Anraat in person to complete the necessary formalities, but you'll be free of the Union's jurisdiction. Anraat has no laws against cloning, so even if your secret is discovered, you'll be able to go anywhere you like in the Universe—"

"I wouldn't want to...now."

"Oh, yes, you would," he said, giving her a very tender look. "I don't reckon you could stop travelling any more than I could. I've seen the expression in your eyes when you watch the stars on the scanner. You love them too much to stay in one place, for a while yet, anyway."

"Perhaps you're right," she agreed. "You know me too well." She laid her head on his chest and sighed contentedly.

"I haven't thanked you for the rose."

He turned his head. The beautiful blue flower stood in a tall transparent case, on a shelf beside the couch, as fresh as the day he'd left it for her.

"I couldn't tell you before, but they're so rare they're considered the sincerest token of love one person can ever give another."

Tenderly, she kissed him, moved by the significance of the rose, which she'd half guessed. "Control won't be expecting me to disembark before dawn now," she whispered, with just a hint of mischief in her voice. "I suppose we might as well stay here and really give them something to wonder about!"

As his lips claimed hers again, the doubts and memories of the past vanished from her mind, in a kiss that promised to fulfill all her dreams of the future.

## A word about the author...

I am intensely proud of being Welsh, although I currently reside in England with my husband Dave and three horses, Sally, Harry and T'pau. I have made up stories in my head for as long as I can remember, inspired by the beautiful Welsh scenery and its legends, and acting out my characters' roles in my mind.

I have always had three great loves—Horses, Reading and Writing, as well as being passionately fond of all animals and the outdoors. I enjoy writing Westerns, but my favourite genre is Science Fiction and Fantasy. I usually manage to have a horse somewhere in my stories, whatever the genre, and it did not take me long to realise that there was another essential element which would always occur in my stories—Romance with a capital 'R'.

I write the kind of stories I like to read: stories that take me, as a writer, into other worlds, where for a while I can forget the problems of the real world—and I hope they will do the same for my readers. Having given up my full time work as an administrator, I am now looking forward to being able to devote a lot more time to writing. My heroines are always strong but feminine—my heroes brave but caring ... love will conquer all.

Contact Hywela at Lyn@Hywelalyn.com
Visit Hywela at www.Hywelalyn.co.uk

www.ingramcontent.com/pod-product-compliance
Lightning Source LLC
La Vergne TN
LVHW020539100826
845148LV00010B/1527

* 9 7 8 1 6 0 1 5 4 3 5 5 4 *